VAMPIRE DEVIL
REBEL ANGELS BOOK THREE

This is why Fallen angels fear the light...

Snatched to the Under World, Violet discovers that the father who abandoned her as a baby is the tyrannical king of hell. She's forced to battle in the Bone Carnival to prove her loyalty in a court of the wildest vampire rebels ever to be cast out of Angel World. Or else she won't be able to save the angels...or her sister.

When she defies the anarchic vampire court, she's tested in three impossible Devil's Quests, which risk letting out the worst monster of them all: and it's inside her. If she fails, she'll be bonded eternally to a tyrannical general, whilst the vampire geek and sexy angel she loves will become the elite army's playthings.

The Apocalypse is coming, and Violet may just be the weapon that destroys the world...

I0629258

FANTASY REBEL

FANTASY REBEL

VAMPIRE DEVIL: REBEL ANGELS BOOK
THREE@copyright2018RosemaryAJohns

ISBN-13: 978-0995557963
ISBN-10: 0995557969

Book Cover Designer: Rebecca Frank
Fantasy Rebel Limited

rosemaryajohns.com

1

Vampires? Angels? I once hunted the bastards.

Now I'm the bitch who rules them.

I reign over a valley of feathers and bones: death, the End, destroyer. Half vampire, half angel, I'm a monster amongst monsters.

My human life of gamers, shanks, and sister burnt on my twenty-first birthday, when my powers arose phoenix-like. They marked me out as anything *but* human. Until tricked into the harem boy Angel World — an angel princess with the vampires' king as dad — I torched the corrupted court, only to become a captive in hell.

Light.

I squinted through the migraine white, stumbling in the heat. My hands clawed around the bars of the Cage; I grimaced at the *slurp*, as gloop clung to my fingertips.

My violet-and-black wings, which had broken from my shoulder blades and flown me free from

Angel World, beat slowly, as I wrinkled my nose at the stink of tar and oil, wiping the ooze down my leather trousers. Then I backed away from the sides of the Cage: a giant birdcage, which swung from chains.

Rattle — clank. Rattle — clank. Rattle — clank.

I peered out at the shadowy vampires beyond the light who were running bones along the bars.

Humans called them vampires, but I'd discovered they were Fallen angels who'd been cast out of Angel World where my mother reigned, leading to centuries of war.

And now?

Captured, I was trapped in the Fanged Wild West: only the most savage rebels survived.

Oh yeah, and my dad was the sheriff.

I spun, whirling my ash-blonde hair like fire, before raising my hands. 'Place your bets, bitches.'

Because this was the Cage: the fighting ring where anything went, and we proved our worth in the Under World through pain to win the prize.

I was a huntress, princess, King of the Under World's daughter and undefeated Champion since I'd been brought here — reluctant guest — eighty-seven fights ago.

How else could I judge time trapped below the City of London in this Fallen Under World?

Alone.

Each time I fought — and won — without the blokes who'd saved me and battled by my side, I couldn't help the worming thought: did I need anyone but myself?

Would I ever be *allowed* to see my fam again?

A shadowy veil of pain, grief, and despair touched me through the bond with Rebel: my bondage Irish angel.

Could he feel it...my rejection?

I shuddered, allowing the ache for only a moment before I shook it off. Exhaustion clung to me like spiderwebs. Then I straightened my throbbing shoulders. The thrill of the fight lit me up, fairyland. I fiddled at the straps on the black leather armour, which was slashed down the back to release my wings, tightening it over my latex top: I was being roasted inside.

Rattle — clank. Rattle — clank. Rattle — clank.

My obsidian wingtips quivered.

It was never a sign of singing unicorns when they got with the bone rattling.

I *eeped* when the steel floor tipped, fairground ride special, and I skidded...towards the tarred cage bars.

I furled my wings behind myself, like a kid curling its hands over its bum to hide itself from a smacking.

Titters and hoots.

I scowled, flushing, but couldn't help closing my eyes and waiting for the *thud*. Only to trip backwards, as the floor gave a metallic *hiccup* and levelled.

I gasped, just as I was caught in a grey-winged embrace; cherry scented feathers swept around me, cloying in their sweetness. A tongue flicked out and, lazy as a cat, licked up my throat.

I arched, wriggling closer.

This cowboy either had a shooter in his pocket or...

I shivered. 'No more fights today, Misrule, this

bitch is toasted to a crisp. Stick a fork in me: I'm done.'

A sigh. 'Your audience awaits, Bone Princess. The show must go on.'

'Then are you stepping up, bro, or can I get with the Fang whomping already? Public groping's not on my to-do-list.'

A deep-throated chuckle.

Then I was swung around.

The Master of Misrule stroked my wings; heat coiled through me, zinging desire in each light caress. His black eyes blazed, as he gazed down at me. I was lost in his towering shadow: a punk god.

The ringmaster of the Cage had bones threaded through his afro like pearls; a frilly lace cravat hung tongue-like over his PVC catsuit and coat.

The ancient vampiric black inside me carolled rejoicing at his hold, even as the angelic violet chanted warnings.

Oomph — I elbowed Misrule in the guts, and he let go.

Misrule bowed, before kissing the tip of my nose. 'We shall hasten to the main act, as the lady desires it.'

I snorted, 'In your dreams.'

He waggled his eyebrows. 'In every Fallen's since our princess so cruelly denies us...entry...'

Whoops and cheers.

I reddened. 'Congratulations. You've just achieved Gold Level Brat.'

Misrule laughed, dodging back, as I dived after him.

The spotlight dimmed, and I could see beyond into the cavern. The fiery violet tips of the vampires' grey wings lit up the gloom, as they hovered in gangs or clutched the sides of the bars like they were the ones in cells.

In Angel World there would've been regimented division: the male Wings kneeling at the female Glories' feet.

Here the gender divide, however, had been torn down. All were equal in the bedlam. Fishnets, leather, bondage. The flash of silver piercings, tattoos, and Mohicans. Below, the sounds of shagging — *slap* of flesh against flesh, howls, and *smacks*.

I guess they didn't have a problem with public groping.

It was a wild chaos of desire, passion, and pain. And I was the star of the show.

You don't know who you are, Feathery-fangs, too lost in the dark.

How sweet does the fight taste? Sweeter than your candy heaven angels? Or has your shank heart forgotten they're held prisoner by their worst enemy, whilst you dance in the mayhem?

Do one. I'm not knocking back tequila shots here, I'm—

Letting the monster out to play.

Trapped, J. I'm fighting for my life.

I sighed. 'J' was the sassy voice in my head who'd plagued me, as well as raising me, since I'd been discovered as a baby on a gravestone in Hackney cemetery, clutching nothing but a violet feather.

So, what if I gank some vampires?

I've survived by myself.

What about your angelic Irish red-head and cutie pie librarian? They're trapped somewhere here too. In the anarchy, you'll need their biteable little asses.

Trusting fam got me betrayed and caged. I'd say I was done with the needing dance. I party alone now.

You're never alone. You have me.

When Misrule twirled, his PVC flying out in bat wings, an expectant hush fell over the vampires.

A slow grin spread over Misrule's face. He unhooked a thin ebony cane, which was topped with a wing bone, waving it around the audience: a ghoulish pointing finger. 'Welcome to the Bone Carnival, where only the bravest enter the Cage! The prize?' He stepped back dramatically, and a skull lowered from the roof. I gagged at the thick scent of human blood that pooled in the centre; Misrule licked his lips, his eyes glazed. Blood: the currency in the Under World and every drop had to be earnt. 'The opponent?'

Clang — the side raised, and a bloke was shoved through.

He stumbled to his knees, blinking up at me through a cascade of shimmering silver hair, which tumbled to his delicate shoulders; his trousers were silver leather with a matching tunic that hung open over his chest.

He could've been a fae.

Except, the glimpse of his eyes through his hair was *violet*.

Why the hell was I battling a captured angel?
And who was he?

Whistles and jeers.

The Fae Angel shrank in on himself, before straightening his shoulders, and tilting up his chin with haughty indifference.

His gaze met mine.

He looked younger than I'd been expecting,

with aristocratic cheekbones sharp as a shank. Then his wings unfurled.

Grey feathers dappled the violet. The angel was *Falling*, becoming a vampire because he'd been away too long from Angel World. In the Under World that made him one of the lowest ranks: The Shadows.

Was that why he'd been put in here to fight?

Misrule snatched the Fae Angel by the scruff of the neck, hauling him into the centre of the ring opposite me, whilst he bristled, cat-like.

I smirked.

The bastard eyed me warily. So, he had some street smarts.

'At the order of the king,' Misrule announced, bopping the angel on the head with his cane, 'the next fight will be between the Bone Princess and Mischief.'

My dad had ordered it?

I twisted round, straining to see if — this once — my dad would be in the crowd, watching. I didn't know how I reckoned I'd recognise him: he could be the bloke in sequin dress and nose stud for all I knew. But with the familiar way two vampires were rubbing against Sequins, I was going with non-royalty.

Eighty-seven fights, and eighty-seven no shows. How was that for Parent of the Year?

Why didn't dad want to see me now that that I was caught? Why the hell didn't my own family love me?

Then my opponent's name hit me: *Mischief.*

Just because the gossips tattle dirty secrets about this new fighter, doesn't mean you have to curb stamp the Lord of Mischief.

Leave some of his pretty white skin for licking, not kicking.

But what the rumours whisper about him—

Is no worse than what they whisper about you, hooker.

What tales do you think he's heard about the king's daughter?

I was awash with oily black that *Mischief* was free, whilst my angels were hidden from me.

I spun, clouting Mischief in the nose.

Mischief yelped, staggering back.

'The bitches around here talk. And the names they have for you...?' I crouched, ready to attack, but I launched it with *words* first because they were the best advantage in any street fight and shanked deeper, '...Shadow, traitor, *whore*... Did you piss off my dad by not bouncing on his lap the way he likes?'

To my surprise, Mischief's lips curled, but he didn't flinch. 'Why, I'm flattered you've heard of me.' He touched his finger to his lips as if in thought, as he cocked his head. 'Remind me: you are *who* again...?'

And that's how you shank with words.

I snarled, launching myself at Mischief; he giggled, side-stepping so quickly that I landed on my face. I scrambled up, sweeping my wings round, but suddenly he was behind me.

My skin prickled: a static *silver* electricity and popping bubbles of...

Magic, Violet-cakes.

I don't believe in fairies; I don't believe in—

He's your daddy's floozy and a powerful mage. Only a jackass trusts their rival.

If he discovers me, you won't be the Vampire Princess, you'll be the freak, even in this world of freaks.

Hide me.

Mischief shoved me forwards, and I hit my

kneecaps — *crack* — on the metal. I growled, before noticing the flaming arrow that sizzled behind me, which had fired from the roof directly to where I'd been standing a moment before.

The Cage was just bag-of-tricks fun.

Why the hell had Mischief saved me?

I ached for my own weapons: Flight and Star. They'd been stolen from me. I couldn't blaze on their ancient light against the Cage's attacks or my opponents'. Instead, I'd learnt new weapons, training through every battle to adapt.

Mischief sauntered forwards, holding out a hand to casually pull me up. What did he think this was, a polite round of fisticuffs?

Bones and blood. Bones and blood. Bones and blood.

I shuddered, as the chant rose around the cavern, animalistic and raw. Mischief had no idea what he was inciting.

Dark blasted through me; it roared to savage Mischief and revel in the battle. I snarled, batting away his hand.

Mischief gave me a cool look, as I crouched ready to spring. 'Oh yes,' he sniffed, 'I remember who you are: the *beast* they keep in this cage.'

I howled. Nothing but darkness filmed my eyes.

I leapt onto Mischief, seizing him by the throat; my wings banded around him in a trap. He struggled, but I choked him. 'Where are the other angels?'

'It almost sounds as if the beast cares.'

Beast...

I quivered. How could words still hurt, when I'd owned the monster inside? A monster that now wanted to crush the angel who'd dared to insult me.

I tightened my grip, and Mischief's long fingers scrabbled at my hands. 'The name's Violet, Feathers, or try *princess* on for size.'

He pursed his lips. 'If you call me Mischief, rather than *whore*.'

Guilt trickled into my fury-soaked brain, and I eased off his throat, nodding.

Mischief lifted his eyebrow. 'So, you keep angels as pets? I'd rather have every feather plucked out than see them under your care.'

I swept his legs out from under him, slamming him to the floor, then pinning him down. He stared up at me with startled eyes. 'How about we start now, bitch? Where are my fam?'

Except, suddenly I wasn't glaring down at Mischief's face but a flame of red hair and thick eyelashes, curling over violet eyes smudged with kohl eyeliner. My hands weren't gripping silver leather but a ripped black t-shirt.

'Rebel,' I breathed, lost in the candy sweetness of his scent. How had I ever reckoned I didn't need my bonded and Marked angel? *Need this?* The feel of him beneath me, whilst he bucked into my touch, his wings pulsing. *Mine...mine...mine...* I kissed Rebel tenderly. 'I promise, you're off my List of Asses to Kick.'

'Can I have that in writing?' Mischief's mocking voice out of Rebel's pink bow lips made me recoil and throw up in my mouth. 'Preferably in blood.'

'What the hell...?'

'Just a trick. A mere glamour.'

'Turn back to your Gandalf self.' I closed my eyes, unable to look at the false Rebel anymore; my bond ached more fiercely than it had in weeks with Rebel's agonised despair.

It wasn't dimmed now through the red haze of the fights or the drugged euphoria of the Bone

Carnival.

The False Rebel fluttered his eyelashes. 'Why should I do that? You'll simply beat me.' I shifted, unable to meet his gaze. This was a fight to prove strength and fearlessness and...I didn't know anymore. Why was it suddenly complicated, when before it'd seemed so clear? 'Also, your father ordered it not because of my...*performance*...but because I spoke out for your pets. Oh, I'm sorry, does that make it harder to despise the cowardly user of magic?'

'One winner, one loser. Then I get to wash, eat, and sleep. You're just a number.' I smashed my fist into his gut, and he doubled over groaning at the same time as he transformed back into his silvery curl of angel.

Mischief peeked up at me. 'Fine, but you pushed me to this.'

In a sizzling spray of sparkles, he changed...into a tiny silver unicorn.

I gaped at the fluffy creature, my fingers cramping to control my urge to stroke.

What. The. Hell?

'Your favourite, I believe?' That same cool voice but from the unicorn's sweet mouth; it blinked its large eyes. I'd always wanted a unicorn toy as a kid. But we don't get what we want. I'd learnt that lesson before I could toddle. *Could this angel read my memories...desires?* 'Surely you couldn't harm a—'

I yanked him up by his adorable twisted horn, dangling him high above the ground. His little hooves kicked, as he mewled.

Guffaws, beating of wings, and clapping.

Yeah, so I was playing to the audience: sue me.

It wasn't enough to simply defeat your opponent. The Bone Carnival demanded blood. I shrank back, however, at the thought of kicking a unicorn's arse...or even Mischief's.

The bloke had played with me like *I* was real and not the freakshow centrepiece.

When his cute pink muzzle attempted to pull back into a snarl, I tried to smother my grin.

'I claim the prize.' I shook Mischief again for good measure.

Misrule edged forwards, twirling his cane. 'Bones and blood...?'

This was the point I should be splaying Mischief's guts across the Cage, unless he truly had transformed into a toy and had stuffing inside him. Mischief was right, however, the black had retreated, and even though he'd been sly, I admired that he was a sneaky bastard.

You found a bloke's weakness and you shanked him sharp.

And he'd found mine.

I wasn't my dad's enforcer, here to mete out his punishments. I was his daughter, yet he wouldn't even see me. That was my weakness, not Mischief's magic.

Me against a toy unicorn? Hell, *I'd* pay to see that fight.

Misrule reluctantly nodded, amidst catcalls.

I dropped Mischief, and by the time he'd hit the floor he was back to his angelic self.

He ran his hand through his hair, smoothing it back, before holding out his wings. 'Go on then, exact your blood revenge on the loser.'

Instinctively, my hand dropped to the leather necklace of fangs around my neck: one pulled from every vampire I'd beaten. I rolled my eyes. 'Colour you dramatic.'

Mischief winced, as I plucked a grey feather from his wing, before hissing, 'Despite all, you're tamed.'

I shrugged, slipping his feather behind my ear jauntily. 'And you're a prick.'

Misrule gripped Mischief by the hair, hauling him to the corner of the Cage.

I sagged. At last, I could return to my bedroom — *cell* — and...

Misrule held up his arms again. 'A double feature!' I shook, my legs buckling: *the bastards.* 'Let us welcome the Seducer. Once the fiercest warrior amongst us, the Seducer is now *owned* by the fiercest warriors amongst us.' A burst of laughter from the vampires, who'd thronged around the Cage; their grins were feral, and their black eyes sparked. I trembled both with rage and fear because I hadn't seen the Seducer — Ash — since he'd betrayed me into the hands of the vampires. Yet he was also fam; he'd fought by my side and knelt for me. How the hell could I battle him, when I didn't know if I wanted to kill or save him? 'Bet on the bones. Then let the battle cleanse with pain!'

Skulls dropped from the roof at each corner, swinging with human blood: *a fortune.*

They wanted us to bastard kill each other.

Clank — the side pulled up, and Ash limped into the cage.

Naked.

His olive skin was paler than normal and purpled with bruises. His ribs showed clearly enough to be counted like he'd been starved. Had he even been fed since we'd been brought here?

Ash didn't raise his head to meet my gaze. I stared at him.

Bastard look at me.

Instead, he scrutinized the grime on his bare feet. Until fires, as bright as the spotlight, blazed in the corners of the Cage. Then he swooped at me, holding me close.

Despite my confusion, a sense of safety and home cocooned me, as his clove-fragranced wings did. He was quivering; little tremors ran through his body. I stroked my hands down his spine: each bone jutted out.

'Bet,' Ash whispered. At last, his gaze found out mine, and I caught my breath at the desperation, which made his eyes gleam. 'I bet I can beat you, Violet. And if I do, you give me all your winnings from tonight and now on.'

I frowned. 'Cool it, gambling-900. This is what you want to say to me?'

He swallowed. 'I'm sorry—'

'Now you're on the approved apology tracks.'

'...But I can't do the whole getting us dragged into the Under World drama thing, gorgeous. We bet, we fight. You probably kick my arse.'

I pouted. 'You've derailed. Apology crash alert.' I stroked the back of his neck with my fingers. Why did we have to be here, under the spotlight and forced to fight? 'So, what do I get if I win?'

Ash stiffened, drawing back from me; I instantly missed the warmth of his wings. 'Me — to punish for the night.' It was my turn to stiffen. 'And there it is, the apology. Burn me, cleanse me, kill me. Your chance to...punish the traitor.' Then he murmured, dropping his gaze, 'How else will you forgive me?'

I shoved him away. 'Who says you get to be forgiven?'

Clatter.

I jumped back, as weapons dropped from the

roof like screwed up confetti: swords, axes, and shanks.

They were serious about us getting down to business.

'Then I guess I am sorry because this is our *Fight Club* moment.' Ash raised a leather crossbow, which had fallen at his feet. It flamed with a hissing arrow.

My eyes widened; the pulse in my throat pounded.

Ash aimed, before firing the blazing bolt at my head.

2

I might have once been the angels' princess, but now I was Mistress of the Cage. And the Geek Fang should've been kissing my violet leather boots...not firing flaming bolts at me.

I twisted to the side, grimacing as I knocked my wrist *clanging* against the bars. When the bolt grazed my right wing, searing the feathers, I howled.

A *roar, gasps, cheers.*

My vampire audience outside in the chamber drove themselves into a fanboy frenzy over the challenger to their Champion.

I panted: *hell, Game On.*

Violet and black blasted in twin volcanos: angelic and vampiric side united in their fury to *punish* the bastard who'd dared damage my new wings, which had only been birthed on the night we'd flown from Angel World.

I growled, glaring at Ash across the heat of the

Cage.

He'd frozen, staring at the crossbow as if he'd never seen it before.

And just as I wanted to boot him in the balls, so I wanted to push back his sable mane and snog him until I'd calmed the clamouring inside to claim him as *mine*. Eighty-eight fights was too long to be without him.

Too long alone.

We'd all been pawns in Angel World's twisted sports. Yet I'd rejected my mum, power, and the Crown for Ash...and he'd been playing me, before betraying me and my angel blokes to the vampires.

He'd bet a night of punishment, hungering to get down with the whip and hairshirt look?

Ash had better prepare himself for penance Hackney-style.

Except, as Ash chucked the crossbow to the side, his charcoal eyes sparking, *he* was the panther ready to strike.

I sprang at him with a high kick, but he caught it, twisting me round. I scratched at his chest, gouging crimson lines, but he clung on, forcing me down. His mouth was set in a grim line; I'd never seen him fight like this. Panic shot through me in icy tendrils.

'I thought you only fought *for* me,' I gritted out.

Ash ground his elbow into my throat, and I choked. 'Funny thing, Violet, I begged you to kill me. You? Told me to *go back and kneel for the Fangs*. Went back, knelt, fangs.' His teeth lengthened, as his lips ghosted across mine. 'Why didn't you kill me?'

Bones and blood. Bones and blood. Bones and blood.

I shivered. I hadn't realized how freaky that tribal chant was until *I* was the poor bitch about to be turned into chunky salsa.

Tingles raced through my fingers, but my violet fire wouldn't ignite. *Why wouldn't my powers work?*

Ash tore back my armour; his hands shook. 'I can make you fly. I'm...different. I won't drink because your blood is precious, but we're the performing lions: I'll have to savage. Look, I wish I could be the hero but I've been stripped and spoiled, until there's nothing left.' He licked down my neck. 'This won't hurt.'

He kissed my throat; his fangs grazed my skin.

'I bet you say that to all the girls, *Seducer*,' I hissed.

He flinched. Why the hell did I still hate it that he flinched?

Let's go: it's violet time, J. Or I'll be the carcass safari-style.

And the Mistress of the Cage becomes Mistress of Scaredy-cat City! All it took was rebellion in the ranks.

Let me read you some realness: your powers only work with righteousness. And what's righteous about curb stamping your dad's enemies?

It's a fair fight. I'm like a prize boxer, yeah?

And I'm Mary Poppins, and you're battling Dick van Dyke.

Then Dick Van Dyke has bitching long teeth.

The king is training you. But it's not your fighting he's soldier drilling, it's your loyalty.

How many vampire fangs will you claim for pots of blood?

Ash hesitated, his lips pressed against my

throat; my pulse fluttered against his mouth.

Bones and blood. Bones and blood. Bones and blood.

Squirming, I reached for an ivory shank that'd been dropped into the Cage; my fingertips grazed the hilt. *Here little shanky, just another inch, you know you want to come to Feathers...*

Suddenly, a skull of blood swayed down from the roof and directly in front of Ash. The coppery scent coated my nostrils, just as Ash stiffened. His gaze darted to the skull; he licked his dry lips.

How long had he been starved?

I grasped the edge of the hilt... *Good little shank....* It thrummed, warm and alive in my palm.

At the same moment, the floor of the Cage heated. Even through my armour, I arched away from the burn. Distracted by the blood, Ash didn't notice the move, until I bucked up my hips, twisting our positions: him beneath and me on top. His naked back and arse pressed against the scorching floor.

Ash screamed.

I winced but pressed my blade to his throat.

Still keening, Ash stilled.

Bones and blood. Bones and blood. Bones and blood.

There'd been no thrill or dance to the fight. Instead, there'd been nothing but a deadly intent, which chilled me. Because for the first time my head was clear of the noise, light, rage...and I'd known what I was doing.

What I'd become.

My eyes burned; I blinked away the tears. No

way was I doing...*this*...again.

My dad could find himself another punisher.

You shake your thing, girl! You're the Mistress of the Carnival.

What about the unrighteous speech you rained down on me?

Where does *righteous* come into it?

You're not in Angel World anymore, Feathery-kitty, and you need to grab your bony pussy and work that thing until you're flooded in black as much as violet.

Cheers for making me chuck up.

If you're a Vampire Princess? This is the price. Choose.

I'd forgotten, J, that I even had a choice. But I'm awake now, and I won't be caged...or cage others.

I won't make anyone else pay the price.

Ash writhed, whimpering against the heat that was blistering him.

Sniggers.

I glanced up at the bars of the cage.

Misrule slumped to the side with his arms crossed. He managed a small smile. His gaze was concerned, however, threaded by a twitching fear.

I blazed to get medieval on the alpha prick who'd reduced Misrule's glorious joy: Supreme Commander Wild.

Wild was top boy of the FF: The First Fallen. The elite bastards were also known as the Feathered, the devoted army unit who'd rebelled first in Angel World with the king and Fallen by his side.

Yeah, I had another 'f' word to describe them and it wasn't only *fanatical*.

Wild, the leader of the Under World's enforcers, sprawled next to Misrule, with one meaty arm against the bars and the other wrapped around Misrule's shoulders, so tightly I could see the imprint of his fingers. Wild's shaved head, which was tattooed with wings, gleamed in the light; he wore nothing but a chocolate blazer open over golden chest, bondage trousers, and a hooped nose ring. When he caught my scrutiny, he winked like a malevolent jinn.

I flushed. Then I jolted.

Fair fight?

Weapons Ash had never fought with before...blood to distract him...heated floor when I was dressed and he was naked...

Wild had rigged it for me to win.

When I glanced around the Cage, I noticed other enforcers dressed in their standard chocolate blazers with leather belts, soaring around like bouncers at a gig.

Was any of this *anarchy* real? Or were the Feathered containing it like a police state?

Ash stared up at me; his eyes large in the spotlight. 'Claim your prize.'

'Bones and blood,' Misrule called.

I dipped my finger in the blood, tracing it over Ash's lips. He licked it off desperately, sighing. Then I wrenched back his head. 'This won't hurt.'

He laughed, but it could've been a sob. 'I bet you say that to all the boys.'

'Only the ones I defang.' I yanked out his canine with a twist.

He yowled.

Yeah, I lied about the not hurting. It'd hurt me like a bitch to do that to him as well.

Tugging out the leather necklace with the other eighty-seven teeth, I knotted on my trophy. Yet now the manic energy had cleared from my mind, I shook at the weight of so many...*manhoods*...strung around my neck.

Why the hell had I worn it with such pride before?

I wiped a tear off Ash's cheek. 'Stop with the kicked puppy routine; it'll grow back. It's not like I chopped off your hands.'

'Florence Nightingale rating? One out of ten. Although, you'd look hot in a nurse's outfit.' Ash struggled to edge off the floor, even though it was cooling.

I didn't miss the wince as he spoke, or the way he poked his tongue into the new gap where his fang had been.

'Not really into the dress up stage of our relationship. You lost the bet.' Something ancient and black inside fluttered at the way his eyes widened, and his breath became ragged. I dragged him closer. 'You're mine to punish for the night.'

Yet why did I wish Ash was mine, rather than owned by the FF, for more than the night? That I simply *owned* him?

The dominant bitch roared inside, as Ash cowered back, and in the close heat of the Cage to the beating wings, stamping feet, and howls of our vampire audience, I snogged him. Because I'd won him.

My prize.

Even as inside *I* was the one cringing, terrified at what I'd unleashed.

3

A Blood Princess, my blood was freedom. Yet in the Under World?

That freedom cost.

I staggered into the 'bedroom' that I'd been assigned as Cage Champion, steadying myself against the central pole from the hard shove to my back. The dust and cast-iron stink caught in the back of my throat.

I rubbed my hand suggestively against my fang necklace as I glared at Mr Pushy. 'Always room for one more, bastard.'

The FF, who had feathers down his cheeks like tears (maybe there was one for each angel he'd killed), snorted. 'By the light, bloodthirsty little thing, aren't you? You already have your prize. He'll be delivered to you once he's been...made pretty.' He leered, before sliding shut the door with a *clank*.

I sank onto a torn blue seat, running a hand through my hair. In a disused station of the London Underground, I slept in an old train carriage, which had derailed at Camden Town. The windows spiderwebbed with cracks, and bold primary colours splashed the walls with the routes beneath London. If the king hadn't shut off the tunnels with guards and darkness, I'd have escaped into the human world that the routes plotted out for me: *way to mock a bitch.*

The punk band, Shame's, aggressive drum and bass throbbed from Misrule's party on the other side of the tunnel: dangerous punk for the fearless outcasts.

When I yawned, stretching, two flashes of red uncurled from the back of the carriage and leapt onto my knee. I giggled, tumbling back beneath handfuls of silky fur, as two noses snuffled up and down me, whilst I writhed.

I waved an imaginary white flag. 'You got me. The Tickle Champion's crown goes to the fox brothers.'

My Blood Familiars, Blaze and Spark, pinned me underneath their paws.

One rust red and heavy, the other sleek and bright red, both were larger than a regular fox. And they'd abandoned me to stand by Ash at the battle of London Fields, even if they'd been returned to me like pets once I'd become Champion.

Yet now I'd glimpsed even a part of this shadow world…?

I soared with joy that Ash hadn't been left alone in his captivity. And that sometimes with them here, I could pretend I was truly a guest, not a prisoner.

Blaze's narrow head shot up and his intelligent amber eyes scrutinized me, before glancing at his brother. 'Away with you, I told you to stop greeting, she'd be returning in one piece with an extra fang around her neck.' His Scottish lilt weaved into my mind, mildly accusing: a telepathic slap.

I grimaced. Yeah, I so wasn't telling him *whose* fang it was, hanging next to the others.

Spark nuzzled at my singed wing. 'She's hurt, hurt, hurt,' he whimpered.

I stroked his brilliant white throat. 'Don't worry, bro. At least I didn't turn into a unicorn.'

'If you weren't our Keeper, numptie, I'd say you were off your head.' Blaze's eyes narrowed.

Spark whined, licking my hand. 'Sorry, sorry, sorry...'

'Hey, it's OK.' I caught his chin, tipping up his head. 'This numptie has a strict non arse kicking policy on foxes...and unicorns.'

Blaze huffed, hopping to the floor. 'Learnt that from Rebel, did you now? You were all for arse kicking when—'

'She wasn't our Keeper then,' Spark peeked over my knee at Blaze. I was tinged with the pride a mum must feel when the shy younger brother finally speaks up to his older one. 'She makes sure we're safe.'

Or maybe the tear-prickling impotency of a mum who knows she can't truly keep her kids safe from the bloke with a bottle of beer and a belt because even though I fought for my survival and my Blood Familiars', *we weren't safe.*

'If you're sulking, Blaze, I guess you don't want a share of the swag...' I reached underneath the seat. Misrule always changed part of my blood into different supplies, which was like the lucky dip at the fair each evening. *Anything but cold baked beans again...* I dragged out the first item, rubbing the sweet balls between the tips of my fingers. 'And the emperors shall eat grapes.'

I rolled one on my palm to Spark, before tossing a second to Blaze, who leapt and caught it.

'You're not going to peel them...?' Blaze raised

his tail.

'What did your last slave die of?' I dropped the grapes onto the floor, rustling back underneath the seat.

I yanked out the packet of chilli tortilla chips with a hoot of victory, startling Spark scurrying to the floor.

Rip — I tore open the packet.

When the hot aroma blasted me, I groaned.

Save your big 'O' moment for the Seducer, Feathery-sweetness, you'll want some pleasure with the punish.

All the pleasure I want is hard, spicy, and bad for you.

You've just read the Seducer's label.

It's not happening. You once told me that I'd destroy Ash if I tamed him.

Did I say tame?

You're the victor gladiator with the whore about to be delivered to your cell. Why waste the sweet ass spoils?

One-handed, I tore off my armour, hurling it across the carriage with a *thunk;* it whacked the Waterloo line.

Then I squirmed down, settling in for a nosh, holding up an orange triangle. 'The food of princesses.' Suddenly, the carriage lurched. I clutched the armrests; my chips sprayed out. 'Bastard...'

The foxes howled, cowering, as the windows rattled. The floor and ceiling pulsed, whilst the *human* underground pounded by in the tunnel on the other side of the wall. My knees rose and fell at the vibrations as if we were on a ghost train. At last, the underground passed, and the noise quietened.

Then two tiny, shuddering vampires crawled out of the bed, which I'd built in the corner out of the foam from inside the seats.

The Bloods.

My carriage had come installed with pets and slaves. I'd have settled for fresh towels and room service.

The Bloods were the lowest vampires in the Under World: Fallen angels who'd been born after the Fall. The Children of the Dark, they were untested and unable to join the higher ranks until they were.

Catch bastard 22.

Whining, the girls shuddered, as they knelt in nothing but the tattoos that covered them head-to-toe: living art.

'The bairns are starving,' Spark huffed, perking his ears and snuffling at the girls' shaved heads.

Blaze clicked comfortingly, circling them. 'Don't just gawk. Where's your real swag?'

I dragged out the bone skull, which had been tucked underneath next to the junk food.

This is my choice, J. If I don't fight, the kids starve.

I didn't say the choice was easy. Your daddy feeds you treats — familiars, slaves, chips — because a skank who has something to lose can be kept in line like a schoolkid.

If you'd been shut up with no one but your pretty little self, could even Hercules have forced *you* to whore yourself in the Cage?

I bristled, pushing the slopping blood towards the girls. They shuffled forward, peering at me.

Silent.

They were always silent. Why didn't Bloods talk? Couldn't they...or weren't they allowed?

Sighing, I dropped to my knees, stroking over the bristles on their shaved heads.

Instantly, they dropped to lap at the blood, cat-like.

I traced over the tattoos on their heads. Intricate tales of battles and the Fallen's myths: living fairy tales.

When I heard the *clank* of the doors, I snatched up my precious tortillas and hustled the Bloods and familiars into the toilet at the back of the carriage, snapping shut the cubicle. Then I twirled to face General Trick, the albino vampire who owned Ash and who'd captured us before *escorting* us to the Under World, who lounged in the carriage's doorway. He studied me, twirling one waist long strand of white hair around his finger. The silver hoops in his ears gleamed.

Crunch — I bit into a chip, licking the chilli dust off my fingers with an exaggerated slurp.

Trick shuddered.

'What's up?' I shook the packet, offering one to Trick who shrank back, dragging his black coat around himself against the spray of chilli. 'A Fang can't live on blood alone; let the sensations blow your mind.'

'I'll decline,' Trick curled his lip. 'Although, *sensation* shall suit you well in your wicked night with the Seducer, our Bone Princess.' I'd forgotten that his words were as cruel as an oiled blade: *congratulations on inciting the psycho*. 'A most interesting condition of such whores is that we allow them to bring delightful pleasure to others...'

Crunch.

Trick gaped at me, as I munched on the chip.

I gestured the universal *go on* with my stained hand. 'With you. Whores...delightful pleasure...?'

Trick shook his head, as if dislodging an

irritating fly. He tapped his fingers against the edge of the carriage door. 'But they're not allowed to find...their own completion...unless their wingtips are touched. As you can imagine, it keeps them in quite the state of readiness and trains them...'

Crunch.

Trick stared at me, then the bag of chips. If we'd been on the battlefield, we'd both have been a fine red mist. He took a deep breath; his foot was tapping now along with his hand. '...Into a state of passion, where even the lightest touch is akin to pain. When they're naughty, it takes little to punish...'

Crunch.

'Will you desist from that infernal feasting, you insufferable creature?' He howled, panting.

I hesitated, chip halfway to my lips. Then I smirked, dropping the tortillas onto the seat. 'What's with the Hulk out? You only had to ask.'

When Trick sidled towards me, sinuous as a snake, I stiffened. 'Then let me ask this, princess, isn't our world what you've always wanted? No rules? Star of our carnival? Dark anarchy to let out your monster? And a world to devour?' He pinched my arm, and I yipped. 'Are you even listening?'

Heat blossomed on my tongue, as I sucked my thumb of crumbs, letting it free from my mouth with a *pop*. 'Carnival, *blah*, anarchy, *blah*, monster, *blah*...'

'World to devour, *blah*, *blah*,' Ash's voice called from outside the carriage.

I sniggered.

Trick glowered, throwing up his bone-white

hands in disgust, as he stormed back to the doorway, yanking in Ash by the silver chain that bound his hands like a leash. He threw Ash to the floor in front of me: sacrificial victim.

And I was King Kong.

Ash sprawled on his side, as if he'd chosen to stretch out on a bed. Kudos on the not looking intimidated.

At least he wasn't naked now: he wore tight black jeans and unbuttoned shirt, with slashes at the back that freed his wings. I instantly missed his red military coat, which I'd ground into the mud on the Snowdonian mountainside.

Ash smiled. 'Hey, babe.'

'Two butter knives and a garlic crusher...is that creative enough on the *babe* death front?'

Ash shrugged. 'So worth it.'

'Butter knife, garlic crusher, or nut cracker, it matters not,' Trick muttered. This time Ash winced. Trick hesitated in the doorway, before slinking back into the frustrated howl of Misrule's party. 'One night to punish him. No one goes back on a bet here.'

At last, I crouched down in front of Ash; he quivered, battling to hold onto the mask of nonchalance.

The ancient possessive powers inside me roared to punish Ash for his betrayal. To force him to be mine again. Even as I touched my knuckles gently to his cheek.

'What's first?' Ash's gaze flickered to mine. 'Castration? Thumbscrews? Pear of anguish? Or straight down to the butter knife?' He touched a tentative thumb to my latex top. 'Although, the kinky bondage look's hot on you.'

Why the hell was the Master of Misrule in charge of dressing me for the Carnival...?

'Hold on there, torture happy, this isn't a medieval dungeon. And you set that bet, not me.' I flapped my seared wing. 'You fired at me. I'm not in the punishing fam business.'

Even if I was shaking with the effort to hold in the bitch.

'If you don't, General Trick'll think I went back on the bet, and *that* means a trip to medieval dungeon land.' Ash rolled onto his back, clasping his hands in front of him, caught in his chains: my spoils. 'I'm ready, Violet.'

'Not a military campaign, Brigadier.'

I hadn't expected the flinch.

When I crouched over Ash, the monster rattled inside, exultant, even as the carriage did with the passing of another train. Our bodies vibrated, joined by the wild thrumming. He gasped: *he truly was hypersensitive.*

I arched a brow, swinging my legs over him. I ran my fingers across his chest; his breath stuttered. 'Enough with the *burn you, cleanse you, kill you* crap. I won't hurt you to order.' My thumb grazed his nipple, tugging at the nub, and he keened. 'Sorry, chilli fingers.'

'Then what's with the Sharon Stone routine?'

I growled, throwing open his shirt and exposing him; he tilted his chin defiantly. 'You can't go back on a bet? And I can't hurt you? But there's no reason I can't *use* you: pleasure is pain. My mum taught me that freaky lesson. Don't worry, you won't even need to be bare arsed.'

I feathered ghost touches down Ash's sides, and he gritted his teeth. Down the fluttering muscles of his stomach, and he hissed as if I was branding him. Then I circled his nipples with a single finger, and he whimpered.

Was I truly scorching him with a touch? And

why did it spiral me higher on the black?

'See?' I murmured, as he tried to scrabble away. 'One finger.'

I clawed my nails into his wing, holding him still, and he bellowed. At the same time, the tenting in his jeans was hard against my thigh; the Seducer had been well *trained*.

'Would Princess Leia use Han like a toy?'

'The problem with that?' I stroked through Ash's feathers. 'You're not Han: you're bastard Lando. And I reckon Leia would do *this*...'

I edged my fingers towards his wingtips.

I burned, as much as he must be burning. My mind was clouded by a berserker rage that twined with an inferno of possessive desire.

What the hell was I doing?

How screwed sideways was it that I no longer knew how to control the beast, which had grown stronger after every fight? I shivered, struggling to battle it down...*to stop it hurting Ash like this...*

No, no, no...

Abruptly, Ash shoved at me with his bound hands, and I stumbled back onto my arse. 'Your eyes...' He stared at me. 'They're doing the fairy glow thing: sparking with light. That's the *king* playing inside your head.'

'Try again, bro,' I snarled.

Frustrated, Ash pinned me with his wings, and I was flooded by their scent, like being wrapped in a clove studded orange. 'The king's power is to spark light...fervour...into your deepest desires. To incite rebellion, anarchy, or...'

'The bitch?'

'You said it. And just so you know: I'm not one of your kinky angels. I don't play games of submission. I can't fight what I've been turned into but I will fight *you* if you touch me like that again.

Note the deadly sincerity.'

The toilet door burst open.

First came the *geekering* guttural chatter, as the Blood Familiars leapt up onto the seats, and then nothing but *hissing* crimson.

Whistle — red whips flashed through the air.

Ash twisted to the side, before the sticky coils of the whip slashed down over my face.

I screamed, as they burnt like jelly fish stings, clinging to my skin. I ripped at the strands, but they glued my hands. Caught in the scarlet, I thrashed, as the Bloods advanced on me. Their tattoos weaved — alive — out of their skin.

I cringed, curling up my knees. I was desperate to look away but when a nightmare comes to life instead of a fairy tale, there's nowhere to hide from the monsters.

'I'm safe,' Ash murmured. Even through my shaking, I could see his eyes gleamed like he was holding back tears. *Why did he care about my Bloods?* 'You can turn off destruction mode. I'm here now.'

When the tattoo whips pulled back, sinking into the Bloods' skin as if it'd never danced to life, I groaned: that was me flayed.

'So, that happened,' I blinked.

Ash held out his arms to the Bloods, and they darted to him, one nuzzling into each shoulder. He shook, and this time I *knew* it was from tears.

My mind was clearer than it'd been...maybe since I'd been brought here. As if the tattoos had sucked the king's light out like poison, freeing me from his fervour.

I touched the fang necklace and I remembered the joy that had zinged through me, whilst I'd held Ash down and tormented him with my touch.

What the hell had I done?

I ripped off the necklace, sickened by the feel of each fang and the memory of every *howl* as they'd been torn from my defeated opponents. Struggling to swallow, I hurled it skittering across the carriage. Then I ducked my head, nudging the skull with what remained of the blood dinner towards Ash. 'If the king-sparked bitch makes another appearance, you take the reins. Until then, the prisoner of war look doesn't suit you.'

Hell, as apologies went it was the best I could manage.

Ash gave a curt nod, but he lifted the skull to each of the Bloods first, stroking their wings, before he drank. I could tell how much it cost him not to guzzle the blood in desperate gulps, instead taking casual sips.

Afterwards, he panted, bending over as if even that much blood pained his guts.

I edged closer. 'You know my Bloods?'

Or the freaky creatures with the epic tattoo whips...

He eyed me coolly. 'They're not yours, Violet.' I pinked. 'They're *my* sisters.'

I jolted, and he hugged his sisters closer.

Hell, had Ash's sisters been placed in my room to control Ash. Or to control me?

'Why aren't they with you?'

Ash's laugh was bitter. 'You free Angel World's slaves, but it's OK for vampires to be kept as pets? Our parents died, but I wasn't allowed to raise my sisters. I can't...save them...but I've sacrificed myself to stop them becoming *me*.'

The Bloods stared at him with wide gazes. Their tattoos glowed, as they burrowed closer.

'I've lost my sister too.' I traced across the pouch around my neck, which held my sister's crystal necklace. *And how had the fang necklace*

34

tricked me into forgetting it? 'She and all the disappeared kids of Hackney could be here. Have you been a good little soldier for the Fangs, or have you found them?'

Ash's eyes narrowed. 'I've been out there *alone*. Kept on a leash by the FF. Now I know where the angels are because Supreme Commander Wild's bedtime routine is less cup of tea, bed, and more whip the angels, bed.'

I didn't miss his anguish at Rebel and Harahel's pain because it smarted through me as well. Ash had savaged Rebel's throat during our escape from Angel World. Had his taste of my bonded angel connected him, even closer than their centuries united *against* each other in the war between angels and vampires had?

Or did they have something else in their entwined pasts that had transformed them from enemies to reluctant mates?

My hands curled into fists. 'If they want the monster out to play, then they can have it on their arses. We're taking back my fam.'

Startled, Ash pushed off his sisters and towered over me, his wings beating. 'Overruled. You thought the Matriarch was an Ice Bitch, she's nothing to your dad's Fire Devil. I want to save Rebel and Harahel too. But if we steal the king's prisoners, he'll burn us and sell seats. And I'm fond of my sexy arse. You think the fights are just entertainment? They're to publicly prove your loyalty and kill your angelic side.' His expression gentled. 'You can't love the enemy.'

'Stick that, bro.' I pushed myself up, tracing his lips. 'I never did well with rules.' At a sudden tugging at my leg, I looked down. The sisters had pressed themselves between Ash and me protectively. I sighed, kneeling down in front of them. 'I'm not going to hurt your bro. Again.'

They glanced at each other out of the corners of their eyes, before nodding. But their tattoos still glowed.

I traced my hand over one, but Ash caught my wrist.

'Ask,' he said tightly, 'before you touch.'

There should be a limit on how many times you can blush in one day.

He was bastard right.

I peered at the crazy mix of lines that told intricate tales. One blazed brighter: an angel on the Blood's back. She held aloft a trident, standing atop a mountain of feathers, above a valley of bones...

I gasped.

The bitch was me.

'Bloods are inked in the tales and prophecies of our people,' Ash whispered, 'like our family photos.'

'Then why am I...?'

Ash tilted his head. 'I thought I was your fam...?'

I pointed a shaky finger at the trident. 'What the hell am I doing with that killer fork?'

Ash dropped his gaze. His voice was clipped. 'You're destroying the world.'

I jerked, knocking back Ash; the Bloods whimpered. I blundered away from the tattoo and every dark desire and fear inked out on flesh.

My chest was tight, as I struggled for breath.

Ash reached for my hand, but I snatched it away. 'Violet...'

'Prophecies jerk you around. I'm not falling for the self-fulfilling trap. I'm rescuing Rebel and Harahel. You wanted punishment? Then you spend one night with me taking on the bastard FF who play fetch with you.'

Ash nodded, holding out his hands.

I undid the chains that chafed his wrists. 'My dad awoke the monster. Now he can meet the bitch.'

Yet I hid my shaking hands in the pockets of my trousers because this was the first time I'd been free to step outside the cage, including the one that'd been built inside my own mind.

We had one night to save the angels from the vampire elite guard, risk Wild's punishment, and defy a king who could cast us into the flames.

4

Obedience had been the doggy trick for the kids in Jerusalem Children's Home who, with tamed smiles, had been conning their way into the adults' hearts.

That is, for the kids who had a chance to be adopted.

With one violet eye and one black...? I was the freaky kid who scared prospective parents away with a look.

Yeah, the world's crappiest super power.

What did *obedience* gain me? No one tamed the Bitch of Utopia because no one wanted her. Or *needed* her.

Now that I had fam, however, mine was the heart that could be split bloody. At last, *I was needed*.

So, could I also be taught to obey?

Misrule's cane *thwapped* on the arched wall, blocking Ash and my way into the Ossuary and the angels' cells.

I jumped; sweat trickled between my shoulder blades in the furnace heat. The air was so thick it stuck in my throat, damp and heavy, like being suffocated by a wet cloth. I choked on my own spittle, backing up.

Ash caught my elbow, wincing as I stepped on his toes in the gloom.

Misrule waggled the wing bones on the end of his cane, as if we were naughty kids caught behind the bike sheds.

So much for our stealthy mission to save the angels.

Ash and I had crept to the deepest FF owned tunnels, only for the Master of the Cage to step out and block our way.

'I thought you had an orgy to run, cravat face?' I shoved at the cane, but Misrule only stepped closer.

'And I thought you had a Seducer to punish?' He shoved Ash against the wall, which was encrusted with fangs, and nibbled up his neck. He smacked his lips. 'Delicious. Is this why my monster has run away from the Bone Carnival? Or...' Ash glared, as Misrule traced down his chest. 'Does that lie within the Ossuary bones?'

'Why? So, you can toss them in the Cage and make me beat on them too?'

Misrule cocked his head. 'The Under World would go wild for an angel vs vampire feature but,' he spun me, catching me in the sweetness of his cherry wings; his lips grazed my ear, 'I Fell with my lover, Tiger, and he was stolen. I know the heart of pain, so how could I steal from you, what I lost?'

Ash smirked, crossing his arms. 'Plus, it helps you have a hard on for angels.'

'What...?' I spluttered.

Misrule drew back, throwing Ash a knowing

look. 'Takes one to know one.'

Then it was Ash's turn to splutter.

Misrule twirled his cane. 'Our new world under the ground was meant to be a fresh start, uncontrolled. But as you may have noticed, the FF squeeze our balls with rules.' He grinned. 'We're rebels. Let's snog rebellion until it swoons.'

'Bitching speech,' I linked my arm with Misrule, as we slipped through the archway. 'I'm tingling with Marlon Brando feels already.' Ash, however, slunk down the narrow tunnel opposite. 'Where are you going? We're having a moment here.'

Ash's smile was tight. 'Guards. Distraction. Seducer. Not drawing you a diagram.'

I jolted towards him, but Misrule held me back. 'It's what he does for the FF. It's what he is.'

'Allow that,' I hissed. 'He's a funny brave geek who loves *Star Wars*, iconic pop culture, and gaming. *That's* what he is. He's not the FF's, you get me?'

Misrule studied me. 'You're different. Something's changed.' I stiffened. Then he leaned in, conspiratorially. 'I love it, and the king's going to hate it.'

'Bring it on.' I marched into the Ossuary. My own dad didn't even want to see me, yet he reckoned he could control me? 'Let's see how *he* likes taking on the Bone Princess.'

I spun in the centre of the cavern, gasping against the suffocating black.

Violet flared from my feathers and Misrule's wingtips before it danced along my skin in skittering sparks: fire goose bumps. I shivered, as it lit the brick walls; the air thrummed, and the roof throbbed.

Crack, crack, crack.

At each step, I crunched over the bones, which were also piled in haphazard pyramids in each corner. At last, I was walking over the land of bones, which had plagued my nightmares and desires since my powers had second puberty stirred within me on my twenty-first birthday. It wasn't trapped within my mind or a tattoo.

What came next? *Did I destroy the world?*

I hadn't realised I was bent over, wheezing, until Misrule had his arms around my waist, soothing me down from the panic attack.

'Where are they?' I panted.

Misrule pointed at the walls.

Yeah, so I had to ask.

The metal doors looked like ovens in a Victorian bakery, and my angels would be just about done by now.

Misrule yanked open a metal door.

There was a sudden desperate breath from the black, before Misrule pulled Harahel out in a sweep of waist length burnet curls, swinging him round in a flurry of apple-scented wings.

I guess Ash was right about Misrule's hard on for angels.

How often had Misrule risked the FF's punishment to visit the prisoners...my fam?

I scanned Harahel for injuries. Although he seemed weak this far under the ground without sunlight — the food an angel needed to survive — his slight body, still only wearing his ash silk harem trousers, was unmarred.

There wasn't even a single welt across his pale back.

So, apart from the buried alive bit, that was one-up on Angel World.

Yet everything had a cost here; I'd been paying

mine in the Cage. What had Misrule's been to protect his pet from the FF? Had that been why he'd allowed Wild's arm to press around his shoulder?

To *rig* the fights?

'Hey, breathing isn't optional,' Harahel sniggered, slapping Misrule's back.

Misrule nuzzled Harahel's neck, before allowing him to stand on his own feet. Not before he'd tenderly kissed the stump of Harahel's missing hand. Harahel blushed, but he didn't pull away, and I didn't miss the gesture.

On Angel World, Harahel had been reduced to the ranks of the Imperfect because of the loss of his hand but here he'd been chosen by the highest-ranking civilian.

Misrule spoke more in that kiss than any words.

'What do you weep in my ear every time I see you? What gift could I conjure to stop your tears?' Misrule murmured.

'Enough with the mocking,' Harahel pouted. 'I'm small but wind me up and watch me explode. BOOM!'

'Pull back on the atomic tantrum, tiny terror. I don't want to be washing you out of my hair all week,' I smirked, pushing past Misrule, who let go of Harahel with a smile.

Harahel's violet eyes widened, before I was enveloped in a koala bear clinging angel who was quivering hard enough to break apart.

Why hadn't I fought harder to find and protect him? Had my dad's angelic power truly been clouding my mind? I could still feel it inside me: the shifting black that snarled with rage and the thirst for battle, which my dad's fervour had incited and controlled. But I'd allowed it. Revelled in it. *Desired* it.

My angelic side had been as buried as the angels.

Harahel stroked my back, before finally lifting his head from my shoulder. 'The perfect gift. Although,' he traced a fading bruise underneath my eye, 'I'd have picked different gift wrap.'

'By the shadows, where's the kneeling?' Misrule tapped his cane on the floor. 'Don't you angels worship her? I'd heard tales of cowering—'

Harahel's eyes twinkled, before he cringed back in mock terror, falling to his knees before me on the bones – *crunch*. He pressed his forehead to the floor, and I rolled my eyes. 'Forgive me, oh powerful and wise one, for I'm only a lowly Imperfect and should never raise my gaze upon the face of my—'

'You say *princess*, I'll boot you in the balls. No fam of mine calls themselves Imperfect. That's a banned word, like *moist* or *butthurt*. And you don't want to see me go BOOM. Get up, bro.'

Misrule's grip tightened on his cane as he watched us, but Harahel only slouched to his feet with a shrug.

Harahel patted Misrule's arm. 'I was her Trainer and her Poly-Wing.' Misrule cast me a glare that made me glad I wasn't still in the Cage. 'She didn't touch me,' he added softly, 'she saved me.'

'How fascinating that it's now *I* who save you,' Misrule dragged Harahel closer again. 'Maybe your *princess*,' *yeah, the bastard was daring a Violet style explosion*, 'is now all monster?'

I winced.

Harahel snorted. 'She was always all monster. You two should play nicely together.'

I scanned the other oven doors, pressing my nails into my palms. 'Which one's Rebel?'

My punk angel hated...feared...the dark. I'd

promised he'd never be put back into it again. Yet he'd been kept in this suffocating black...

'So, the Bone Princess wants her pet angel?' Wild's gruff Brummie accent startled me from the mouth of the Ossuary.

I spun, but Wild barred the entrance, his arms crossed over his broad chest. FF guards ranked behind him, clutching Ash between them.

Hell.

Ash's gaze met mine, before he forced himself to offer a brittle smile.

It couldn't hide his swollen eye or cut lip.

Wild had just lit up the bitches inside me, and soon *he'd* be the one lit up.

You're in the heart of Fascists Are Us homeland. You don't have your tickled punk yet. And you don't even know what Daddy Devil wants.

Think before you choose the angelic prisoners over the asshole gaolers who hold the shiny keys.

Allow that, J. These assholes hurt my fam.

They also run this underground pageant where you wear the sash for Miss Vampire.

Sometimes being on the inside works better than being on the outside.

What? I should go undercover? Pretend I'm all vampire?

The Supreme Commander expects a throw down. What better reason to deny the shady dick?

The ancient powers inside howled, twisting up my throat, until I choked to spew out my fire and barbeque the smug face of the bastard lounging in the doorway.

Instead, I forced the flames back down to sizzling embers before meeting Wild's scrutiny.

'Cheers, I need a punching bag between fights.'

Ash's smile faltered; I hated the wariness lurking behind his gaze.

'Princess...' Misrule tugged my sleeve.

Smack — I slapped him across the cheek.

Misrule raised his hand to the hot mark, staring at me through shocked eyes.

'What did I just say about calling me *princess*?' I steeled myself not to look back as I stalked towards Wild. I'd never have been able to keep up the lie if I had. *Undercover was harder than it looked.* 'Let's bounce, yeah?'

Snap.

I glowered down at the cuffs that Wild had locked around my wrists. I pulled at them, but there was no budge: angel and vampire proof.

Wild winked. 'It's not that I don't trust you...' When he leaned closer, patting my cheek, I flinched. '...But I don't trust you.'

'Back at you, times a thousand, no returns.' Something about Wild brought out the kid in me. I only just fought the urge to stick out my tongue.

Nonplussed, Wild stared down. 'I see there's much training to do before you become my Bonded, wench.'

Bonded? As in, his vampire bitch?

'Hold the wedding bells,' I choked, my heart thundering worse than in any fight in the Bone Carnival.

Wild petted my hair, before prowling to Misrule. 'We had an arrangement, and you've broken it by bringing *her* here.'

Misrule's arm tightened around Harahel. 'You think you *bring* the Bone Princess anywhere?' He scoffed. 'By my blood, if you want pain for this, then punish me. I'm sure it'll put on quite a thrilling spectacle in the Cage.'

'You're half-soaked if you don't know what I want.' Wild leant over Harahel, ruffling his feathers; Harahel trembled. 'The FF have been clamouring for him. The price for his arse alone has gone up, and you can no longer pay it.'

Violet surged through me: why had I imprisoned myself? Now I couldn't save Harahel.

'Please...' For the first time, Misrule's charisma waned, and I glimpsed the bloke underneath who was as fragile as he was tough.

'Begging?' Wild's lips curled. 'How many beg in your bones and blood show? How many are granted mercy?'

'None,' Misrule's voice was hard, 'but I didn't set the rules. Just like this one.'

I jolted, as Misrule's teeth sank into Harahel's throat with a *crunch*; Harahel shrieked.

'*Bastard no.*' I fell to my knees.

Crack — the bones broke, dusting me in white.

Wild dragged Misrule off Harahel, slamming him against the wall.

Harahel fell next to me amongst the bones, and I cocooned him in my wings. The scent of his spring orchard blood juddered through me, as it dribbled down his neck onto his chest. Tears soaked his cheeks.

I clutched him tighter. 'Way to protect a bloke, bastard.' I hissed at Misrule.

'Actually, that'd be a yes,' Misrule panted. Wild's long black claws pinned him through the shoulders against the brick. 'I've claimed him as my sole Blood Lover. I'm owed one, since mine has been missing so long. I'd only wished to take the willing but.... Well, who's willing in this dance?'

Wild withdrew his claws with a *squelch*, and

Misrule slumped. 'The gaffer will have something to say about this.'

Misrule sighed. 'Doesn't he always?'

Wild wound his fingers in my hair before I could pull away, wrenching me to my feet.

Still dazed, Harahel tried to hold onto my legs, but was booted back.

'Come on, wench, let's leave the happy couple together.' Wild leered. 'I have a pet to break and a princess to tame.'

'This monster won't be domesticated,' I growled, struggling.

Yeah, undercover wasn't my thing.

Wild only chuckled as he dragged me out of the gloom of the Ossuary and into the dark.

Trussed in chains, *I'd* become the sacrifice for the top boss of the elite guard.

When Wild Bonded with me, I'd be forever trapped in the Under World.

5

A violet feather floated in the copper rich air of the Charnel House. I batted it away with my manacled hands as I shifted on the floor. Wild nudged me onto a steel stool in the corner, and my back scraped against the wall, which was pitted with fangs.

How many enemies of the FF had they been ripped from? Had they all been tortured in this Charnel House?

I couldn't look anywhere but the wooden slab, which was suspended on chains from the centre of the room, waiting for gingerbread men fresh from the oven and ready for decorating.

And Rebel was the gingerbread man — bare arsed, of course, apart from the spiked black collar around his throat. Chained faceup, with his violet wings spread wide and his skin translucent in the spectre light of our feathers alone, he was just waiting for the baker...

I tugged on my own chains, bruising my wrists,

as I stared at Rebel, hungering for the *slam* of his sugar blood after so long apart.

Craving all of him.

Why wasn't Rebel moving?

I catalogued the yellow, green, and purple of past beatings, healing blister burns, and scabbed slashes.

What gave me the Mythically Screwed tingles, however, was his stillness. Rebel was a bouncing, unpredictable, volatile ball of energy that had torn through my life and thrown it into chaos.

He shouldn't be *motionless*, as Wild teasingly stroked his wingtips.

'Enough with the wandering hands. This one's mine,' I snarled.

My pulse pounding, I reached through our bond: *silence.*

What the hell have they done to Rebel?

How about worrying about what Supreme Commander Jinn will do to your hoochie mama ass?

If he Blood Bonds with you, he'll be the one with the reins. Nothing but death will separate you.

The bastard can't force a bond. There's no way I'm offering up my neck.

Like tall, dark, and caney sank his fangs into our sweet apple thing? Now Harahel's his Blood Lover, no permission needed.

A Blood Bond *can* be forced.

But if bonds only go one way, they're tricky things: consent's a shady whore. She sells herself for bargains.

Wild stared down at Rebel, before petting his red hair. 'No need to throw a wobbly, wench, the whole world knows he's *yours*. After all, you Marked him as your bed slave.'

I flushed.

Wild pushed aside the hair on Rebel's neck: **VZ** stood out in a blood tattoo. I couldn't deny I'd had Rebel Marked to claim and control him.

To force him to kneel.

Except, I'd been under the influence of my mum's — the Matriarch's — poisoned love at the time.

I wasn't as blind to my dad's world as I'd been to hers. The dreams I'd had of my parents growing up alone in the children's home? They'd been chased away by the nightmares.

Parents, they screw you sideways.

My true fam was lying on the wooden slab and he still hadn't moved.

When Wild traced his fingers over the Mark, I growled. Only the owner of a Mark could touch them in that intimate place.

Wild chuckled. 'Possessive? We're well matched.'

'Are you going to share with the rest of the class or cling to your Big Bad posturing?'

When Wild clawed his nails into the Mark, I jolted.

Thank hell Rebel wasn't conscious or he'd be a screaming puddle.

'After all, you only want him as your *punching bag...?*' Wild traced the **V** with his nail until it beaded with blood. I winced, unable to dodge my own words thrown back at me. I was more Austin Powers than Nick Fury. *Underhand bastard.* 'The good behaviour you see here is a dead handy mind control I've been training. The soft babby's bawling was giving me a worse migraine than sunlight. I warned him. Now, he can hear and see us, but he can't move so much as a feather....'

'Feel us...?' I quivered.

Wild leant his strong forearms on the slab. 'How would he learn if he didn't feel?'

Hell, hell, hell...

When Wild unwound the belt around his waist, doubling it over, before tying the buckle end around his fist, I recoiled against the wall. 'Call me a feminist, but my dream dates don't start with a bloke wielding a strap. I blame *50 Shades of Grey.*'

Wild stared at me blankly, before glancing down at his hand as if he hadn't even realised there was a belt hanging from it. 'Oh, bab, I'd never strike *you.*'

Crack, crack, crack.

The leather *thwapped* across Rebel's chest, marking him with livid welts.

I leapt up, but Rebel didn't move. There wasn't even a flicker across the bond. He was trapped in his own body, however, and I knew he felt it.

And that was bastard worse.

'Sit down,' Wild thundered.

'Do one,' I grasped Rebel's limp hand between my manacled ones, massaging his palm with my thumb.

He could hear me, see me, feel me...please let him feel me...

'I said,' suddenly Wild's voice was cold as ice water, and I shivered, 'sit down.'

Crack.

The belt whipped across Rebel's nipples. A fiery weal stained dusk across the nubs.

But I didn't let go of Rebel's hand. Instead, I hissed at Wild, 'Bones, blood, bodies like corpses...it's all freaky morbid. Either you're a thwarted mortician or a closet necrophiliac.'

Wild's calm shattered, and the next barrage of blows criss-crossed scarlet lines. 'I said,' he clenched his jaw, 'sit. Down.'

I craved to shoot calming emotions through the Mark to Rebel and show him my joy of being with him again...*my love*...that I couldn't say in front of Wild.

I'd sacrificed Rebel's little brother, leaving him behind in the cruel arms of the Matriarch, to save the slaves and my fam in Angel World. I'd never had a chance to talk to Rebel alone about it, or help him grieve, before the vampires had caught us, and I'd been dragged away from him.

Despite what Wild thought, however, I could learn, and the Mark was a violation. I wouldn't force myself on Rebel, like Wild was now, or control him.

I wouldn't be the same as these bastards.

I clutched Rebel's hand more tightly.

Then Wild rested the leather across Rebel's vulnerable prick, before raising the belt behind his shoulder.

Check mate.

I took a shuddering breath before I stumbled back to the stool.

I booted the wall behind me, as Wild eyed me, hesitating. 'It seems the princess can be tamed.'

'You want me tame? I thought you'd been playing my manager in the Cage to turn me feral.'

Wild opened his mouth as if to say something, before shutting it again.

I grinned. 'Yeah, the bitch isn't just a pretty arse.'

Wild hurled the strap along the floor. 'Savage by my side, tamed in bed.'

The black beast, which had been growing monstrous inside me trapped underground, roared.

My skin prickled, my insides burned, and my eyes flooded with shadows.

I would never kneel for another. I was the Bone Princess.

'I'd take that back if I were you,' I whispered, fidgeting in my seat. My nerves were grated raw.

'Why?' Wild scrutinised me. 'Stop riling like a kid with a whipped behind. I'm not the Master of Misrule: I won't force you. You'll Blood Bond willingly.'

I lifted an eyebrow. 'Not even if you pissed rainbows.'

'You're a strange one, but I'll get Mischief working on the rainbows. For now...?' Wild stabbed a claw into Rebel's wing; I missed the way Rebel should've yowled.

And the way I knew he must be inside.

'Enough with the Pincushion Game. If consent's forced it stops being consent, Brainiac.'

Wild dug in a second claw, and I flinched. 'It's a bargain. That's willing enough for me. Your pet for your bond.'

Hell, hadn't J warned me?

I panted, rubbing my sweaty palms together.

How could I leave Rebel to this? I'd claimed him, and he'd fought by my side, kneeling for me.

No way I was abandoning my fam.

When Wild's third claw shot out, I hollered, 'Allow it. Don't touch him, and I'll—'

'Supreme Commander,' Trick's head popped through the archway like an albino mole, 'you're needed on the battlefield. There's been an attack—'

Wild bellowed, spinning to Trick with such ferocity even Trick's lounge lizard arrogance slipped. 'One more moment...*just* one... This was a bargain...'

'And this is *war*,' Trick held up a thin finger.

'The angels attack at our very heart.' His scrutiny slid to me, before he sneered, 'You had one night to punish my Seducer, yet I find you here with an angel: fascinating. How many worlds will you devour, destroyer?'

'How about just yours?'

Trick huffed, wrenching at his hair that'd been braided ready for battle. 'Commander Drake and the Glories have attacked our Blood Lovers.'

Drake?

I grinned. My harem angel Commander Drake was still alive. My guard and Rebel's gaoler, Drake had been gifted by his dad, the Mage, as Marked Wing to my mum. She'd shown me every version of twisted love on him, but he'd still helped us to escape.

I'd mourned him because the Matriarch wasn't the forgive and forget type, more the string up, torture, and then flay alive type. If Drake was leading his kid army, then he'd survived her punishment. And I couldn't help the squirming inside at how much I'd *missed* him.

When Trick slunk towards me, Wild blocked him, playing the possessive husband. Trick rolled his eyes. 'You brighten at the name of our darkest enemy, princess. Are you naughtily still traitor? Loyal to the angel world that you shook from your sandals? And here I was mistakenly believing you cared for humans...'

'Humans, bro?'

Trick examined his nails. 'Blood Lovers can be claimed from angels, vampires, mages, witches...or humans. The cowardly angels have launched their wicked attack against the Blood Lovers' quarters. The Matriarch does love to sacrifice her pawns and she's baiting you by attacking our weakest.'

I pushed myself up, glancing between the two

vampires. I didn't trust the bastards but couldn't leave humans unprotected. Rebel had always taught me as a huntress to save lives.

Yet could I fight against Drake and the kid army I'd promised would always be my fam when I'd fought on their side?

Kill those I'd risked my life to save?

'New bargain,' I muttered.

'Wait,' Wild grabbed for my arm, but I smacked away his hand: no touchy feely for him. 'You were just about to—'

'Kick your arse? Sprout horns? Dance the fandango?' I bounced on the balls of my feet, as the ancient powers built within me. 'The bargain's this: I'll fight to protect the Blood Lovers from the angelic horde. But you free the captive angels into my care.'

Trick glanced at the grey feather behind my ear. 'Deals are precise. We're not freeing every angel. So, which prisoners?'

'*My fam*. Free my blokes.'

'On my bones and blood, deal,' Trick touched the fanged necklace around his neck, and I copied him, touching the pouch with my sister's crystal angel necklace instead. 'Although, be aware that the king is the ultimate arbitrator: judge, jury and...you can whistle the rest. If he wishes to overturn our little bargain, his power is such—'

'He can juggle twelve virgins, whilst battling the angelic hordes with only his death glare and yodelling "Slap My Bitch Up"?'

'I'll give you a right lamping when this...crisis...is over for your dealings with my wench,' Wild barked at Trick.

Trick airily waved his hand. 'Let us save the Blood Lovers first, or the king shall have all our wings. Now we have the Champion as mascot: our tamed beast.'

I swallowed, running my hand along Rebel's welted chest, before dipping to kiss him on the cheek.

I'd bargained for his freedom and Harahel's. Allied myself with the vampires against the angels for my fam.

But freedom had a price.

I had to be the savage the Bone Carnival had trained but tamed under the FF's leash.

I was going to war.

6

War had never tasted so candy sweet.

If I'd paid for freedom, then why shouldn't I sample the wares?

Slam.

I shuddered, swept up in Rebel's coppery sweetness. Then I swooped, crushing Rebel against the wall of the underground tunnel, shivering in the shadows.

The king's cold lights showed us the route in ranks of flickering fireflies. The railway line and the tunnel walls stank of oil, but the only scent, as we'd flown towards the battle to save the Blood Lovers, that had called to me had been the *slam* of Rebel's blood.

Slam.

I licked up Rebel's neck, quivering at the sugar

tingles, which zinged through me. I pushed his arms this way and that, running my fingers through his bent wing and his unbroken one, to see them arch and flex, *move* at last, freed from the mind control. Even if it was me holding him up, as if he was able to fully fly.

Like that hadn't been stolen from him.

Joy, desire, and a pissed off tinge at being treated like a puppet...

Yeah, that was my Rebel.

I could feel him again, throbbing through my bond. I soared on the emotions erasing the bastard *silence.*

Slam.

Treacled passion slid down my throat.

I stroked my fingers over Rebel's harness and scabbard with his sword — Eclipse — and his ripped black t-shirt, pressing my fingers against the punk safety pins, just to feel he was *real.*

To hell with being alone.

When I pressed my hands lower towards his red bondage trousers, however, Rebel caught my hands between his. 'Sweet Jesus, woman, would you take it easy? Trapped as I was in my own head, I heard every word, including how close you were to bonding with the git just to save my idiot self. Fair play to you, but a princess doesn't sign away her life for a bad angel.'

I touched my lips to his: tender and chaste. 'What about for fam?'

A polite — or not so polite — cough behind me.

I twirled: a pair of narrowed violet eyes sparked at me in the gloom.

I smirked at Mischief, as he flapped his wings, hovering in the middle of the tunnel: A Silver Fairy playing gooseberry.

My False Rebel didn't like being a shadow to the real thing.

It's called karma, bitch.

'When one bargains in the Under World,' Mischief lifted his head regally, 'one should choose one's words carefully, not like a troll with mashed turnip for brains. *Free the captive angels*? *My blokes?* As if my life was not enough of a nightmare, it appears I am now *yours* because of a battle lost in the Cage and my grey feather worn in your hair.'

'And when *one* pisses off the Bitch of Utopia,' I flew closer to Mischief, tugging the straps of my armour tighter; Rebel dropped, holding himself just above the ground with his bad wing, 'one gets turned into a unicorn sparkler.'

I couldn't help remembering plucking the feather from Mischief's wing, and the way it'd rubbed silkily behind my ear. I'd tossed it away whilst I'd prepared for battle and now I missed it. *What the hell was wrong with me?*

Trick had warned deals were *precise*... I should've listened. Now I had Mischief *in my care*, whilst Harahel remained in Misrule's because according to vampire law, being made into a Blood Lover, whether forced or not, officially changed your family like marriage. Harahel belonged to Misrule, meaning he hadn't been covered in my bargain.

Lucky me, I received Mischief instead.

Violet flames danced on the tips of my fingers.

Mischief shank back. 'Get on with it. At least I won't have to fight in this farce.'

I scrutinised Mischief. The bloke had some balls, even if his hands trembled. I trooped the sparks along the arms of his tunic and onto the strands of his hair.

I grinned; so that's how to make a supernatural *sparkle*.

Mischief hissed, but the fire wasn't burning him, only playfully tingling like static.

Except, if I wanted to, it could…

Mischief didn't move, however, because he was a smart bloke. I liked that.

'I'll make a note of it,' Mischief breathed, 'just before we die battling…oh yes, *our own side*.'

'Screw that brand of pessimism. We're throwing ourselves into the meat grinder but we'll gank the Bad Guys and save the damsels.'

'And which is which again?'

I flared the flames brighter, and he gasped. 'Whichever I tell you.'

'Democracies: don't you just love them?'

'Kings and queens don't rule with a vote. I didn't elect the Matriarch or the King of the Under World and I didn't bastard ask to be made the princess of both worlds.' I laughed but I knew it sounded manic.

How the hell could Mischief piss me off with only the poison of a softly spoken sentence? The bloke wielded words as a weapon but he shanked himself.

The flames leapt again, and Mischief keened.

Cool your juices, Violet-sweets, turn down the gas because the unicorn is all cooked.

Why? If he provokes the <u>*beast*</u>*, then he knows he's going to get dashed.*

And the prize goes to the freaky girl in violet and black!

He *knows*…

The sly mage *wants* to have his pretty ass

whipped. He's jumping up and down on your buttons like it's a party game.

I don't figure him for a kinky angel, so why's he tempting my inner sadist?

You *own* him, girl.

What would it prove if you burnt him on your first day...?

That the Bone Princess can't look after her pets, that's what.

Plus, our sweet Sugar Plum wouldn't be able to fight... Who's he so afraid of seeing that he'd rather be roasted?

I clenched my fist, snuffing out the flames.

Mischief didn't sag with relief, instead he glared at me.

He truly *was* trying to get his arse whipped. *Well, who was I to disappoint...?*

Oomph — I slammed Mischief against the tunnel wall.

'I can't wait to see my dad beside me at last.' Mischief's pale chest tensed under my hands: *direct hit*. Why was he terrified of seeing the king? Weren't they lovers? 'Unless he's a coward like my mum and hides away in his Bone Palace.'

Mischief smacked away my hands. 'If you want to be burnt from the inside out over eons of agonized suffering, then you only had to ask. You do not, however, have to bring down the king on *all* our heads.'

'We're in an underground tunnel, Mr Paranoid, how big are his ears?'

Mischief rolled his eyes, before pointing at the firefly lights. 'Spies,' he whispered. 'Our words are never free, nor are we.' I gaped at the lights, which guttered as if listening...or *thinking*...and caught my breath. 'Be careful what you wish for,' Mischief's words wound smooth and dangerous, as he leant closer, his breath cooling the heat of my cheeks. 'Because now you've gained a shadow. How sweet that you consider me *fam*.'

Rebel grabbed my arm, yanking me away from the inviting spell woven in the melody of Mischief's voice.

I shook my head to clear it.

'Fam is earnt,' Rebel bit out; his eyes flamed, even as he quivered from the strain of flying. 'Wise up! You're nothing more than the pain in the hole free gift.'

Mischief pouted, touching his hand to his chest as if his heart had been broken. 'You wound me.'

'Not yet, git,' Rebel's shoulders stiffened. 'Give me time.'

I blinked, tumbling back to myself away from the safety of Mischief's words, before flushing. 'You bastard whammied me, spell lobber.'

Mischief smirked. 'How did it feel? Divine?'

Crunch — Rebel smashed the heel of his palm into Mischief's nose.

Mischief grunted, nonchalantly wiping away the blood. 'Why should I expect better from an Addict?'

'Dry up,' Rebel's wings flamed. 'Should *we* be after expecting anything better from a Brother of the Phoenix? Sweet Christ, did you think I didn't recognise your muppet arse, Zophia?'

I stared between them, hands on hips. 'And why, McSecretPants,' Rebel blushed; his pink tongue swiped his lips, 'didn't you tell me he's a member of the Legion? A Mage's boy?'

'When? During the touching or the kissing...?'

'Anytime, Master of Avoidance.'

Rebel gazed down at his boots. 'Even bad angels deserve a chance. Once you knew he worked for our enemy...?'

'I'd do this?' I choked Mischief; he gagged,

beating his wings.

Whish — thud.

Numb, I shook at the remembered sound of the guillotine echoing in the waterfall cavern: the corrupted sweetness that had clung to me, the terrified wails of the slave twins, and the wing bones *snapping* underfoot. And I remembered Nathanael, the silver-haired Discipliner from the Legion who'd trained the Broken slaves...and chopped off their wings.

My hands tightened around Mischief's neck. 'How many wings have you stolen, Discipliner?'

Mischief coughed, rubbing at his forearms. He blanched as if he was as queasy as me — and I was close to hurling all over his glittery trousers. 'S-stolen...wings? I've never...*none.* That's not my department.'

Rebel's voice was quiet in the gloom. 'And how many did you *save*?'

Mischief's gaze darkened. 'We can't all be heroes. I didn't choose the Legion; it chose me.'

Suddenly, Rebel grasped Mischief's hair, tugging it; he yipped. 'Holy saints, Nathanael's your little brother...?'

As if I'd been the one burned, I let go of Mischief's neck, and he hissed, wrenching away his hair from Rebel and twirling free across the tunnel with deadly grace.

Mischief pushed his hair behind his ears as he panted. 'What consequence could my delightful brother possibly be to you?'

Everything — because in the escape from Angel World the Lightning Angel we'd rescued had killed the teen assassin.

And Mischief didn't know.

My gaze caught with Rebel who gave a quick shake of his head. 'He was a brutal git to *my* brother, Haman. I wonder if it runs in the family?'

Even I could catch *that* meaning: hide the death of the bloke's psycho brother. And Rebel should know: I'd sacrificed *his* brother too.

Mischief's head bowed; his hair hung over his face. 'Haman has potential. He's powerful. I've never wished...for him to be harmed, far from it. But if you wonder if I am like my family, then I can reassure you.' His laugh was bitter. 'I'm the black sheep, who they would have sent for slaughter if my wool were not so valuable.'

'You knew Haman?' Rebel's smile was dazzling. 'That grants you one chance, Shadow.'

'I'm honoured,' Mischief inclined his head with a sneer, only to be bowled out of the way by a tumble of vampire.

Ash: lit up will-o'-the-wisp style by the Spy Lights. His face had been painted by the fists of the FF, but I grinned because he was *free* and...

Yeah, a bitch had to choose her words more carefully.

Captive angels...

Ash caught my expression and shook his head. 'Still owned, and it still sucks. What happened to the Free the Vampires campaign?'

I grimaced. 'It brought out a charity single and a t-shirt: *A Fang isn't only for Christmas.*'

Ash fiddled with the holster of his shooter. It thrilled me that he'd be fighting at my side.

'But I am your *fam*. So, double ownership: the FF and their princess. Who knew I'd be in such demand? Except,' he glanced down the tunnel, tilting his head as if listening for something, 'your refusing to sit up and beg for the Supreme Commander has twisted him Joker to your

Batman.'

'I'd say I was more of a Deadpool—'

Mischief snorted. 'Is not Wolverine more fitting?'

'Shut your bitch mouth, Doctor Strange. Still with the *beast* jokes?'

Mischief fluttered his eyelashes. 'Why, I meant it as a compliment.'

I growled. *How could I fight, when my blokes were so divided?*

Ash's gaze became flinty. 'You freed *him*? You'd trust your father's whore?'

Mischief's smile was venomous. 'Yet she trusts the whore of the entire Under World.'

Ash dived towards Mischief, but in a burst of red-and-black Rebel caught Ash around the waist and dashed him to the tunnel floor between the steel rails and sleepers.

Crack.

I flinched, as they hit the earth; the lights flickered, casting wild shadows. They rolled in a snarl of fangs, fists, and feathers.

I fidgeted, hiding my hands under my armpits to stop myself leaping in and pulling them apart like it was a schoolyard squabble.

This was between two ancient enemies who'd allied because of me. I wasn't part of the tangled centuries they'd spent warring before me. Even if I howled inside at knowing *I* was the outsider.

'I wouldn't do that if I were you,' Mischief singsonged as he watched them on the rails, his smile widening.

What did the bastard know that we didn't, when he was as much a prisoner as the rest of us?

Rebel pinned Ash with his wrists above him;

Ash panted but didn't struggle. 'I don't forgive you.' Rebel banged Ash's head against the girder as he whispered, 'By all the saints, you promised you wouldn't leave me alone in the dark. Wouldn't...abandon me.' His voice hitched. '*I don't forgive you, Brigadier.*'

'That's all right, angel,' Ash murmured, 'because I don't forgive myself.'

My eyes prickled, but as I wiped my sleeve across them, I sniffed at the sudden whiff of ozone, followed by the gust of wind hot across my face.

Can you say Screwed Choo-Choo?

Not now, J, busy dying.

'The Joker wouldn't send me onto a real, human...unabandoned...Tube Line...?' I spun to Ash.

Ash had paled as he struggled out from under Rebel. 'He would. In a heartbeat. Tried to tell you.'

I soared down to snatch Rebel up into my arms, but my foot skidded out from under me on a slippery rail.

'I truly wouldn't do that...' Mischief called, in genuine warning this time.

But it was too late: I reached out with my palm to steady myself on the central rail, only to be hit by the *live* current coursing through it.

As the first rumblings of the underground coming towards us vibrated through the tunnel walls, I was shocked to death.

7

When I first touched the live railway track, the shadowed tunnel that was lit only by the king's lights vanished as if my brain had been fried and all that was left were the fragmented flashes of my life.

And it'd make a bitching movie.

My heart stopped.

Then like a boot to the gut, a sensory overload hit me: my nerves screamed with the searing pain, just as I couldn't open my spasming jaw to utter even a whimper against the agony burning me from the inside.

I juddered under the intense heat, as my chest tightened and ached. *Hell, could your heart explode bloody?*

Rumble, rattle, rumble.

Even through my haze, the dissonant rumble of the tube train, blasting with it a whisper of ozone and cast-iron, shocked me out of the pain.

I yanked at my hand; the roasted scent of my smoking palm filled my nostrils. I was stuck, as the rails trembled.

J, I'm asking, help us.

What do I look like, Miracle Workers For Hire? You're fused, like a kid who lollipop licks a frozen lamppost, to a live rail, whilst a train roars towards you.

Who needs a villain to tie down your ass? You tie yourself in knots.

Don't take up motivational speaking. Those could be the last words you ever speak to me.

Then if these are my last words: You're more than feathers, blood, or bones. You're the Protector. And you've always been mine.

I was hoping for more along the lines of: Wait, I've just thought of a kickass escape plan...

Not this time, Feathery-love.

I wrenched again at my blistering hand. The blokes hollered, the tracks rattled, and the train thundered.

Why hadn't the others flown away and left me? Why had the current frozen shut my jaw, so I couldn't scream at them to *leave me...*?

Then I caught the shadow of the metal fiend out of the corner of my eye.

Hell, this couldn't be it... *This was bastard it...*

I braced for impact. Only to lurch, as everything vanished in a rain of silver fire.

Death smelt of tequila...?

I sniffed: the funky pungent whiff of Blue Nectar, mixed with lime and sweat. I could've been back in the dive of a bar that played live rock gigs with my mate Gizem, before my twenty-first birthday and the supernatural world that'd fallen from the sky. I licked my lips, before realising that meant I could move again...

Maybe I *was* back there...? And that would mean I had a lame arsed choice for my eternal reward.

Figured.

A mouth, soft against mine. It worshipped with gentle kisses, before tonguing open my lips and pressing deeper, insistent.

My eternal reward wasn't so lame arsed, after all.

I blinked awake.

Rebel drew back, smiling down at me. He pushed a strand of hair from my forehead, before rubbing it between his fingers as if checking I wasn't an illusion or burnt to a crisp.

'Angel kisses,' he touched the back of his hand to my forehead like he was testing for a fever, 'fierce powerful, remember?'

I ached: *electrocution was a bitch.*

The plum and black mosaic floor dug into my back; it stretched in a map of the world picked out in the British Empire, under the marble arches of a grand abandoned Victorian station. One that'd been transformed into a bar with those taste bud exploding tequila smells and bohemian sofas.

Humans huddled in glinting eyed gangs, watching *us* like we were the Big Bads.

Blood Lovers?

'Even more powerful than vomit inducing fairy tales...' Mischief shoved Rebel off me; his hair hung into my face, tickling my nose. '...is true magic.'

When Mischief snatched my burnt hand, I hissed. Then I jolted: a silver trail quested through my body, like sweet popcorn, it crackled through me and then just as suddenly...it fizzled out.

'Stop with the whammying...' I snarled, but

before I could grab Mischief, his legs buckled, and Rebel caught him.

Mischief had healed me.

A sheen of sweat coated Mischief's forehead. Pale as he always was, he looked more sickly than normal, as if he was the one who needed healing.

An unexpected jolt of concern shot through me. 'What the hell's up with your fae arse? Why the hell aren't we crimson grease under the train's wheels? And where the hell are we?'

'Are all princesses so demanding?' Mischief panted. I shoved myself up, exchanging a glance with Rebel that was more anxious than I'd intended: near death experiences do that to you. 'I find that healing you has taken more energy than sensible, since I was already indisposed from saving our lives.'

'All right, you win brownie points.'

'Oh goodie, whatever shall I spend them on? After all, I'm bursting with the joys of life... Oh no, I'm gasping for breath explaining this to you, after expending my meagre reserves restoring you after your moronic playing on the tracks moment and—'

Tap – tap – tap.

I rapped my boot against the mosaic floor like an impatient headmistress. 'Tantrum over?'

Mischief took a breath, before nodding.

'We. Alive. The. Hell. How?'

Mischief swiped a bead of sweat off his upper lip. 'Multi person teleportation.'

I bounced up and down like I'd become the kid. Rebel lifted his eyebrow at me. But teleportation brought out the inner geek. The Mage had told me his boys had mutant superpowers and he hadn't been bastard lying. 'You just...magicked us out of there?'

Mischief inclined his head, which would have made more of an impact if he hadn't been shaking as if he had flu. 'Of course, that means it was *Legion* magic that saved you...'

'Better not use up all your brownie points at once.'

Thud — Rebel dropped Mischief, and he yelped as his head hit the floor.

'If you could do a flit whenever you wanted, why are you still here, pretending to be trapped like the rest of us?' Rebel booted Mischief, and he rolled into a ball.

Unicorn Boy was on his own with my enraged punk.

'It only works...' Mischief gasped, 'when I'm with others.' He glanced up, as if gauging whether I believed him. *I wished I bastard believed him.* Then I remembered that Drake on Angel World had shielded us with invisibility but hadn't been able to hide himself. There were rules to the angels' mental powers that I didn't know. Maybe this was one of them? 'And the king has magics woven over the Under World...I can't teleport outside it without his permission.'

When I glanced up, I caught sight of Ash; messiah-like, Ash strode amongst the humans, who stroked and pawed at him like his touch alone was as healing as Mischief's.

It was only when Rebel caught my hand that I realised I'd been growling. 'Don't get narky, but this is the Brigadier's world. It's nothing to think on before a fight, but these young ones are his too.' I jerked, but Rebel held me steady. 'He's a Seducer, and that's worse than me being an Addict because I was weak and chose that path. But he was forced.'

'I'm not following, Riddle Master.'

Rebel clasped my hand tighter. 'The fib is that Blood Lifers are human: they were, once. But now they're stronger and faster. They're tied to the vampires. We go to war for the vampires' eternal lovers.'

Yet it was Ash who'd seduced them into the dark...

Shaking, I stared at Ash across the shadows of the platform. He sprawled against the bar, whilst a skank in a sheer satin dress, which was held together at the side with chains, clung around his neck.

I craved to claw out her eyes.

The ancient powers inside burst to life in a volcanic explosion that shook me away from Rebel. I clenched my jaw until it ached to keep in the *howl.*

'I'm a muppet. You know I'm no good at this blathering, I should never have—'

'Don't you dare take it back. For once you're Mr Honesty and no way you're regretting that.'

Above, the roof shook; the roars of battle blasted down the far stairway.

Flight whined, humming against my back in the gold-threaded harness and scabbard.

'I missed you too, bitch,' I murmured, 'looks like we're on.'

Trick must truly be terrified he'd lose his wings if the Blood Lovers fell to the angelic army because my weapons — Flight, a huge sword with a hilt of feathers, which had once belonged to Commander Drake's mother, and Star — had appeared in my room alongside my armour.

When I'd held them again, it'd been like waking up.

I drew Star, my dagger that Rebel had gifted me, and stalked towards the stairs.

Rebel drifted after me, but I held him back with a hand on his chest. 'You have a sassy mage to watch.' I studied Mischief who was still curled up on the floor. 'Plus, the freaky Blood Lifers, human or not, to protect down here.' I glanced at Ash, who'd tensed, considering me back. 'Ash too.'

'And who's going to be at your side, or your back, or bleeding at your feet? Because that's my—'

I silenced Rebel with a kiss because angel kisses are fierce powerful and sometimes they say more than words.

Rebel melted into the kiss, accepting.

I'd fight for the vampires, but I wouldn't risk my angels — or my Seducer.

Now I went to war alone.

When the red-haired howl of a Glory — the female dominant bitches who ruled over the blokes in Angel World — dived at me, resplendent in gold armour over silk lavender dress, she expected to carry me off in triumph to Angel World, Helen of Troy style.

She didn't expect me to spin kick her hero arse skidding across the sapphire floor.

Around the giant chamber, angel warriors clashed in *clangs* that hissed with violet fire against the vampire elite who tore at them with fangs and claws. Growls and groans, roars and moans: the two sides ripped each other bloody. Grey and violet feathers drifted on the draughts like party decorations.

Here was the true carnival, everything else had only ever been playing.

I'd protect the Blood Lovers but how could I fight for either side, when I was nothing but swag to them?

I edged to the corner of the room, wincing when my back hit the wall. I forgot how much these two supernaturals hated each other. Just wind them up and let them go.

Did the Matriarch truly want me back, or was she terrified of what would happen if I remained with the vampires?

When a charred hand flew past my nose, hewn from its wailing owner, and waggled tarantula-like at my feet, I cringed back.

I rolled my eyes, however, as the would-be Glory hero shook herself down dog-like and charged towards me again. I snatched her braids, swinging her round facefirst into the wall.

Slam.

'What the hell are you?' *Slam.* 'A Valkyrie?'

'I shall rip out your disrespecting tongue,' Valkyrie scratched at my hands, as I — *slam* — smashed her forehead into the wall again. 'Then I shall pierce my blazing fire through—'

Slam.

'Primary kids on Utopia Estate are more creative with their death threats.' I shook her. 'Why attack now?'

The Valkyrie bit back a laugh. 'The Matriarch does not allow her *possessions* to be stolen, or escape, even a traitorous daughter such as you.'

I couldn't hide the flinch at *traitorous*. 'It's what happens when two parents split up, then fight over the kid. Things get messy.'

I clouted her in the guts, and she doubled over.

A *scream*: higher-pitched than the rest.

I twirled round, then wished I hadn't.

Trapped at the far side were a small gang of trembling angel boys; Trick and the FF surrounded them. The gang were the same Lost Boys I'd fought side-by-side with and protected when everything had been reversed, and I'd been fighting *with* the angels. I'd promised these kids that they were my fam.

Why the hell would the Matriarch send them on this mission?

Except, I knew why: they were the pawns. A sacrifice to test if my vampiric side had fattened enough to kill the kids who'd hero worshipped me.

And I didn't bastard know whether it had.

I slashed my way across the writhing mass of feathers and sweating bodies. Flight shot out flaming white feathers across the battle.

I shuddered at each *wail*. Trick was playing with the boys. Tempting each out to one-on-one combat, he danced around them in his swirl of leather. As they swiped at him with their sword, he hacked them to ribbons with his claws.

A struggle arose beside him, and suddenly I faltered: *Commander Drake.*

The angel's slim body hung in the brutal grip of two FF, who towered over him. His bare toes barely touched the floor. His creamy back and chest were scored with gashes, which wept scarlet as if he'd been flayed, staining his indigo silk harem trousers until they clung to him like red skin.

So, Trick had played his game with Drake first.

Drake lifted his bowed head; his golden curls stuck to his forehead with sweat, but his violet eyes met mine. They widened with a desperate hope, before shuttering as if he'd sensed something in me.

And it wasn't rainbows and pixie dreams.

Slowly, Drake turned away his head, his shoulders slumping.

I was going medieval on Trick's arse.

I raised Flight, and she howled, heating lava-like.

How many fights has it taken to win the title *Champion of the Under World*?

The Genie and his Night of a Thousand Cuts is your mummy's Marked Wing, and although his ass is for the gods, his dick is the Matriarch's.

If you save him and his kid army, you'll be branding ANGEL across your forehead. And girl, in the land of the vampires, that's not a good look.

What were your last words to me?

I'm a Protector...?

I won't leave kids to be sliced. They need protecting, and I'm their Monster Princess. I'm no one's branded bitch.

Not yet...

The bolt of winged fire shot from Flight. The FF shrieked, as it sizzled across his arms, falling back from Drake.

Drake collapsed, before struggling towards the gang of boys.

When the remaining giant spun to me, I booted him in the balls. Then I slashed Flight in a hissing arc across his chest. Blood bubbled up and sprayed out, before I hooked him across the chin, stumbling him into a wall of Glories.

Trick gawked at me, his claws still raking across the chest of a weeping boy. When I raised my eyebrow at him — blood splattered across my cheeks — Trick dropped the kid and raised his hands in mock defeat.

I smirked but then caught Drake's panicked gaze.

'Princess, turn around,' he commanded. '*Now*.

Do not trust...'

I twirled, staggering back at the searing shock of the flames from the arrow that'd shot through my shoulder.

I dropped to my knees, keening.

The Valkyrie grinned, stroking her golden bow. Her threats hadn't been empty after all, she *had* pierced me through with blazing fire.

8

Fire coursed through my shoulder, sealing the arrow's wound and arching my back in agony.

I blinked at the cold on my cheeks: tears that'd been conjured by the heat.

In the roar of the battle, I curled around myself, swaying on my knees. I couldn't raise my right arm; numbness snaked down it. Flight had clattered away from me, and I couldn't reach her hilt. When she moaned, I looked up...into the smug grin of the vengeful Valkyrie.

The Glory had only messed me up when I'd started the Norse myth trolling. *Maybe I shouldn't...?*

I pulled myself straighter. 'Newbie mistake, bitch. This isn't Valhalla...'

A cool hand muffled my taunts, just as blood-stained silk patted out the flames around the arrow.

I recoiled, but Drake's quiet words stilled me, 'Hush, now. Extraordinary, I believe you've cracked the honour of our latest Supreme Commander.'

The Valkyrie tipped back her head and howled: Drake had a point.

And no trousers.

Like a kid, I licked Drake's palm, and he squirmed, shaking away his hand from my mouth. 'Cheers for the ultimate sacrifice, harem boy.'

Drake blushed, folding his wings over his prick, like I hadn't seen him bare arsed before or stripped from him those *same trousers* that'd put out the flames. The rich scent of frankincense wound around me, intoxicating.

'You know little of sacrifice.' He closed his eyes, but his shoulder brushed against mine. 'I am now the lamb, am I not?'

I stroked across Drake's eyelids with my left hand, and his eyes opened. His gaze shot to mine, startled. 'You're fam, yeah? I'll protect you, no different to the rest of my blokes.'

'Lie,' he whispered; his smile was sad. 'Although, a pretty one.'

When he pushed himself up, like an exotic bird caught and butchered, blood rain dropped from his gashed skin onto my lips. I gasped at the zing of brilliant candyfloss that tripped through me: magic, sex, and Drake's heady power.

Hell, I'd more than missed him: I'd *mourned* him.

I grasped Drake's hand, as the boys, clawed and tattered, stumbled to stand around me.

I snorted: the mighty Bone Champion shielded by angel kids, the same ones I'd once saved on the battlefield from the FF vampires.

Drake glanced down uncertainly at where our hands linked. Then he pressed his free hand to his forehead as he murmured, 'Allow me to remind you how you burnt me, during my attempt to stop your escape from Angel World. One of us, however, can follow your *mother's* orders and still save you from the fire now.'

Not spy level stealthy, yet even through the pain of *still having an arrow through my shoulder*, I caught onto Drake's stiffly rehearsed script: *The Matriarch was watching*. Just as she had at the battle with Drake's kid army, although she'd chosen to hide in the mountainous Angel World, whilst we'd battled and used *my* eyes to spy. This time she was inside Drake's mind, however, and if we survived, he'd be the *lamb* roasted if I snuggled with him and let slip how he'd saved me.

Instead, I snatched back my hand. 'I'd forgotten what a girlie brat you were.' Drake winced; I hoped he didn't believe *my* act. But then, I'd spent most of my time in the Matriarch's poisoned court hurting him, so why would I've stopped now? 'You can cry all the way back to my mummy. I'm not running home with my tail between my legs because I'm not a loyal bitch, like you.'

Drake gazed at me coldly. 'Enough. The Supreme Commander shall not care whether you're a...*bitch*...or not.'

I swallowed, as the Valkyrie stalked towards me with her bow still raised. And she didn't look the type to take *no* for an answer.

My breaths were harsh and ragged.

Which was worse: to be shot in the face or dragged back to my mum's toxic court as spoils?

I'd have to take the arrow to the head.

I reached for my violet fire, but the shaking pain of the arrow's fire had subdued it. I tilted my chin, as the Valkyrie drew her bow, only for Drake to step in front of me.

I yanked him down, and he yelped. 'Way to break our cover.'

He shrugged. 'I apologise for attempting to save

your life.' He tilted his head; his curls fell over his eyes. 'I forget quite how many times that is now.'

Then a crackling arrow flared against my cheek, the Valkyrie's shadow dyed me in black, and I screwed closed my eyes, preparing to have my head set alight.

Screams, hollers, roars.

I cracked open my eyes, only to hiss against the swirling living *light* that tore whirlwind through the centre of the chamber in a rumbling rush. Blindingly bright and yet chillingly cold, it caught each angel in its cruel embrace, before incinerating them in a blast of ashes.

I tumbled backwards, hissing at the jolt to my shoulder.

'The king,' Drake breathed, quivering. 'Behind me!' He bellowed at the cowering boys, clutching at them with trembling hands.

But this wasn't an enemy that could be protected against. It was judgement and death.

And it was coming for us.

A sobbing boy clung to my leg; he peered up at me. 'Monster Princess,' he wailed, as if my name alone could make this elemental terror of light, which had been born out of the dark, fade back into the shadows.

I *was* his Monster Princess: his saviour.

It jolted me because since I'd been stuck in the Under World, I'd fought for nothing but my own pride, celebrity, and blood. I'd been more than that before, and I bastard would be again.

The light twisted towards us — screams and ashes filled the chamber. Even the vampires cringed, as the tornado passed.

Violet me up, before I'm cremated alive.

You wanted to meet your daddy, Feathery-face, and here he is in all his glory.

The bastard just had his custody revoked.

There's a reason the Fallen fear the light. And it's not their migraines in the sun.

It's the Light-bringer.

Right now, he's bringing it not on your arse but the Ice Commander's. Let him cleanse Drake and his kids from the Under World, and that ANGEL brand on your forehead will be burnt off.

You're the Ice Bitch, J, because that's cold.

If that's what it takes to prove my loyalty, then I'd rather be a traitor.

How did that work out for your Seducer soldier?

Just remember, I offered you a way out.

I juddered, my stomach roiling.

When I tipped back my head, my throat tingled, before an arc of flames exploded from my mouth in a snaking stream, falling over the heads of Drake and his boys and shielding us in a spitting bubble.

Staggering backwards, the Valkyrie dropped her bow. Her face became pinched, as she hammered on the bubble, even though it seared her fists, begging to be let in.

Despite the arrow in my shoulder...and the one she'd held to my head...if I'd been able to break the flames, I'd have pulled the Valkyrie inside.

Because no one deserved to die like that.

The Valkyrie was torn up into the arms of the light's wind and became nothing but ash, falling onto the top of our fire shield.

The boys wailed, clutching onto Drake and me, as if we were dysfunctional parents on a vacation gone wrong. My gaze met Drake's over their heads.

Us next.

Except, the light battered against my fire, howling in its outrage at being denied its treat, and although my shield flickered, it didn't break.

Please, bastard hold...

I stared down the light, even though it haloed against my retinas, burning. I jumped, as just for a moment, fiery coal eyes scrutinised mine from the centre of the light.

The king: *my dad.*

As the light winked out with a final furious wail, I shook because I'd defied the King of the Under World to fight on the side of the angels.

I'd made an enemy who was so dangerous he could burn armies to ash.

9

I shook, trapped in the darkness.

And I couldn't bastard move.

Taking panicked breaths, I could feel something soft underneath me and...delicate hands *touching* me.

I fought to pull away but I was frozen in the shadows, trapped in their touch. Tears burned.

J, help me, what's...?

Nothing but a muffled bass guitar throbbing over a tom-tom like a heartbeat and low laughter.

Don't rage quit on me because I saved the angels. Please....

Another sweep of slim but strong fingers across my shoulder, followed by a flare of stinging pain, before it dulled.

Don't abandon me.

I was wrong, yeah? Is that what you want to hear? I don't want to be alone.

Finally! Give that girl a crown.

With a wild gasp, my eyes flew open, and I was

hit with the Savage's ferocious punk, loud enough that I cringed from the battle cries and manic chanting, along with the funky whiff of tequila.

The Blood Lover's bar on the abandoned station.

I tried to sit up, my arse sinking into the shaggy sofa, which I'd been laid onto, but a pale hand pushed me down: the hand that'd been *touching* me.

'I'd take Mr Naughty Feels away if you don't want me to bite it off.'

Mischief snatched away his hand. 'I see our ball of beastly sunshine is with us again. I'm delighted my magic could yet again save your life.'

Oh yeah: violet fire, pissed off light dad, shielding Drake and his kids until they escaped, and then...nothing but black.

An arrow will to do that, even to a Monster Princess.

Mischief knelt next to the sofa. Shadows darkened the skin underneath his eyes like bruises, and he swayed, struggling to hide it by bracing himself against the mosaic floor.

Mischief looked like *he'd* been the one who'd been shot.

Hell, was that how his Angelic Power worked?

'Why didn't you tell me that you take pain? Heal by transferring it? That's screwed-up.'

Mischief raised an eyebrow. 'Why would you care? There are reasons I don't offer out this service to everyone. Among other things, it hastens the speed that I Fall. Will you now award extra brownie points?'

I stroked his sweating forehead. 'As long as you're not plotting to save them up and spend them all at once on something fiendish.'

He smirked through his agony. 'You know me so

well already. But I shan't have the time to do that...yet.' He dropped his voice to a whisper. 'We find ourselves in a tricky situation.'

For the first time, I glanced around the bar, across the imperial map and through the glistening arches. And realised that *everything had changed*.

The Blood Lovers were no longer cowering humans, but a sensual, subversive, *terrifying* tribe.

And this was their yard.

Fishnets, bondage, and piercings. The Blood Lovers blazed with an energy that wasn't human, not anymore. It buzzed in every swing of their hips, tangle of naked limbs bent over tables as natural as any orgy, or smash of shot glasses on the bar. It also lurked in the darkness of their eyes, as they watched *us*: the outsiders in their private world.

Maybe a parade would've been too much for saving them but how about a medal? Or I'd settle for a tequila on the house and for them to stop staring at us with those *Village of the Damned* eyes.

Ash had been stripped down to his jeans, stretched out across the length of the bar. Two girls in matching patent leather catsuits and black lipstick sucked love bites across his chest, whilst he squirmed, biting at his swollen nipples as they held him down by the neck.

Unlike when I'd first seen Ash with the Blood Lovers, however, this wasn't worship: it was ownership.

And I should know.

I hadn't left Ash down here for this *abuse*.

I surged up, but Mischief tugged at my leg. 'It is even trickier yet for your Irish angel.'

I spun round, but I couldn't see Rebel through the heaving carnal celebration. When I twisted back to Mischief, he merely jerked his head upwards.

I gasped.

Rebel had been pinned against the roof; his bent wing weakly flapped. Without feeding from sunlight for so long, which all angels needed, would he even be able to fly to save himself if he was dropped...?

How did Mischief still have the strength for his Angelic Powers? Unless someone *was* feeding him light...?

Rebel's lip was split. He shook, but he didn't fight back because the Commander who shoved him in the chest by his elbows, holding him precariously high above my head, was his older brother: Wings.

In faded black denim jacket over emerald shirt, and a short buzz of red hair, Wings was just like Rebel and yet nothing like him: his eyes held the killer edge of a soldier, whereas Rebel's still blinked with a soft innocence.

Even though I *knew* Rebel was a killer too.

And, of course, Wings had no hands. Not since I'd burnt them off in our last battle.

Rebel didn't know I'd done that, however, because I'd kept it secret.

I couldn't help the sigh of relief that Wings had survived, and I hadn't killed Rebel's family. Yet that family was slamming Rebel into the roof, and my wings were beating before I could engage brain.

'How many times, git angel?' *Oomph* — Wings smashed Rebel against the marble, his elbow grinding into Rebel's throat. 'Traitor.' *Oomph*. 'Coward.' *Oomph*. '*Our da is dead because of you.*'

I caught Wings before he could crack Rebel's head back again; scarlet snaked behind Rebel's ears, matting his hair.

'Time out,' I snarled, shoving Wings next to Rebel with one hand, as I pulled Rebel's shaky arms around my neck. 'If you can't play nicely with your bro, then you can't play at all.'

Rebel didn't look away from Wings. 'Briathos... If you can't forgive me then... Sweet Jesus, please, let me...just let me, this once, explain...'

'Why?' Wings shrugged one careful shoulder. 'So you can fib as you've always done? Slink your way back into my life as a Shadow? Pretend you're a real fellah, when you're nothing but a banjaxed Addict?' Rebel flinched on each jibe as if he was still being slammed into the roof. 'I don't have hands now.' My heart thudded, as Wings met my gaze, before he sneered, 'But I'm a hundred times the warrior you'll ever be. Da knew that. Your *owner* does too, or she wouldn't have torn me to tatters. A predator knows a predator.'

Rebel whined, panting.

I expected him to pull away — *who wouldn't?* — but instead his arms tightened around my neck. His cheek rested against mine: wet and cold.

I quivered; Rebel's silent grief sang to the possessive powers inside, who growled for vengeance. Except, the bitch who'd hurt him was *me*.

Rebel drew back; his gaze was desperate and despairing, as if I could deny the truth that I'd taken his brother's hands.

When I nodded, however, because at least I could admit it now, he bit his lip.

'Never mind, git angel,' Wings swung, catching me unbalanced in the sweep of his wings. 'The princess just isn't that into you. I don't know what all the swooning over her is about anyway.' When he shrouded us in his grey wings, I struggled, my jaw clenching against the panic, as he rocked us backwards. Then he whispered, hot and vicious into my ear, 'I wouldn't ride her into battle.'

He wrenched backwards.

Finally, we were falling.

I tried to open my wings in an instinctive attempt to fly. *And when had it become so natural?* But Wings kept them trapped, and we plummeted to the floor.

Bang — I screamed when we hit, rolling in a crunch of bones and blood.

Rebel hollered, trapped beneath me in a feathered tumble. And Wings? When we stilled, lying in a dazed pile, the psycho *laughed.*

'Now *that* was a ride,' Wings grinned.

Groaning, I straddled Wings, surging with adrenaline that soared me as high as my battered wings had in imagined flight. 'If there's any riding? I'll be the bitch doing it. And your brother's name,' I twisted Wings' head by the ear, and he squealed, 'is Rebel.'

An explosion of pink and black tumbled me off Wings and onto my back. I stared up at the small teen who was now straddling *me*.

Then the world imploded, as I forgot to breathe.

Jade.

The sister who'd disappeared on the night I'd been dragged into the supernatural world by Rebel: not a sister by blood but a sister from the street who I'd adopted to save. My boyfriend had threatened to sell her to settle a debt, and since Jade and I had both fallen out of the children's home at sixteen, I'd been terrified to lose her to a worse world of slavery.

Except, had I?

Because here in the Under Word was the sister I'd been searching for ever since. The sister Drake had tricked me up into Angel World to find.

Now here she was in candy pink shorts and black satin top, a sulk of Emo, with her pink-and-black striped fringe brushing against my cheeks...scowling at me and effortlessly holding me down.

How was she so strong? Plus, her eyes were just a shade too blue, like the other cuckoo kids'.

She was a Blood Lover: no longer mine, human, *or free.*

Did you expect anything in this world to be free?

Jade...she's changed.

And you're not? You were human when she last saw you, Violet-peeps.

Were you ever trying to save her? Or a perfect image of a life before the angel fell into your lap?

The joy that'd burst through me at discovering Jade tasted bitter sweet.

I clasped onto her arm in case she vanished again. 'Hell, you've no idea what... How long I've been searching... What do you call disappearing like that? Since when did you go off with some bloke without sending me a text?'

Yeah, so over anxious sister mode had kicked in sooner than expected.

Jade rolled her eyes, stroking her fingers through my feathers. 'You have wings.'

'And you're a blood donor to Fangs.'

Smack — Jade slapped me.

My head snapped to the side.

'That's for his first hand,' she hissed.

Smack — she slapped me again.

'And that's for his second.'

'I didn't take any more body parts, did I?' I rubbed at the crimson handprints.

Then Jade was sobbing in a way I'd never heard her cry before because if you wanted respect in Hackney you hid the pain. She clung to me, and it hit me in a heady rush: I'd found Jade, and she was in my arms.

But how the hell did I keep her?

There was also a trembling ache, however, which rose to a shanking crescendo when her supernaturally bright gaze met mine: Rebel had once told me that I was no longer *connected* to her. I'd raged against it, but now I knew it'd been the truth.

The vampires had stolen her away from me. Stolen her humanity.

I'd gank the bastard who'd violated her, just like I'd always sworn I'd kill any bastard who'd made her suffer.

Wings slipped his arms around her shoulders, swinging her onto his lap, as he sat up, before lifting an eyebrow at me. 'You stopped at the hands, although you did take my bollocks for a while there.' I froze, gawking at Jade, whilst Wings mouthed kisses down her neck. Then he lazily glanced at me over her head. 'Here's the thing of it, princess, she's mine.'

'You're a fine red mist, bro.' I launched myself towards Wings, but a fizzing invisible blast blew me backwards.

That hadn't come from Wings.

I stared at Jade, who scowled at me like I was trying to borrow her favourite skull t-shirt.

Yeah, not fully human anymore.

But I had tricks too.

I stormed back towards them, before cool hands banded around my waist. I looked into Rebel's troubled gaze.

'Mind yourself, princess. This is your sister. The human we gave everything for...remember?'

And I did.

I shuddered, calming the violet, as I relaxed into Rebel's hold.

Jade dragged Wings up by the elbow, pacing to face us. She slung her arm around his shoulders, as if we were in a Mexican standoff for siblings.

Rebel stiffened at the same moment as I did at the shock of seeing his brother and my sister together.

'He's mine too,' Jade mouthed down Wings' cheek, and I cringed. 'How this works? If you kill him, I die too. How's it feel to know you almost killed me in London Fields? I suffer the phantom pain of his hands. Does it haunt you? That *you* did that?'

I'd have taken a step back, if it hadn't been for Rebel's steadying arm around my waist.

I remembered those times Rebel had faced his brother's humiliating rejection — once in front of an entire vampire army — and I blanched because my sister's wounded deeper than the Valkyrie's arrow.

The other Blood Lovers were watching now.

'I've done a lot of things. It's ghost central in my head. Your lover, however, must be the engine driver on his own spook train.'

Jade's eyes narrowed. I'd forgotten that disapproving of her boyfriend only led to the Romeo and Juliet effect. 'He's a war hero. A courageous leader of a rebellion—'

'Yeah, and can turn water into blood, pisses penicillin, and wears a mask and tights to play superhero at the weekends. He still bites and feeds from you.'

'I knew you'd be like this. That you wouldn't understand. Why do you think I left?'

I hissed. This time it truly was only Rebel holding me up. I rubbed my tears away on my shoulder. I wouldn't let Wings see me cry. 'I'm sorry you didn't think you could come to me. But I'm here now—'

'And you still don't get it.'

'I never stopped looking,' I tried again, although it was as if the Jade I'd known less than a year ago had faded away, and this was someone new speaking with her voice. 'Rebel and me both searched. I kept this...' Eagerly, I unclasped the pouch around my neck, which I'd worn since the witches' house, taking out Jade's crystal angel necklace. I'd discovered it the day I'd gone back to the apartment searching for Jade. I held it out for Jade on my palm like an offering to appease a furious spirit. 'Take it.'

Smack — Jade slapped my knuckles, and I curled my hand around the necklace, yelping in shock.

'I left that behind because I didn't want an *angel* around my neck. I'm not the bitch with the angel obsession. I like my blokes dark, powerful, and Fallen.'

She swayed in Wings' arms, and he snogged her.

Rebel trembled with rage, and suddenly it was *me* holding *him* back. 'Wise up! Treat your sister with some respect; she loves your ungrateful arse.'

'She's an *angel* lover,' Jade spat; her eyes were glassy and unfocused.

Hell, it was like looking at a stranger and a bespelled one too.

'What do you want me to do?' I asked, slipping the necklace back into the pouch and tying it around my neck as reverentially as if it contained my sister's ashes.

Jade lifted Wings' arm, even though he squirmed, flushing. 'Can you give back my lover's hands?' I looked away. 'Didn't reckon so.'

Had she *chosen* this? I'd been dragged into the

supernatural world but had my sister *embraced* it? If she had — mental, destructive, and unhealthy as I reckoned it was — did I have any right to go against that choice?

Suddenly, I realised that the other Blood Lovers weren't merely watching anymore, they'd moved closer, circling us along the outline of the empire map. Their eyes had darkened: guarded and malevolent.

Were they connected behind those eyes: their thoughts and emotions?

I shuddered.

Ash and Mischief hung between them, passed like a spliff to be toyed with. Mischief was barely conscious.

I growled: no bastard way they were treating *my* fam like that. *At what point had Mischief wriggled under my skin to earn that title?*

'Whatever's happened...we were raised human. I struggle with this too, Jade, but you've more humanity in you than I have. You can't think this is—'

'They're captured angels. A Seducer. We're allowed to play with them,' she pouted.

The Blood Lovers slunk closer.

Was my baby sister their leader?

Jade had always had swag. Except, now she was auditioning for my *nemesis*, so maybe I shouldn't have worked so hard on building her self-esteem.

'And I want to play with your punk.' Jade snatched for Rebel.

Rebel jumped, alarmed, and I blocked Jade's hand, only for her to wrench my arm up behind my back.

'You love him?' She asked, surprised.

'Let's put my love life in the *none of your business* drawer, shut it, lock it tight, and never speak of it again.'

She huffed. 'But you're not drinking from him?'

'Because nothing says *I love you* like ripping out someone's throat.'

When Jade twisted my arm, I stilled; it was almost like she was young again, and we were back in Jerusalem Children's Home fighting over a Marvel comic.

'Wings feeds from me because he loves me. He'd die without me. Literally. And if I die, so does he.' She frowned. 'I've never been needed like that. Romance is for kids. But being needed...'

I winced. Because I got it then.

To be needed...

As orphans, we hadn't even been wanted. Jade's search had always been for some purpose, identity, *meaning*...and she'd found it in the arms of a vampire.

How could I break her belief that she'd found her place — become something special — with someone who *needed* her at last? Even if she'd been brainwashed with lies and hope?

Maybe that was better than being human for her?

'Epic,' I murmured. 'I'm happy for you, you get me?'

Jade's expression softened. She finally shoved me back towards Rebel. 'Why aren't you feeding from your sissy boy? Angel Blood Lovers are meant to be hot.'

I glared at her. 'Not happening. Plus, I don't have pointy teeth in the fang department.'

Jade stroked down Wings' jeans, and he arched. 'Not yet. But you're half vampire. They told me.'

'Then what's up with not seeing me...?' I burst out.

Jade brushed her fingers through her fringe.

'Don't they tell you anything, *princess*? We can't leave. This is our home. Where we're safe.'

Your bastard prison...

Because the king wouldn't want the Blood Lovers, lost in their whirl of sex and blood, to discover the truth of the Under World: The Bone Carnival, Cage, Ossuary, and Charnel House...

A sudden murmuring flurry amongst the Blood Lovers, before they parted, and Wild, streaked in scarlet and ashes (the cremated remains of the angels who'd showered down under the king's light), marched so close to me that his copper breath blew across my nose.

'You big soft babby,' he chided, crossing his brawny arms, 'saving those angel kids. Our deal was that you fought on the side of the Fallen, but you broke that. There's nothing more serious in the Under World than breaking a bargain or a bet.'

'Did you just come here to lecture the pants off me or...?' I grasped Rebel's hand, however, and the way he encircled me with his arms, told me more than any words Wild could say.

I was screwed.

'I'm here to take you to your father.' Wild nodded, and a gang of FF flooded into the bar. 'Congratulations, wench, you've won an invitation to the Bone Palace. Let King Lucifer cleanse you with his light.'

Lucifer?

I'd known my dad was *king* but not that he was the original Fallen angel — Lucifer himself.

I shook, backing away, as Wild advanced. I glanced at my sister, but she'd pressed her face against Wild's chest.

Was she...crying?

I remembered the light, burning everything before it into ashes and quailed.

At last, I'd meet the bastard who'd abandoned me.

Except, he was Lucifer, he lived in a Bone Palace, and I'd pissed him off enough to be burnt alive.

10

Two things I'd always known about blokes: they were bastards and they were bastards who ditched you.

My dad had left me on a gravestone as a baby and had never appeared in the sparkling perfection I'd dreamed to rescue me from the children's home.

There was a fortune to be made from a vaccination jab against blokes: *safe from abandonment with a tiny prick.*

And it turned out, my dad — Lucifer — was also a *tiny prick.*

I shifted from foot-to-foot on the polished skull floor of the Bone Palace. The heat in the graffitied bedroom baked me like *I* was the gingerbread man toasty in the oven. I stared at my boots, ignoring the vast white bed in the centre of the room and my dad who was sprawled on it. Sweat collected at the base of my neck. My hand itched towards Star.

ANARCHY, CHAOS, LIGHT.

The spray-painted words blazed across the stark walls, between femurs and ribs, which stuck out of the concrete and *glowed*.

When a chill prickled my neck, *I was trapped in my vision again.*

My land: violet feathers above glowing bones. Here in the Under World it was made life.

Real.

Was I truly doomed to rule a world of blood and feathers? A tyrant like my parents?

I sank beneath the soft waves, choking on the feathers. They were in my lungs. I couldn't breathe...

J, I'm suffocating on my own Disney kingdom.

And I'm quaking in my fabulousness. This is the King of the Under World: Lucifer, the Light-bringer.

I'm hiding myself deep where the light doesn't shine.

Disturbing as you've made that sound, how about saving me first?

J...? Are you that much of a scaredy-cat? Is Lucifer that much more terrifying than the Matriarch?

I let out a sob, spluttering feathers. My chest burned. And I was alone.

Until I wasn't.

'On my fangs, we'll have to teach you to control your little dreams,' a seductive murmur, which ended on a giggle, broke sharply into my vision like a shank popping a bubble.

Then I was tumbling out of mid-air with a *squawk*, landing on the centre of the satin four-poster bed, and Lucifer was scrambling onto me, every miniature incubus-like slink of him.

Lucifer's tiny legs (in even tinier black leather

shorts), rested either side of me. His leather shirt hung open, revealing the word **FIRE** branded from one pink nipple to the other. I flinched, but it was true: he even smelled of bonfires. The warmth of his wings rested against my cheek; the autumnal aroma was so comforting, I rubbed against him.

His bare toes curled, as he purred.

I stiffened: why the hell was I so drawn to him? *What had he done?*

I wished his spiky ash-blond hair didn't match my own, and I could pretend he wasn't my real dad.

Especially after my mum had told me he'd *forced* her...

Crack — I backhanded him, and he fell to the side with a startled yelp.

I shuddered: how often did you bitchslap Lucifer?

Lucifer pushed himself up amongst the silk pillows, wiping the blood away with his thumb, before sucking at it. He eyed me with pride. '*Badass*. You're full of tricks, aren't you, champ? Not many can resist my spark. I'd always hoped...' He wrung the edges of the pillow between his delicate fingers. Was this truly the same bloke who'd decimated the angel army? Who'd petrified J into hiding? 'Huh, I didn't think I'd come over all cry-baby about it, but it's been hell watching the Bone Carnival and not, you know...'

'You watched me?' I shoved myself onto my elbows, hating the whining hope in my voice.

The Matriarch hadn't been the warm maternal sort; she'd been an Ice Bitch. No matter how I'd tried to change to be the princess she'd wanted, I'd never have been the *daughter* she'd wanted.

And hell did *that* smart.

But Lucifer...? What he seemed to be offering was everything the Matriarch hadn't...but I knew there'd be a price.

If Lucifer could hold sway over you with a spark, how long had I been under its control?

'You think I'd have missed my own daughter's debut? You were the show's greatest spectacle!' Lucifer rose onto his knees in excitement.

He looked no older than me, although I knew he must be centuries old. Only when I caught the flames flaring in his eyes — twin suns — did I recognise the howling power that transformed angels to ash. I shuddered: it was like peering into infinity.

'I'm not a freakshow,' I muttered.

Lucifer pressed his hand to my cheek; I couldn't help the way I leant into its heat. 'I know that. You're my beautiful, perfect, good daughter.'

I trembled at each word, as if he'd struck me with each one.

Too much, too much, too much...

Why couldn't he have been cruel? Hated me? Punished me like Wild had been expecting?

Then I could've hated him: the bastard who'd abandoned me.

Hate myself.

Lucifer sighed. 'You never should've been left with the humans. Tell your daddy: those little creatures didn't treat you kindly...? No matter, you're with me now. Safe. And on my bones, you'll never doubt your glory again. Although,' he grinned, 'it's interesting to know what makes you cry. Praise: is that a kink or...?'

I snarled, booting him away from me, as I jumped off the bed. My heart thudded, and I pulled my clothes straight with shaky hands.

How had he broken me down so fast?

I couldn't think. Confused, I opened my mouth, only to snap it shut.

'I'm messing with you.' Lucifer reclined on the sheets, wriggling his leather clad arse. 'Come on, loosen up. Have some fun.'

'I'll have some fun,' I flexed my fist, 'going medieval on your arse.'

'Always so dramatic.' Lucifer waved his hands in the air, before lifting his pale eyebrow. 'Did your *mother* teach you that?'

Suddenly, Mischief plummeted through the roof of the four-poster in a swirl of silver, landing with a *squeak* in Lucifer's arms.

I stiffened: Mischief had said Lucifer was waiting for him to Fall to Blood Bond with him.

No way in this freaky-glowing-bones-hell was *that* happening.

Lucifer cooed at Mischief, who was breathing so rapidly his chest rose and fell like a horse that'd run the Grand National. He was slicked in enough sweat for it too; ashen and shaking. The angel was still suffering from using his magic to help me and would Fall faster because of it.

Screw it, he was fam.

'What's wrong, rascal?' Lucifer rested his hand across Mischief's forehead, as if lovingly taking his temperature. He *tutted*. 'You've taken your masochistic streak a little far, wouldn't you say?'

Mischief's smile was tight. 'I'm certain I shall still be able to service you, Your Majesty. I wouldn't wish my pain to inconvenience you.'

Lucifer tightened one arm around Mischief's chest, locking his small leg around his hips. When he slipped his fingers beneath Mischief's tunic, Mischief's breath hitched. 'So sassy; you know, it's lucky I love fire in my pets. Still...'

When Lucifer's gaze met mine, my hands curled into fists, and my wings stretched out, beating violently. 'He's Mr Sassy Bitch, but he's also on the

No Touching List. See, the humans might've been bastards but they had a thing called *consent*. I reckon that's what should've been branded across your chest.'

The bones blazed fiercer, and the room shook. I swayed, before steadying myself.

Then the bastard giggled.

Lucifer pressed the heel of his foot against Mischief's balls, and he moaned. 'You truly are my daughter: a rebel. Good, good. But you see, there's only power and pain and...' His expression became flat and distant, as if he was remembering just such pain, before he shook his head. 'Here in the Under World, we've broken the shackles of Angel World. But *we're not human.*' His gaze darkened. 'Angels are pets to be killed or played with.' He ground his heel harder, and Mischief keened. 'Kill or play, champ?'

I blinked. Hell, he meant it. Right here, I chose Mischief's fate.

Power and pain...

Did I deserve to wield it? *Did anyone?*

'I believe you were asked a question,' Mischief bit out, strained. He clasped onto Lucifer's forearms, almost for comfort, even though Lucifer was the one hurting him. 'It's a simple choice.'

But it wasn't.

To kill Mischief or turn him into a pet against his will? To have that guilt on *my* shoulders?

'Added bonus,' Lucifer clucked his tongue, 'if you choose *play*, which will after all mean we can indulge ourselves in so many angelic fantasies...' *I was going to hurl.* '...Then you have permission to ask me three questions.'

I froze, my breath caught. For a moment, I even forgot Mischief. 'Anything?'

'Well, no questions about how you escape, kill

me, or...you know? Come on, this is a onetime offer and your deepest desire, hmmm?'

The top boy on the Estate didn't rise through the gang's ranks because of his shank or shooter but because he could read your desires and fears, before turning them against you...until you lay chained at his feet.

Lucifer had wound chains around me, until I stood shackled because he'd dangled the one thing I'd always wanted.

Answers.

It was no longer a choice, and he knew it.

He'd never wanted to gank his pet; he'd been making me perform instead.

'Play,' I whispered.

Mischief grunted with relief, but Lucifer only smirked. 'I knew you'd make the right choice. Come, let's play now.' He bounced on the bed, pulling Mischief with him like they were toddlers hyped up on sugar, before smacking a kiss onto Mischief's cheek. 'What? Pouting? Like I'd let you be harmed by the big bad monster.'

I bristled.

My dad had been threatening Mischief like he was no more than a fly waiting to be swatted, but now *I* was the wolf stalking in the shadows...?

'You're the one with the fangs, bitch.' I booted the bed, and it shook.

Lucifer's canines curved to gleaming fangs, as he hissed, yanking Mischief off the bed by his hair and twisting his head to the side to gouge scarlet lines up and down his slender throat.

Bitch move to remind a vampire of his fangs: I wasn't a wolf, I was a wallad.

Lucifer peered at me over Mischief's neck, as if to check I was watching his performance; I almost rolled my eyes. 'Fangs, claws, spark... The things I can do would perk up this party a treat.' He licked up the blood dribbling down Mischief's neck, before hurling him to his knees. Mischief winced. 'We already have our hunt, however, and a Quiz of the Day.'

'Hunt?' I licked my lips, unclenching my hands.

Why did my blood sing at the word, even as the powers inside uncoiled, like scorpion tails tensing to strike?

Trained as a huntress, it'd been too long since I'd hunted even for sport.

Mischief's gaze flitted between us, his eyebrows raised. He edged himself to his feet, backing away until he hit the graffitied wall.

'Uh-huh,' Lucifer tutted, 'no escaping. We want to play...*hunt*...don't we?'

I nodded, biting down on a smile. My vision blurred like fireworks were *pop* — *pop* — *popping* in my brain.

'The light, you witless beast, the king's spark...it's inside you...' Mischief smacked his hands together, as if attempting to awaken me.

Crack — Lucifer darted to Mischief, smashing his head against the wall.

'Naughty... Who said you were invited to play? The prey is silent, see?' He chucked Mischief towards me.

Mischief dived under my arms, dodging behind the bed.

Yet Mischief's words had been enough to darken the lightshow in my head. I squinted at Lucifer. 'My three questions, bro. Time to pay up.'

Lucifer swung his arms, limbering up. 'Give me your best shot.'

I swallowed.

I could do this. I *had* to bastard do it...

'Why did you abandon me?'

Lucifer doubled up with a pained groan. 'Straight for the balls.' Then he straightened with a grin. 'I didn't. Your mummy did. Next question.'

'Wait...what?' I gaped at him.

Unconcerned that he'd shattered my world into a thousand-piece jigsaw and stolen all but a single piece, Lucifer launched himself over the bed, clutching at Mischief, who stumbled away with a gasp.

Absentmindedly, I caught Mischief as he passed, pulling him close and feeling the panicked *thud* of his heart against mine. I stroked down his back; he trembled.

Lucifer stalked towards me. 'If I could've sensed you before your powers came in, I'd have ridden to your rescue. Didn't I fight to get you back? To have you by my side? How much do you like the men in your life to sacrifice for you? It seems to me a hot topic...?' He ripped Mischief out of my arms. 'Next question.'

'Why'd you fight at all?' I tugged Mischief back: a gazelle between two lions. His sleeve ripped. 'When you raped my mother? And all I am is—'

'All you are is *glorious*,' Lucifer hissed. His arm around my shoulders was hot and comforting in a way I knew it shouldn't have been. His wings wrapped both Mischief and me in their bonfire scent. 'By the shadows, I didn't...force...the Matriarch. *She* forced *me*. And you're the perfect gift from the union. I've missed you.'

I struggled, pushing to be free of Lucifer's suddenly suffocating embrace. But he only held on tighter. Mischief whimpered.

Violet crackled beneath my skin, stinging to burst out and mess up Lucifer for daring to lie about *this*. But when my gaze met his...the flames died. Because he meant it.

He bastard meant it.

Tears streaked my cheeks. 'Don't...'

'What?'

'Pretend I'm anything more than a Bone Princess in a cage.'

'That's your mother's poison,' Lucifer sneered. I didn't miss the tremor that ran through him. 'She kidnapped me, after I'd thought myself free. All because she wanted an heir: that'd be *you*, my monstrous daughter. A weapon.' I flinched. That's all I'd been? From the moment of conception? Nothing more than a shank to kill? 'I play, you know, but she's a whole other league of twisted. She wanted you to win the war for her but have me see it was my own daughter who'd defeated me. Dog doubly beaten and all that jazz.' His expression softened. 'The Brigadier didn't get off on such methods. He was my angelic shining knight, sweeping me to safety and Falling because of it. He became my most honoured and darkest soldier.'

Ash had told me he didn't fight. Yet once he'd been the *darkest soldier* at Lucifer's side...? He'd fallen to save Lucifer from the Matriarch...?

Yeah, I couldn't even think about that, as I'd witnessed first-hand what she'd done to Drake.

Slam — I headbutted Lucifer, and he stumbled backwards.

Mischief tripped to the floor between us; his hair was stuck at angles, his clothes dishevelled, and he was still a sickly grey colour.

Less a hunt than a mauling.

'If Ash saved you, then why is your ungrateful leather arse punishing him now? He stopped you from being a bed slave to my psycho mum, but you've made him bed slave to your psycho army. What the hell gives?'

'Oh goodie, third question!' Lucifer steadied

himself against the bedpost, which was carved with the rays of the sun, whilst massaging his bruising temple.

I sighed.

Epic fail on the Trick Three Questions Game.

Lucifer's expression hardened, dangerous and deadly. 'We both have a power; you'll learn it. We enflame — *spark* — loyalty in others. Some we can catch and pull more deeply, and the fun to be had with those...fervent followers. They'll walk into the fire for you. But here's the problem: what happens if someone disobeys? Breaks your hold?'

'You stop being a control freak before you're slapped with a restraining order?'

'Huh, you're not really seeing the parallels yet, are you? See, when you're a ruler, you can't just spank and forget. You have to make an example. And the Brigadier, our sweet Seducer, started obeying someone else more than me. His loyalty belonged to them. And when the spark fades...then so must your follower.'

My gaze became as hard as flint. 'You'll be fading, sparky.'

Lucifer shook his head. 'You wanted answers. Afraid of a little honesty?' I swallowed, looking away: *bastard.* 'It's been just splendid to catch up, but now I must put on my official face.'

Mischief scrambled back against my legs for protection, and I frowned.

Lucifer waved his hand once, and his leather boy outfit changed into sleek black armour that covered him, as much as he'd been on display before. His wings surged on demon fire. A flaming horned helmet flared on his head.

It had to be bastard horns, of course.

My dad was as much a drama queen as J.

In a moment, my dad transformed himself into

a terrifying vision: exactly the ancient supernatural I'd imagined lurked in the Bone Palace as King of the Under World.

He smirked. 'Impressive?'

'You're smaller than I was expecting; more Satan's Little Helper, than Beelzebub himself. The Matriarch's taller than you.'

Lucifer's smirk faltered. Then he touched his helmet; a flame leapt from the horn onto the palm of his hand, pirouetting like a fire fairy. 'Size isn't everything.' He crushed his fist, killing the fairy. 'How'd you like the taste of my light?' *The swirling living light that'd torn whirlwind through the battle, chillingly cold and bright.* I shuddered. 'Isn't it chaos in its most pure form?' He blinked, as if steadying himself. 'A spark must be fostered and helped to grow. Like a daughter. You fought against me. Protected the angels. Defied me in front of my army. See what a bind you've put me in? How can my followers trust you? Your loyalty? They think you're a wild traitor who's a danger to us, and now I'll have to take you into the Crypt to be sentenced and tested.'

'What is it with you and your tests?'

'Option two is execution...'

'Test away.'

Lucifer snatched my arm, marching towards the wall. The bones glowed violently, before peeling back, like ribs in an autopsy.

Bones and blood. Bones and blood. Bones and blood.

I steeled myself, as the chants grew louder from the Crypt beyond.

The vampires had been there, waiting for us, all the time I'd been with Lucifer. Had he always been planning this?

Lucifer leaned closer. 'A leader doesn't get what they want, oh no. You have us pinned as the enemy because you've been brainwashed by the angels. We're the freedom fighters, however, and I put my people first. Even if my daughter must be the one to prove herself. Remember, whatever happens, I love you.'

I gawked at the King of the Under World — Lucifer, Light-bringer, *dad* — clutching my arm in Big Bad of Comic Con outfit and shook.

Because the bloke who I'd always thought the biggest bastard of them all hadn't ditched me at birth: I'd been stolen from him. And maybe...*please, please, maybe*...he wasn't a bastard because he loved me.

Yet, despite that, he was a king, and he was dragging me before his court in the Crypt to be sentenced as a traitor.

11

Even I knew that a bitch didn't laugh when she was being tried as a traitor.

Yet terrified as I was of the sentence, I was being convicted to the cheers of my fanboys.

Bones and blood. Bones and blood. Bones and blood.

I bowed my head in an attempt to look contrite, snuffling on the stuffy dust, but the vampires who sprawled across the stone floor of the Crypt, pawing at each other like they were at a hippie party, weren't chanting to have my guts sprayed over the marble walls. Rather *for* their favourite Bone

Carnival Champion in excited fervour, as if this was just another fight.

I peeked a glance around the medieval arched court room, with gold inscriptions on its walls and Lucifer's lights hovering along the dipped roof, and I finally got that we were below a human cathedral, which had been abandoned or bombed out in the Blitz.

The vampires had built their kingdom on the human dead.

And I was their Champion.

I buzzed, giving up on the sombre and throwing back my head to grin. The temptation to snatch this *celebrity...power...acceptance* flooded me.

Along with a desperate desire to *snigger*.

I preened, until I caught Lucifer's eye.

Lucifer crouched on a tomb, his eyes flaring as dazzlingly as his wings and horned helmet. And jealousy...? Move over, because your new name was Lucifer.

I guess Devil Daddy hadn't been the one who'd sweetened the audience towards me...

Misrule sprawled against the far wall, clutching Harahel to his chest in comfort. I scanned Harahel as I'd once done when he'd been owned by a sadistic Glory, expecting to find the same evidence of bruises now he'd become a Blood Lover.

Misrule had forced the Blood Bond with Harahel, and I knew from Marking Rebel how wrong that was. But Harahel's skin was still unmarred. Perfect. And right now? *Harahel was safer than I was.*

The Feathered prowled between my new worshippers like security guards at a festival, whilst Wild stood akimbo behind Lucifer, sending me a *nana nana na* sneer.

No one can be everybody's cup of tea.

'Crack on with it, bro. Do I get multiple choice?' I tilted back my chin.

When Lucifer gaped at me, I chuckled.

'On my heart of pain, you *do* have spark. But you see, we must be fair, huh? All those who aren't First Fallen are tested, if they wish to escape the Bones...'

Suddenly, the chanting stopped. That one word — *Bones* — conjured an eerie silence.

I shivered. 'Why haven't I been shown that part of the freaky Carnival? How much more of the Under World are you hiding?' When I marched up to Lucifer, Wild blocked me.

Lucifer waved back Wild, however, who reluctantly retreated.

Lucifer's fire wings beat, blowing warm air across my cheeks. 'You know, hiding is such a strong word. When you stop hiding from me, maybe you'll earn my secrets, and they're a cartload of fun.'

'We may have different definitions of fun.'

Lucifer smiled, tapping at his lips. 'Wow, I do hope so, or what will I have to teach my daughter? Now...'

Rizzz — Lucifer pulled down a hidden zipper in the front of his armour, exposing his chest.

I recoiled. '*Different definitions*, kinky bastard Fang. And there's going to be no teaching if this is your fun.'

Lucifer clutched his chest like a violated maiden. 'Yikes, you didn't think...? Those kinky angels have poisoned your mind, missy.' He wagged his finger at me, and I blushed. Then he slipped his hand under the tight leather and drew out a toy, proffering it to me like it was a relic. 'This is your inheritance.'

I stared at the doll's house fork, whilst the

vampire court stared at me.

I clenched my fists.

Was this whole thing a windup?

'You missed the playing with dolls stage by about fifteen years,' I hissed. 'Plus, if you knew me at all, then you'd get that I was the geek you'd impress with a comic, computer game, or...'

Lucifer flicked his wrist. The fork grew in the instant. Living bone, it twisted outwards: long, thin shimmering bone, with three forked prongs at one end and at the other, a point as sharp as a shank.

As tall as Lucifer, it was a bastard of a weapon.

It was also the killer fork that'd been inked onto the Blood's back, which I held aloft, whilst I destroyed the world.

Yet I wanted it.

Awoken, the ancient powers crackled as they crashed against each other, disturbed. They smelled my inheritance and they craved it: a sweet yet sulphurous, charcoal-like musk that spoke only of death. It was so rich, I could taste it, coating my tongue. It didn't choke me, however, it liberated the monster inside. Even though, buried beneath the haze of *want want want,* I shook at what it meant.

'Your Devil's Trident,' Lucifer breathed. 'I just call him Devil. Take him.'

'*Yours, always, touch me...*' The Devil's Trident whispered, insidious and yearning.

I raised my shaking hand towards the shaft.

'Stop with the Percy Jackson action: it's *death.*' Ash's bellow from behind me, sliced through the silence, which hummed with only the honeyed murmurs from the bone trident.

Shocked out of my haze, I spun round.

In the shadows at the back of the Crypt, Ash...and *Rebel*...had been chained side by side to a column, as if it was an ossified tree, and they were waiting for the dragon to barbecue them.

I didn't miss the way their hands were linked.

Trick watched them from the gloom. His long hair swung loose, and he played with it, as if imagining playing with my blokes.

I stiffened.

'The Brigadier's not fibbing,' Rebel pleaded, torturing his lower lip with his teeth. 'On all that's holy, don't touch that bleeding thing. He's after changing you...'

Trick slunk away from the wall at a nod from Wild, sliding a strap from his belt. He hefted it over his shoulder, before whacking it down over Rebel.

Whish — crack.

It caught Rebel's cheek.

Rebel let out a broken sob. The leather had split his skin; scarlet teared down his face. 'Battle it. Whatever the gits do.'

I flinched.

Why wouldn't Rebel stop talking? Why was he always...walking into the fire for me...?

Hell, I wasn't like my dad, was I?

'Princess...don't...'

Whish — crack.

Rebel keened.

Devil was calling to me again; I was already lost to him. I quivered as I turned back, reaching out my hand.

Bones, Devil whispered, *feathers and blood...*

The tips of my fingers almost grazed the bone.

'Don't touch him,' Rebel gasped, 'please...'

Whish — crack.

Rebel's cry, and Ash's murmured comfort, were muffled by the pounding pulse in my ears and the carolling of my new weapon: *I'm yours...hold me...*

I closed my hand around the shaft, my fingers sparking static-light next to Lucifer's, *and touched death.*

I gasped, throwing back my head in a wild howl.

Lucifer's smile was triumphant, as he beat his wings, rising with the trident between us like a war standard. I rose next to him. Dad and daughter in the thrall of death, and it was better than the moment when a shank sliced through skin or the taste of candy blood.

It was coming home to my birthright and it *was* glorious.

'It's a lie,' Ash's voice was haunted. 'Devil latches onto your desires. Twists them, so you'll follow like a good puppy. You can fight it, Violet.'

'Says the green-eyed Seducer who's only having a tantrum because I took away his toy,' Lucifer smirked.

Devil had been *Ash's* weapon?

My fingers loosened on the trident, but a burst of light snaked out, wrapping them back around with a warning *zap*.

'*Free, strengthen, save you. Never abandon. Yours...*' My hand tightened at Devil's pleading whisper.

'Listen up, you gorgeous Fallen: see how the Devil's Trident chooses your Bone Princess?' Lucifer struck a pose for the audience, hand on hip.

And he'd called *me* dramatic.

Awed murmurs.

'Let it be known on Lucifer's Light that if my

daughter passes the tests, then she'll win the trident and reign by my side as Queen of Chaos!' Lucifer grinned, his wings and helmet leaping with flames.

Cheers, beating of wings, and stamping of feet.

As the vampires leapt up and twirled each other round in savage celebration, my heart thundered at the crazy arsed coronation with my name on it: Queen of Chaos.

And yet...for the trident to be mine? For dad to *want* me to rule not as his shadow but *by his side*...?

It *was* my every desire. And that terrified me.

When Lucifer shrunk Devil back to toy size, I panicked.

'*Help, I need you, take me,*' Devil begged like fire blazing over oil.

I snarled, snatching for the trident, as Lucifer tucked him back under his leather outfit and sharply zipped it up.

When I grasped the zip, ramming Lucifer against the roof, I almost missed the instant silence in the Crypt.

Almost.

Lucifer's eyes twinkled. He gave a high laugh, as he prised me away from his zip with an ease that shook me. 'I'm just bursting with pride. Look, I'm positively glowing. See what you can do, when your darkest desires are brought into the light?'

I squirmed. I couldn't help the thrum of joy that he was proud of me. Yet also the rush of fury that it was only because he'd dragged out my inner monster.

He didn't know what he was messing with: my fire had blasted whole battlefields, and I hadn't been the bitch in charge of the power. I was the monster that even the King of Hell should fear. If he let me out of my cage, none of his illusionist tricks could put me back. I remembered then in a shocking rush that in the prophecies inked on Ash's sisters those monsters ended the world.

'You don't know me,' I muttered. 'Dark isn't the way to go.'

Lucifer cocked his head. 'That's why I'm testing you with pain to really get to know the heart of you. After all, Devil desires *you* for a reason.'

'That'll be because he's feeding from you, Violet,' Ash banged his head — *crack* — against the column; the sound cut across the tripped-out daze that'd connected me with Lucifer, and I glanced over at him. 'Dark thoughts, power, killing. He's taken you on a date, and you're the dinner. An all-you-can-eat buffet since you've been sparked with the king's light.'

Lucifer growled, clutching my arm, as he swooped us down to Ash. He landed lightly, stalking towards him. 'Tsk, bite your tongue, Seducer.' He touched his hand to his helmet, before tripping sparks off his palm and across Ash's flinching lips.

I shifted because how many times had I burnt others with my fire...even their lips?

'Are you done gagging him? What do I have to do to win Devil?'

Lucifer wagged his finger at me. 'I love it: straight and to the point. But first, you need to keep up your strength.' He swept to Rebel, wrenching back his head to expose his long white neck. 'Feed.'

First my sister and now my dad? What was up with the angel blood fetish?

'Not happening, moving on, and a kick in the balls for the first person who gets fangy around my angel.' I paced closer.

Lucifer sighed like I'd broken curfew. 'You have to eat, champ, to grow up big and strong.' He grinned. 'Seriously, angel blood is the magic ingredient to your super mix. Just sprinkle in a dash of Fallen blood as well and...voila!' He shook Rebel's neck at me again with an encouraging grin.

'No way on your little horned head.'

Lucifer touched his helmet self-consciously, then frowned.

I suddenly remembered just who I was sassing.

Hell...literally.

Crunch — skeletons exploded out of the ground beneath me.

I screamed, but they clung to my legs and arms. My heart pounded so hard it hurt. I bit my tongue to stop myself shrieking again.

The skeletons moulded around my limbs, pulling me down as they shaped themselves into a chair, wrapping their bony fingerbones around my throat to hold me still.

I drew panicked breaths through my nostrils, catching the skeleton chair's musty stench. 'Let me bastard go.' I struggled against the bones, and the skeletons' fingers tightened.

Lucifer crossed his arms as if in thought. 'That'd be a *no way on your little violet-and-black-eyed head*. My patience is like a flame.' He crushed his fist, and the lights dancing over Ash's mouth died. 'Soon put out. But I'm all in favour of *puppies* learning tricks. So...' He yanked the chains away from Ash and caught him in his arms. 'Show my daughter how to be a *good puppy.*'

Lucifer knew how to make your own words bite you in the arse.

Ash cast a desperate look at me, before forcing himself to relax into Lucifer's hold. I tensed, hating that Lucifer was touching him. 'Don't ask me to do this, Your Majesty. Not in front of—'

'The angels stole our light,' Lucifer's agonized howl ran a shiver of dread through me, even as his sparking glare — flaring with cold light — met Ash's. That they'd saved each other and fought in battles for centuries was unexpectedly real and raw. 'They stole *me*. Just because we wanted to be free. You remember, right?'

'It's hard to remember anything when you're a whore,' Ash spat, his eyes glistening.

Smack — Lucifer slapped Ash across the cheek but he was shaking too.

Then he thrust Ash away, backing up a step, as if realising they were putting on a Soap Special for the rapt vampire audience. 'If you don't obey me, *whore*, then I'll do it.'

What the hell were they talking about?

Ash startled, before shaking his head; his mouth set in a grim line.

Wild shoved through the vampires to drag off Rebel's chains. Rebel collapsed to his knees, curling over. The purple welt stood out across his cheek. Ash dropped down next to him, fiddling with the belt of Rebel's jeans. Rebel scrabbled at Ash's hands in alarm.

My eyes widened; I fought against the skeleton chair. 'No playing without permission.'

Ash patted Rebel's shoulder: two soldiers about to go into battle. 'We're to put on a show, mate. Let me, and I'll take it easy on you. This is for Violet. Pretend we're alone.'

Rebel nodded, but his head was turned away, his arm over his eyes to hide his face. His voice, however, was tear-tinged. 'Just do it, muppet. And don't say you'll make it good because there's nothing bleeding good about this.'

Ash wet his lips, before sliding his hand down

again to the waistband of Rebel's jeans.

Outrage, fear, humiliation: they shrouded me through our bond. I retched at the sticky shame of it.

'Jesus Christ, please...just my wings...' Rebel begged.

Ash pulled away his hand, dipping his head to feather kisses along Rebel's fluttering neck. I could hear both their harsh breaths even bound in my bone chair.

I curled my toes, as my jaw clenched. If Ash bastard touched my Mark on Rebel's neck...

But Ash skirted around it. Instead, he placed a single chaste kiss on Rebel's trembling lips: two men-at-arms.

'Gather round! Here's a special spectacle: our Seducer showing off his tricks.' Wild gestured to the FF who flanked the vampires, trapping them closer.

Hoots, guffaws, jeers.

Bets called out on *me*: how many minutes before the Champion pulled her wrists bloody against the chair (already happened), stopped watching...*cried*. Even though my eyes already burnt with tears, I gritted my teeth together: *they were all bastard losing that one.*

The vampires were addicts to gambling and pain.

I caught a glimpse of Harahel's brunet curls; he'd hidden his face on the Master of Misrule's shoulder. Misrule's expression was carefully blank. Shouldn't he be leading the show? Except, the vampires around him all wore the same shuttered expressions and stiff shoulders. They weren't betting or laughing.

Maybe not all of the Under World revelled in

the pain of Seducers and angels. Or were as loyal as Lucifer thought?

Rebel gasped, as Ash caressed his wings, circling each feather. Mortified shame wept through the bond at the forced pleasure.

I closed my eyes, but Lucifer whispered with shocking intimacy into my ear, 'Naughty naughty, you're missing the performance, and when I went to such lengths to have it put on in your honour. Are you bored, huh? Are the boys not being...adventurous enough?' My eyes shot open, and he chuckled. 'There you are. And today's lesson? Look how willingly they'll walk into the fire for you. They're just begging to be sacrificed.'

What...?

I startled, my skin tingled.

He'd set me up. Yet here my fam were, acting just like Lucifer had known they would. I'd reckoned it was because they loved me.

But...now?

No one was winning that bet about me crying.

Ash kissed Rebel's wingtips, sucking, as Rebel arched and purred. Then Rebel shuddered, stilling. His head lolled back, as he blacked out.

Ash crouched over Rebel, wiping away the tears underneath his eyes. Then he juddered, licking Rebel's neck: an addict coming back for his next taste of heaven.

Hell, Rebel's blood was mine. What would happen if Ash Bonded with my angel?

Ash turned Rebel's head to the side, lowering his fangs to his neck...

'I'll bastard do it. I'll feed from him,' I hollered.

Silence.

The vampires had been well trained, like kids in

school assembly.

Ash's star sparking eyes were cold. 'You couldn't have had this revelation before we...?' He hung his head. 'Before *I* did this? Before you made me feel...'

Lucifer drew in a mock shocked breath.

Ash glowered, cradling Rebel to his chest, before carrying him to lay on my knee; he held Rebel's throat up to my lips.

I hadn't realised just how much larger Ash was than Rebel, until I saw him carry him in his arms. I couldn't meet Ash's gaze.

Awkwardly, I worried at Rebel's skin with my blunt teeth. Then the candy blood hit.

Slam.

Sugary copper heaven hit me in a tsunami wave: life, strength, *mine*. I zinged with the new world opening before me, written in my angel's blood.

I gulped, sucking down my own addiction.

'*This* is your home,' Lucifer's voice broke through my blood daze. 'But you still need to pass the test. Rescue a Fallen from a human hunter's lair. Prove your loyalty's with me, rather than the human world. Consequences: a test can be failed, see? No one wants a trip to the Bones. You're my daughter, however, so...if you fail, you'll be Bonded to the Supreme Commander. He'll keep you on a tight leash.' I jolted, spitting out a mouthful of blood. It sprayed over Lucifer's face; he wiped away dripping scarlet. 'My, you truly don't wish the honour of my most trusted fighter's fangs...? That's not the spirit I like to see. Here's the bonus: if you fail, Wild will also get your pet angel and Fallen as playthings. Large appetite, know what I mean?'

'I'll gank the bastard first.'

'Then here's a novel thought: pass the test.' Lucifer patted my head.

My dad wanted to turn me against the human world.

Even as Rebel's blood buzzed through me, I knew it wasn't enough that I'd violated my angel by drinking from him and forcing him to become my Blood Lover. Now I had to risk fighting human hunters and if I failed, I'd lose everything to the Feathered bullies.

12

When I'd trained as a vampire huntress, I'd wondered what would happen if humans worked out that supernaturals shared the shadows of their world. Would they become hunters too?

What I'd never guessed? *That the human hunters would be the Big Bads.*

I curled on the ripped seat of my carriage bedroom, with Blaze and Spark both resting their heads in my lap. I stroked their satin ears like stress relievers.

No throb of drum-and-bass or roared punk from Misrule's next-door: my performance in the Bone Palace had killed the music.

Our performance.

I peeked at Rebel, who was clutching onto the central pole like it was all that was holding him up. His wings were hidden again underneath his studded leather jacket; I hadn't realised how much I'd missed that.

Would he think it crazy stalker territory if I buried my nose in his shoulder just to sniff the familiar leather and metal?

Considering the way he wouldn't even lift his scrutiny from his boots — either to me or to Ash — I'd go with a stalkerlicious: *hell, yeah.*

Publicly seduced by one of us, then changed into a Blood Lover by the other...?

I was waiting for the explosion of killer angel.

As was Ash, who sprawled on my foam bed. His gaze was wary, as he shielded his huddled sisters. He ducked his head. 'It's a trick—'

'Holy Mary will you stop it, you great muppets,' Rebel said softly. At last, he raised his head. His eyes were red-rimmed; the kohl smudged. 'Treating me like *I'm* the lion about to eat off your idiot heads. We're all prisoners. And after how I was treated in Angel World: Addict, Imperfect, Marked...' I pinked. 'I understand between bad choices and worse. You both...tried. Now we have to get ourselves out of this trident bollocks. Human hunters are vigilante gits.'

Ash swung himself up with a grin. He gripped Rebel's shoulders, before kissing him loudly on the cheek.

Rebel flailed his arms, rubbing at his face. 'I'll boot your Fallen arse, Brigadier.'

'How about a pole dance first, retro angel?' Ash ducked Rebel's clout. 'Although...' Ash raised his eyebrow at me.

'If the next words out of your mouth have *Violet*

in them, *I'll* be the lion ripping off your head,' I snarled.

Both familiars balefully glared at Ash on my behalf.

Ash slid up and down the pole with a smirk. 'I'm the sexy dancer who's trained, *Violet.*'

When he twisted sinuous and sinful up the pole, I held my breath.

No time for the happy tingles, Feathery-dark, even if he could ride my pole any day.

Give me a moment, J, concentrating.

The hot Seducer is distracting you. Because this test? It's not just about flaying your humanity. It's about the Seducer's for the gods ass.

'*It's a trick*,' I blurted. Ash stilled, upside down on the pole, before slowly sliding down and facing me. 'What did you mean?'

'The hunters who play at *Supernatural* are vicious gang members, but it's all a game. No human hunter has ever caught a Fallen.'

The familiars whined, as I pushed them to the floor. I paced, whilst they wound around my ankles. 'Why set an impossible test?'

'It's more like a no-win, Kobayashi Maru type situation. This is about sacrifice. Allow one of us to be caught by the humans. Then you'll have a Fallen to be rescued.'

'The cold bastard.'

Ash shrugged. 'Lucifer is hot, in all senses. The question is, whether we can hack the situation beforehand. Stop it being no-win.'

Rebel looked away. 'Who's the sacrifice?'

I studied him — my Blood Lover — his blood still sweet as it tangled with my own.

Look at me.

The thought blasted through our Blood Bond, even though I didn't know I had the new power.

Rebel's head shot round, his eyes widening as they met mine.

He'd obeyed.

I thrilled at the connection. With the Mark I could force emotions, but now I could also force *thoughts*.

Yet a wave of despair washed over me from Rebel, and suddenly I was aware of the darkening horror in his gaze.

If he'd become my Blood Lover willingly, would he have been free? Equal?

I drew back within myself, sensing the moment our connection *snapped*. Rebel staggered, his hand pressing to his forehead as if it ached. It was forced submission like the Mark, and I craved the true kind.

I touched the tender skin on the back of my neck.

...Screaming...held down in the skeleton chair as the bone needle tattooed the feather-shaped blood ward to protect me and all those who were mine from the angels' sight.

The Devil's Mark.

Ash took a brisk step forward, back to army mode. 'Volunteer Brigadier at your command.'

'Hold up, soldier, who says running into the fire — twice — will make everything—'

'I won't ever be clean, you mean?' Ash caught me by the arm, crushing me against the window's shattered glass. His lips grazed against mine. 'Reminder not necessary. Anyone here with grey wings flap them.' His wings beat; their breath spectred across my cheeks. 'Only me then? We plan, sacrifice, rescue. Just don't forget the rescue.'

'I can't wait to see what type of bastard becomes a human hunter. Although, don't you think that makes it sound like they should be hanging up human pelts? But I won't let these thug Batmans hurt you.'

'They'll hurt me.' Ash's smile was tight. 'You only need the wankers not to have worked out how to kill me.'

'How do you know...?'

'They'll want to experiment. I'll be the rat.' Ash sauntered to his sisters, pulling them closer to kiss their heads.

Rebel assessed him for a moment. 'We can't balls this up. So, what aren't you telling us, Brigadier?'

Ash stiffened, before slinking to Rebel. He trailed his hand down his chest. 'Bet: Violet, for your account of blood, I bet...my kiss rates higher out of ten right now than Leprechaun Angel's.'

'Cop on!' Rebel growled, although his shoulders slumped. 'She wouldn't even want to kiss a filthy thing like you.'

Ash flinched, but his gaze never left mine.

Why the hell did he want to bet? Didn't he still trust me?

'I'm not in the gambling mood, Addict-5000.'

'Do you think I am?' Ash burst out, before striding to the carriage door and swinging it open. The rumble of a train approaching vibrated through the dusty air. 'Then I'll have to fight in the Cage before we leave.'

'No way in Psychoville.'

The windows rattled; the carriage lurched. My head pounded.

'There's something worse than being a Shadow, Seducer, or a Blood,' Ash's eyes sparked fallen stars, as he stalked towards me. I fell back on the chair.

'*The Bones*.' I shivered at the tremble in his voice. 'Anything you've ever feared: the dark, pain, starvation, or loneliness... That's what it means. Being trapped. You're the future Queen of Chaos, the Champion, and the king's daughter: you think *this* is losing your freedom?'

I huddled, drawing up my knees. I turned away my head, but Ash grabbed my chin, forcing me to look at him.

Sobs caught in my throat. 'I didn't know—'

'What about those you beat? Who couldn't earn enough blood? Or didn't pass the tests? They're the ones who suffer in the Bones. Like...Anarchy's little brother, Key.' I gasped, squirming to escape Ash's intent gaze, but he didn't let go. Anarchy was a Fallen who'd been captured by the Pure: fanatical vampires. He was also Ash's best mate and a decent kid who'd helped me. And who I'd failed to rescue. 'Everything I earn goes to Key. To buying his freedom. If I hadn't betrayed you, I wouldn't have been able to...'

This time, it was Ash who looked away.

I brushed Ash's cheek, and he reluctantly raised his gaze. 'My blood is your blood. And we'll bastard save the Bones, all of them, the same as I'll save you.'

'Pinkie promise?' Ash grinned.

'Geek,' I sniggered.

Except, my mouth was dry at the thought: I'd have to gift-wrap Ash for brutal human hunters, when I was myself just another monster they'd love to bag for their collection.

To win the test we'd have to become the hunted.

A satin cobalt blue top, which rode up Ash's hips over jeans that were tight enough not to leave anything to the imagination, was trapped beneath a black military jacket: a slutty toy soldier.

Ash completed the impression by lounging against the brick wall with one arm slung behind his head and the other smartly behind his back.

I crouched at the end of the alley behind the burger bar on the Utopia Estate in the shadow of the tower blocks that had dominated my human life, in the cover of the stinking bins.

My fists clenched on my knees, which were dampened by the fat summer drizzle, as I watched Ash.

Our bait.

I choked on the greasy clouds from the burger bar, which warred with spicy ones from the kebab shop opposite. My eyes watered. Grime music pounded across the evening estate.

To hell with adding hunters into the mix: hanging around alleys at night in Hackney, you were either shanked or the bastard with the shank. And Lucifer had made one rule before he'd allowed Trick to lead Ash and me — blindfolded — from the Under World.

This was a game played without fangs. If Ash was a sacrifice, he was a lamb, not a wolf.

Although, I'd always reckoned him more of a panther.

Mischief had come up with the hack to put us one ahead of the no-win game. He'd airily waved a hand and informed us that humans' technology was little different to magic. Then he'd burrowed a tracker under the skin of Ash's neck. As he hadn't warned him, Ash had howled, before shoving Mischief away and swinging for him.

Mischief, however, had blocked Ash's hook, holding up an earpiece instead. 'Since I've been dragged into this travesty, I find myself intrigued as to what the *beast*...' Ash had snarled and this time had managed to split Mischief's lip. '...What the *princess* will pay for the pretty three-pronged bauble.'

'Ash,' I whispered into the earpiece, suddenly frozen with the need to hear him because *something wasn't right.*

Ash's gaze flicked to the bins, before his voice murmured through the earpiece, 'I'm not the stealthiest, but I thought the point of this undercover was...I was undercover?'

'It can wait. Why'd you pick this alley?'

Ash tensed. He wasn't as practised a liar as Rebel. His top rippled snake-like, as he shrugged.

Then realisation hit me. And I wanted to hurl. 'This is where you seduce them. Trap the humans, before you take them back to your flat...and the same bed as you slept in with me...'

'*No*,' Ash straightened, before closing his eyes. 'Yes. Not always...? It's my job, Violet, my punishment. It's not like I... And I don't sleep with them, not most of them, I just introduce them to this world. They're not forced, they choose—'

'The Fang idea of choice is as messed up as the angels'.'

Ash opened his eyes, crossing his arms. 'I don't make the rules.'

'But you're legendary at following them, aren't you, soldier?'

'Not recently, Violet, not since I met you.'

I shuddered, taking a deep breath, '*My sister.*'

Ash broke position, reaching out to me as he strode towards the end of the alley. 'I never touched your sister. I didn't even know she was in the Blood Lovers. On my anime collectible collection, I swear: I didn't seduce her.'

I dived out from behind the bins, ramming Ash

against the wall, and he let me. My fingers bunched in his shirt; I hated that I leaned into his aromatic fragrance. 'On your Lara Croft poster: how did you know the hunters would even come sniffing down this alley?'

Ash squirmed, booting against the wall. 'Because they always do. It's part of the *Paranormal Slayers'* patrol.'

The sneaky bastard.

I said this was about that sweet slice of ass.

I'll buy you an I told You So t-shirt in sequins.

I shook Ash.

Thud — his head whacked against the brick, but he was too busy avoiding my gaze to wince.

'You know them? These wannabe slayers have hunted you before?'

'Look at me,' Ash sneered, shoving me away at last and wiping his hand down his slut soldier outfit in disgust. 'The Para Gang heard the whispers about the whore vampire on the Estate. I'm the only Fallen out amongst the humans long enough to be targeted and I'm meant to be making soft and cuddly with the natives, not ripping out their throats. So, what do I say to them? Please stop spitting on me, kicking my head in, and trying to out me...?'

My stare was hard. 'They're been beating on you for years? I never thought—'

'What?' Ash's voice was deceptively calm. 'I was weak like your angel?' His glower was as hard as mine; I shrank back. 'I obey orders. This was part of my punishment. The hunters wanted proof, and I was strong enough never to give them the satisfaction. Except, tonight I will, for you.' His smile was bitter. 'Hasn't everything been for you?'

I slammed my fist against the wall; drizzle

streaked down my cheeks, warm and suffocating. 'I didn't ask you to...'

'Love you?' Ash wound his arm around my waist, pulling me close. He ran his fangs up my neck, pressing kisses in their wake; I trembled. 'It's not something you ask. You just have to accept it, gorgeous, and don't...forget.'

Then he pushed me away, and I stumbled, tripping into the pile of black bins.

What the hell...?

Three large blokes in hoodies with orange stripes on their sleeves, hollered and dashed towards Ash down the alley.

Humans. But Ash shrank back like they were an orc horde.

I was going to kill those bastards for making Ash look like that.

'Where have you been, pansy boy?' The tallest Para Number One jeered, grabbing Ash by the scruff of the neck, before kneeing him in the balls.

I sprawled in the shadows, tears pricking my eyes, and waited. The moment the Paranormal Slayers hauled Ash to their hunter hideout, I'd kick their arses. I just had to push down on the violet that swirled in furious eddies.

'You're going to get dashed, Edward.' Para Number Two, channelling the *Twilight* prejudice, jumped up and down on his toes like a boxer. Then he clutched Ash, hurling him into the centre of his circling mates.

I'd wanted to see human hunters.

Now I bastard had.

They had no righteousness, only a sadistic joy in the vampire's suffering. Why had I expected humans to be different? They were protecting their own from the Big Bads in the shadows.

Would I've been any different, before I'd known

the truth of my monster inside, when this had been *my* yard?

Smack, thump, whack.

I flinched at each clout to the face and each boot to the ribs and kidneys. When they took turns stamping on Ash's face, violet burst in a spray from my fingertips, lighting up the gloomy alleyway, but the gang were too busy curb stamping the vampire to notice the monster behind them.

Breathing hard, I forced myself not to drag them off Ash. He had to be caught, fangs out, before he could be rescued.

'Oh, my days, did you see that, bro?' The scrawny runt of the pack, Para Number Three, leapt back before leaning closer again and pushing Ash onto his back.

Ash sprawled as if unconscious, but I knew better: The Brigadier was making his play.

Fangs glistened in his bloodied mouth.

The gang fist pumped in jubilation at breaking and catching the monster. Only then did I notice the backpacks that they dropped with disturbing *clunks* next to Ash's head.

And when they opened them…?

An Aladdin's treasure trove of machetes, Zombie Slayer shanks, shooters, bottles of acid and bleach, garlic and crosses spilled out. These bastards didn't know what they were playing with. Except, they weren't playing.

Ash had known.

As soon as I saved him, I'd stomp on his anime collectibles to show him what I thought of *that*.

Para Number One snatched out a bottle of bleach, holding it over Ash's eyes, laughing.

And what made my chest tighten?

Ash didn't even try to pull away, even though his jaw clenched, and he swallowed.

'Don't want you seeing our yard,' Para Number One mocked. 'It's time to take you to your cage.'

To hell with waiting until they had Ash at their lair.

I burst out of the bins, like vengeance, fire, death...with violet blazing on my fingertips. 'Get away from him.'

My wings spread, flaming. The tips pulsed obsidian.

I'd expected awe, unmanly squeals, maybe even puddles of piss, if I'd been lucky.

What I hadn't expected...?

'Safe! Another monster stepping-up!' What was this, paranormal investigations Hackney style? 'Roast the bitch.'

Hose, nozzle, fuel tank... *They bastard hadn't...?*

My pulse pounded; I backed up a step.

Para Number Two grinned. He hefted the DIY flamethrower onto his hip. 'Burn, freak.'

Then he sparked the flamethrower, and the fire roared.

13

My singed wings trembled under the assault of silver sparks; popcorn sweetness crackled along each feather. I panted, curled up on the freezing concrete floor of Mischief's cell, which was a scarlet bomb proof bunker from World War Two.

I was still battling a war, but this time the enemy were in my own yard. The humans from the Estate, which I'd saved from vampires at Christmas, had taken *my* vampire, whilst turning their fire on me.

Welcome to the Bone Carnival, bitches, the beast is about to break out of her cage.

Tune down the Revenge-O-Metre. Lucifer wants your humanity stripped to the bones. Why let your own fire do the stripping?

Do these hunters even count as humans?

Assholes **may have their whole own**

evolutionary branch of the shady tree.

So, why are you turning Miss Judgey Girl on the rest of the species because the hunters fought dirty...like you once did?

They tried to flame me, J, and they kidnapped my fam.

Of course they did, Feathers-mine, because that was your play: Sacrifice the Geek Fang before rescuing his ass.

Did you think any test your two horns of crazy daddy set would be a waltz in the sunshine?

When I twisted, slapping Mischief's hands away from my wings, he tumbled backwards from his crouch over me onto his arse. His eyes were blown wide; he panted as loudly as me. I gripped his hands, dragging him closer again.

The bomb shelter was crammed floor to ceiling with gadgets: An Apple iMac had been split open like Mischief had been puzzling out its *magic*, and a spider drone lay next to Hermione's Hogwarts wand.

Gifts from Lucifer, his sugar daddy...?

Either way, this bunker was *Ash's heaven*. If Ash could see past the *angel whore* label, Mischief was his geek mate.

Tears pricked, as I shoved myself up.

... Furling my wings around myself, as the roaring wall of flame hit... Violet shooting out to shield my wings but just too late... Screaming...scorching...stumbling...and then silence...

Cool fingers cupped my cheek; gentle wings wrapped around me. 'Your half of the tracker melted,' Mischief's voice had lost its hard edge, like ice chipped smooth. 'There's no guilt in being outwitted. Your father knew you wouldn't be able to sense Ash...'

I yanked away from Mischief's hold. 'How many new toys does my dad give you to whisper his praises into my ear?'

Mischief bristled, pulling himself up as tall as he could. '*None*. With his ego, the king hardly believes he needs my word on his genius.' Then he bit his lip, glancing at the shut door of the bunker, as if Lucifer's spies could hear him even through that and report him. 'I'll burn for you,' he hissed, 'as certainly as your Brigadier shall.'

With a growl, I snatched a thin piece of wood, backing Mischief into the corner, as I held it to his chest.

He raised an eyebrow. 'Should I be arching in excruciating agony? Oh wait, you haven't cast the imaginary spell yet.'

I blinked at him, before staring down at the wood in my hand: Hermione's wand. When I whipped it across Mischief's cheek, he yelped. 'Can you feel the magic yet?'

'A little tingle,' Mischief seethed. 'It fizzled out. Now *true* magic...'

Crack — the wand snapped in a shower of sparks and splinters, soaring across his cell that masqueraded as a bunker and smacking against the far wall.

Why had he been hiding that power?

'You could blow me to itty pieces,' I breathed, staring at where I'd been holding the wand.

'And give up trading insults? Death threats. Blows to the head...?' Mischief rubbed at his cheek. 'Still so beastly, I see.'

'Track Ash,' I pushed my nails into my palms hard enough to cut the soft flesh; my own voice sounded too loud in my ears. 'He's done nothing to you.'

'The Fallen's done nothing *for* me,' Mischief gave a moue of distaste. 'But that's hardly the point. The thugs took out the tracker in his neck. Maybe not so thuggish after all.'

I howled, ramming Mischief against the wall. 'You are one word away from becoming a fried Gandalf.'

'*Lair*,' Mischief turned up his aristocratic nose, 'my one word. What type of leader do you wish to become? Because this was always about sacrifice. Are you protector of one or all? The king chooses his words as carefully as one picks up a snake: *rescued from a hunter's lair*. Not saved from requiring the assistance of a Guide Dog. You almost lost the test because of your mawkish heart.' I tried to slap him, but he caught my wrist. 'Please, always with the violence. Are you trying to prove me right or wrong about the beast inside?'

'I don't sacrifice fam.'

'Yet *you have*,' Mischief tilted his head; his hair veiled his face. 'Is all this sound and fury because someone has finally bested you, *Champion*? And a human at that. Truth slips in the soft parts of us and pulls us to pieces.'

I staggered back, breathing harshly. 'This was always your plan. Did you know I'd fail?'

Mischief twirled, falling with the elegance of a fairy dancer and the air of a prince, into a PVC computer chair. 'Have you failed? Surely that's your choice? I'm many things but I don't claim to be all-knowing.'

'But you are Falling?' When I plucked a grey feather from his wing, Mischief winced, curling around himself. 'And your gamble is to Blood Bond with my dad. I guess that makes me Snow White stepdaughter in the way of your wicked stepmother?'

'What would you have me do? *I survive*, and freedom is earnt.' Mischief gripped the chair's armrests so hard they squeaked. 'There are more ways to earn it than through fighting.'

Fury and grief raged in a swirling maelstrom; my fingers twitched.

'I'd have you offer up your arse as my *sacrifice*,' I rapped his knuckles. 'I'll find this gang, and when you Fall, I'll exchange you for Ash.'

Mischief paled; he gave me a searching look. 'Hold that thought...' He rootled amongst his pile of gadgets, pulling out an iPad. He swiped it to a clip on YouTube, which stuttered my heart. My head jerked back, as I gasped. My fingers clutched Mischief's knuckles, so tightly *he* gasped.

Please...hell...no...don't...bastard...please...

Ash: he sprawled in arched pain. His wings were furled around himself, as if he could hide from the camera.

He'd been chained on an elegant sofa, which was covered in faded pictures of the Garden of Eden, as the trophy. Three hooded figures stood behind him: the hunters after the safari.

And they'd bagged their wild cat.

'When...? What...?' I whispered, reaching out for the screen.

Mischief pulled it away from me. 'Did you think *I'd* given up on your boy? That *I* fail? This is the humans' moment of triumph. Of course they'd trumpet if online. Watch.'

'In one hour, we — the Para Gang — will show the world the truth.' Para Number One's voice boomed, gleeful as a bloke who'd discovered wanking. His two minions gripped Ash's wings, stretching them out; Ash whined. 'This is for all those who've disrespected and the unbelievers...' *What was this: a warped Justin Bieber concert?*

'We're the real deal. Hunters, yeah? In an hour, you come correct, ready to watch all the ways to hurt and kill a vampire. We'll be making history, brothers and sisters.'

When he spun a wooden stake dramatically over Ash's chest, I tensed. It couldn't kill Ash, but it'd hurt like a bitch.

Just as it did, when the hunter plunged it into Ash's guts.

The video cut out on Ash's howl.

Smash — I flipped the iPad to the floor.

'Constructive,' Mischief muttered.

'How long ago was it posted?' I shook as I stood over Mischief; furious waves of my vampiric power howled as loudly as Ash had to lift this *angel* from his seat and break him as I had in the Cage. 'Do you get off when I go medieval on your unicorn arse? Tell me you only just found out...?'

'Twenty-six minutes ago...' Mischief scrambled back off his chair, holding out his hand to ward me off. 'And I didn't tell you until talk turned to *hostage exchange* because it's evidently a trap.'

I took a deep breath, unclenching my hands. 'One sentence, bro, before I violet up your arse.'

He pulled a face. 'Unpleasant. Anyway, the Seducer knew the risks; he didn't expect you to rescue him.'

Fire sparked along my arms. 'Wrong answer.'

Yet then I remembered the way Ash had known the hunters, what was coming, and still had accepted it. How he'd told me that he loved me and not to *forget*.

Ash *had* sacrificed himself for me. And I hadn't even realised.

I met Mischief's steady gaze. 'Does this look like a bitch who gives a flying fairy toss whether it's a trap, or Ash has come over all martyr? This is *my* test, and I'll take it.'

Mischief sighed. 'How will we discover where they are?'

I stared at the screen, which was frozen at a shot of Ash silent in his agony. 'Animals,' I muttered.

'Quite. That's a George III tapestry sofa he's bleeding all over.'

I froze.

You lived twenty-one years on these streets, Violet-honey, your daddy's testing your knowledge of the human world.

Ask yourself why Lucifer's shining a light on the humans...? If he's testing whether you still rule them, then you better believe he has a shady ass reason.

I peered at the screen again: marble floors, soft lighting, and that sofa...

What the hell type of gang had lairs like that?

Only one I'd ever heard of...

'Here's a London story for you: a dick Russian oligarch buys up a rundown block of houses. Then he has them built up as a mansion that he only visits once in a blue moon. And a creepy-arsed *trio* squats there, making snuff films.' I shuddered. 'I guess they were practising.' I took a final look at Ash on the screen. 'How long...?'

'Half an hour. You'll need me to come with you to the surface and teleport—'

'Then move your arse. But only I go in because if this *is* a trap...it's for me alone. Cheers, for not giving up on Ash...' When I pressed a kiss to Mischief's high cheekbone, he pinked.

Then we dived out of Mischief's cell.

Thirty minutes to save Ash. Thirty minutes to run into a trap. Thirty minutes to take on the human hunters.

The hunters hadn't been expecting me to boot through the line of salt or swagger through the Devil's Traps hidden on the crystal-embedded ceilings and daubed over the black-and-white chessboard floor of the mansion's deserted hallway.

These were kids playing out warped fantasies. But this time they'd invited in a real monster.

They'd even switched off the security system. *Eager little bastards.*

Four minutes, Violet-cheeks, until the Hackney Paranormal Slayers start with the torture games.

I crept through the hallway, which blazed with light from the crystal chandelier that hung in its centre, towards the glass spiral staircase.

It stank of damp.

Creak — the chandelier swayed like a giant pendulum.

I glanced upwards, only for my eyes to widen, as the gleaming lights hurtled down.

I flung myself to the side.

Crash.

The chandelier smashed against the marble, catching my ankle. I hissed, hugging my knee to my chest.

Bastard booby traps.... Wait...weren't they rigged up to trigger each other...?

Squirt — liquid shot out of blasters that'd popped out of a cabinet.

I scrunched up my face against the acid or...?

I licked my lips, savouring the *garlic water*, as my hair dripped into my eyes. I'd always wondered whether holy water tasted *holier*. I didn't feel any saintlier. And if that was the worst weapon they had...?

Three minutes...

I wiped my face, swooping for the staircase.

Slam — a giant steel cross sprang out of the wall, Indiana Jones style.

The cross swung, ramming into my shoulder with a *thud*. I yelped, as I was pinned to the plaster: a butterfly trapped by its wing.

Then the steel began to heat.

14

In Jerusalem Children's Home we hadn't believed in fairy tales. Magic had been stolen by the ugly truth of an adult world forced on us before most kids had stopped searching for fairies.

Vampires? Devils? Monsters?

They already came to our beds at night in the guise of our carers or beat us in jeering crowds in the playground for being *orphan freaks*.

Yet here was the irony of being the outcast: even when you didn't believe in fairy tales, you spent your life searching for a fantasy, in which to lose yourself.

Because anything is better than being alone with harsh reality.

The steel cross burnt across my left wing, pinning it

to the wall of the mansion.

I panted, shoving at it with my palms, even as they blistered; lights danced firework across my vision. I took deep breaths through my nostrils, which were still coated with garlic-laced holy water. In the stinking haze, my skin blackened, as my boots gouged the plaster, pushing in frantic scrabbles.

Two minutes...

Enough with the nuclear countdown, J, I'm being melted by a cross.

This is me asking—

For my fabulousness' help? Why? You drank the angel blood; you have the power.

What is this, Her-Woman, the Most Feminist Woman in London?

It's the Bone Princess realising that her Blood Lover has granted her more strength than she ever dreamed.

I braced myself against the wall, slowing my breathing.

Was J's sassy arse right? Had Rebel's blood strengthened me?

I pushed: *nothing.*

I shrank from the scorching heat. Then I closed my eyes, sinking down into my new Blood Lover bond. I reached out, throwing a single forceful thought across to Rebel: *push.*

Instantly, my hands jerked, doubled in strength. Rebel was in me, through my blood, Mark, and Blood Bond. He was enslaved even through thought; I stole his power.

And I pushed.

Creak — inch by inch the cross edged backwards.

I slipped out my wing, dropping the white-hot metal again with a *clang.*

One minute...

Tremoring with rage, I stalked up the staircase: the beast arrived to rescue Beauty.

Inside my mind, the Devil's Trident sang: '*Fight, win, kill...*'

I booted in the door at the top of the staircase in a spray of splinters, high kicking the camera that perched on a tripod to record the trio's next snuff film. The cream carpet had been covered in black sheeting: *the bastards were pro psychos.*

Ash was laid bare arsed in the middle of the sheeting, his clothes neatly stacked to the side, whilst the trio had scarves over their faces, like they deserved to be anonymous, whilst Ash had been stripped of all dignity.

Ash's body was already a map of the hunters' torture. Their machetes and baseball bats rested over his body, like he was a blow-up doll at a bachelor's party waiting to be passed around.

As Ash turned to the doorway at the sound, my breath hitched: his eyelids were swollen by chemical burns, his pupils were too large, and a cloudy film whited over his eyes. He twisted this way and that sniffing...

The humans had blinded him.

My knees buckled, but black rose up, coiling through me higher than it'd ever blazed before. It didn't demand righteousness but *vengeance.*

'*Feed me,*' Devil hissed, '*take them.*'

With a *whoop*, the Para Gang drew their shooters, grinning.

Para Number One barked, 'Silver bullets, hell bitch.'

'I'm not a werewolf, bastard.' I dodged, as they shot, soaring over their heads.

Ash rose in panther glory, fangs and claws shooting out.

The humans' sweating fear was intoxicating. Their shooters nothing but toys.

I raised my hands, which crackled with furious fire. 'I am a bitch though: The Bitch of Utopia.' My voice rumbled with flames; they erupted from my lips. 'Protector of these streets, and you'll never bring violence to them again.'

Light, fiercer than my violet fire, blasted from me. It melted the hunters' guns. Then it melted the humans, as they screamed, twisting like I had under the cross.

I was as lost as they were, however, lost to the beast inside.

When I slammed into my carriage room, dragging Ash stumbling after me, I still rode on the heady mix of fear and triumph: The Champion of the Devil's test.

Hunter of hunters.

Even if my hair stank of melted flesh.

Rebel had been stretched out on the floor in a circle with the Bloods and familiars, each with a pile of poker cards and grapes in the place of cash. Blaze had just nosed in an extra grape, tapping his pile.

I blinked.

Then Rebel twirled round — towering killer angel bathed in righteousness — with the Bloods whipping scarlet out of their tattoos Medusa style at his heels. The fox brothers sniffed, before backing away and baring their fangs.

What the hell's wrong with them?

Here's the satanic reality: what the hell's wrong with you? You feed from death, then you can bet your breath stinks.

They had it coming.

The Trident wants you. And when the Devil comes calling? The answer's: *not tonight, darling, I have a headache.*

I yanked Ash further into the room.

Rebel's eyes widened, before narrowing dangerously at me.

'What? He's a rescued Fallen.' I shrugged, flapping my burnt wing for sympathy. 'They fought dirty; I fought dirtier.'

Rebel stomped to Ash, guiding him to the seat, before kneeling in front of him as he scrutinised his cloudy eyes.

Ash's sisters whimpered, crawling onto Ash's knee. He snuffled at them, before kissing their shoulders.

'You smell minging,' Blaze shook his head, as if to shake away the stench. 'Who did you fry?'

Spark whined. 'Killed, killed, killed—'

'Enough of the horror movie vibe. I *saved* our fam. Saved Ash.'

'Not all of him,' Rebel's voice shook. 'Not his eyes.'

Blind: I forced myself to think it. But vampires and angels could regain their sight, couldn't they?

I closed my own eyes, wringing my hands in my lap.

Bastard, please...

'Any reason you're giving me the finger, angel?' Ash's amused voice broke across my pain. 'I'd like to know why I'm breaking it.'

My eyes shot open.

'You can see!' Rebel's middle finger was frozen between us just in front of Ash's nose: not a known therapy method but it'd worked. 'And get on with you, when did I need a reason to swear at my mortal enemy?'

'Point taken.' Yet Ash raised his hand, as if

waiting for it to be clasped; Rebel linked their fingers. 'And it's more like: blurry, movement, *turn off the lights because — ow — they hurt.*'

'If you ever leave me like that again,' my breath hitched, and by the way Ash's did as well, I knew he understood what I meant, 'I'll make those hunters look like babies with bath toys.'

Ash quivered, before nodding.

He hadn't *seen* what I'd done but he'd sensed it and that was enough.

I hadn't realised until I'd almost lost him how close to Bonded I was with him. Yet also how many responsibilities he had: sisters and Anarchy's brother, Key.

What would've happened to *them* if he hadn't come back? *If I escaped without them?*

Suddenly, the Bloods turned towards me, and I recoiled. My skin stung with the remembered feel of their sticky whips. Instead of lashing me, however, they wrapped their arms around my neck.

They couldn't speak, but they were bright sparks.

Rebel gave a delighted laugh. 'Holy Mary, you look like a hedgehog has been shoved right up... It's called a hug: you put your arms—'

'Do one,' I sniggered.

I clasped my arms around the Bloods' small bodies; they tremored, burrowing closer.

Why wouldn't they talk? I craved to free their voices, which were as trapped as the rest of us.

I swung them across the carriage, spinning them.

Was that a breathy giggle?

'They threatened my sisters,' Ash burst out, his jaw set. 'If I didn't seduce you back to the Fallen from my cell in Angel World. If I gave the game away and told you the truth. Trick would've taken my sisters as Seducers.'

I nodded, holding the Bloods closer to my chest. 'I understand but I thought I was sacrificing my sister, and Rebel's sacrificed his brother. Why do you get to keep your fam?'

'I don't,' Ash tore at his bloodstained jeans, his gaze anguished. 'I never did. But sacrificing and giving up anyone to be Trick's...?' He shivered. 'I had to save my sisters; I owed my parents that.'

The Bloods stiffened in my arms. I spun them again to still their tears: *they understood*.

Did they remember their lost parents?

'If you ever need me,' I whispered in their ears, 'call for me. Your *fam*. You can talk, I don't care what the bastards have told you. I'll find a way to free all of you. You can trust me... I don't want your fear. I'm not the Vampire or Bone Princess. I'm your Protector first, yeah?'

'Dead sweet,' Wild chuckled, swaggering through the open carriage door. 'You'll make a fine mom to our babbies.'

I dropped the Bloods on the back of the familiars as if they were riders at the Derby. The fox brothers crouched, growling.

'I won Lucifer's test, Supreme Commander Birdbrain. No mom, babbies, or sweetness for you.' When I turned away, however, he kicked my ankle, tumbling me onto my face. 'What the hell...?'

Gekkering, hollers, roars.

'I knew turning savage would get you into trouble, wench. Now I'm taking you and your pets to see the gaffer. If you make a fuss, your daddy will be giving them a taste of the light.' He booted my burnt wing; I howled.

Wild held me down with a knee between my

shoulder blades.

Had he always been this strong?

I quailed. 'Don't touch me.'

My heartbeat raced; I couldn't even turn my head to see the others. I booted my legs ineffectually, squirming.

'When you're mine, I'll give you to General Trick to train,' Wild's hot breath tickled the back of my neck; I stilled. 'If he can break a dark Brigadier, turning him *whore*,' his lips smiled against my neck, 'then he can do the same for you, bab.'

When I'd held Ash down like this on the floor on his night of punishment, had he felt this powerless?

Then hard fingers pressed into the back of my neck. White-hot pain lanced down my spine. And I was swallowed by violet.

15

The worst sound in the world?

It's not the scrape of nails on a blackboard, the screech of Tasmanian Devils, or even the yodel-like battle cry of Xena Warrior Princess.

It's an angel's tears.

I awoke groggily to a wave of anguished fear through the bond, which like a shot of black coffee, blasted away the darkness.

I'd been forced into unconsciousness by Wild...but after that I'd been drugged.

Fragments arose, breaking the surface of a savage sapphire sea: arches of an abandoned station, map of a lost empire, and tequila.

I shoved myself to my knees to the soundtrack of angel tears and I tingled with the agonising grief of it. I could've torn down the world to make it stop and save Rebel from the torment, but my thighs wobbled like a new-born lamb's.

Breathing hard through the stone dust of the Crypt, my kneecaps shifted on the bed of femurs nested beneath me.

'Morning, champ.' I startled, falling on my arse. Lucifer sprawled next to me, casually sharing my bone bed. He wore full regalia; his horns tipped towards me like candles in the gloom. He waved like we were best mates on a sleepover. I didn't know whether he needed a kick to the balls or a cuddle — maybe both. 'My Blood Lovers, why, those tykes sure like to play. I hate to spoil their fun and I've never been the spanky guy with the *strict* face unless it's a scene and all in play. What? Is that *your* strict face? Am I in for a spanking?'

I tried to turn my head — *jeers, laughter, and Rebel's sobs* — but Lucifer caught my chin.

I shook, fisting my hands. 'What did they do to me?'

'Aw, you still think I'd let any of my people hurt you? Your sister was getting antsy. She's a feisty little thing, isn't she? Keeps the Blood Lovers in line. A real Queen bee. She wanted to see you but...' His lips quirked. '...She didn't trust you. The clever creature had General Wings...borrow you...before your trial.'

'Trial?' I jolted.

'Yikes, someone's tense.' Lucifer stroked a strand of my hair behind my ear. 'By the Light, relax. You're safe with me.'

I unclenched my hands, which was a mistake because then flash shot images broke through me in a tidal wave.

I'd been spread-eagled on the plum and black mosaic floor, tripping out on the invisible force Jade had pressed into my mind. Her hand hovered over my forehead, and the force had surged, flooding me until I'd been paralyzed and dazed, under her command.

Numb, I'd battered at my mind. But I'd been locked away. Nothing but a body to be petted and pawed by the Blood Lovers, who'd swayed in hazy blurs above me.

Eel's ethereal "Trouble with Dreams" had caught me in its unnerving spell: dime-store keyboards, layering over drums and ticking clocks, until I hadn't known whether I'd been truly asleep.

Then Jade's pink-and-black fringe had swept across my cheek, and I'd tremored with enough awareness to know she'd crouched over me with the iPod plugged in each of our ears. The intimacy of sharing the song — as I had with Rebel in times of grief and triumph but always joined in the search for *Jade* — had roused me like the lancing of a needle.

It'd been almost as sharp as Jade's words. 'You never saw it with your fancy job at that gaming company. Lost in your computers and angels. The *perfect worlds* you created. But a girl like me at college...? I was the outcast: the bitch even the geeks bullied.' *How hadn't I known? Had I always been that blind?* Jade's expression had darkened. 'No one bullies me now. My bloke's the Commander, and I can do this.'

Jade's Blood Lover power had rushed though me, dragging me down into an LSD whirlpool.

I'd managed to force out a whimper.

Why hadn't she let me talk? Or maybe, for once, she'd wanted me to *listen*.

'*Shhh*,' Jade had raised her finger to my lips. 'I just want you to know...you don't have to worry about me anymore or do the big sis thing. Because no one's a misfit here; the vampires accept us. There are no outcasts because the Fallen are outcasts too.'

I'd choked at her twisted, romanticized narrative of the Fall.

Yet she'd never had the chance to believe in

Santa as a kid and now she'd been making up for it with an adult fantasy.

Hadn't everyone the right to lose themselves?

Jade had dragged a bloke to her side who wore nothing but a plaid kilt, fishnets, and war paint that streaked his cheeks. He had the beautiful androgyny of a teen David Bowie. He'd ducked his head, grinning. 'Remember Ben from Jerusalem's? How he was so anxious he couldn't even speak?' *Ben*: the silent kid who'd crept around the home with armfuls of schoolbooks like they'd been a shield...? *What the hell...?* 'And Zoe...Ella...Connor...'

The pulse had pounded in my ears.

The disappeared kids from Hackney. The vampires had stolen them as Blood Lovers.

Because of me? Because *I'd* been there?

'The Fallen own Jerusalem's.' I'd startled out of my daze, as Jade had stroked my hair: *had she read my mind?* 'They watch over it like...guardians. Then they choose the special ones to become their eternal lovers. It's a dark fairy tale, and we're the princes and princesses.'

Lucifer wiped the tears from my cheeks, holding me to his chest. *When had I started crying?* 'Tell daddy all about it.' The leather was hard and hot: black armour moulded now over the PVC. 'Mortals are such funny...*little*...beings. Sticks and stones may break my bones, but a Blood Lover's words can never hurt me.'

'Don't mess with me: *you knew*.' I pulled back, swiping at my own cheeks. 'You wanted me to—'

'Get over your human fetish? See your adopted sister for what she is and not what you pretended because...hooray for us...you have new pets to play with.'

Lucifer rose in a roar of light, yanking me to my feet and spinning me.

I yelped, before stilling.

This time the Crypt was empty apart from a gang of FF, who circled my *pets* and were already playing.

A female FF wearing snake earrings through her enlarged earlobes and inked with feather tattoos across her chin, held Rebel under her as she ground against him, clouting him between kisses. Her tongue, as long and thick as her piercings, forced between his sobbing lips.

His tears, shredding me across the Blood Lover bond, were the worst sound in the bastard world.

Ash's cloudy eyes remained defiantly dry.

Catcalls and whistles.

Wild held out a skeleton, dancing it around Ash and rubbing it against him in a grotesque parody of seduction.

Ash struck out clumsily, confused in his near blindness, as he was baited.

'Stop this,' I snarled, shaking. 'This is a one-bitch show.'

Lucifer's arm trapped me in place; the bonfire ash of his wings curled around me. 'Uh-huh, they're playthings, see? Hiding from the light — truth — is that a family trait? Because I have to say, it's appealing in a Blood Lover, but not in a true princess.' When I flinched, Lucifer giggled. 'Only my daughter could be such a rebel that she can't be won over with the *be a princess of the night* line.'

Oomph – I elbowed him in the guts.

When Lucifer doubled over, I twisted to him. 'Listen here, Your Creepy Highness, I won the test, the Devil's Trident, and my blokes. I'm no one's princess of the night — or their bitch.'

'Did you?' Lucifer soared up, blocking the way between me and my fam. Suddenly, he appeared to have grown, his helmet and wings blazed brighter, and his armour gleamed. 'This is a trial. Not really much point to that, if the jury's not out....'

'And where's this invisible jury? The same place as the imaginary barristers and pretend judge?'

Lucifer pirouetted. 'Here, and all in one and the same glorious person! You see...' Suddenly he became sombre, steepling his hands. 'We have few rules, but one of the biggies is: Don't kill humans. At least, without permission.' My stomach roiled. 'You were meant to rescue the Fallen from the hunters. But did you also...?'

'Cut the Old Bailey dramatics. The bitches filmed torture porn, for real, because it got them off. There's no superhero who wouldn't have gone supernova.'

Lucifer smiled sadly, and all I wanted was for him to say he was *proud* of me again. He waved his hand at Wild, however, who reluctantly dropped the skeleton, before hauling the Snake Bitch off Rebel.

Rebel staggered up, clasping Ash, who booted him with a growl, until Rebel curled his wings around him. Ash sniffed. Then he settled into Rebel's arms, as they rocked.

Hell, I wished I was in their arms.

Lucifer tapped me on the nose. 'You reckon you're a superhero? Let me break this to you: you're the villain. In fact, after that...KABOOM...you're the supervillain.' When I recoiled, Lucifer's smile wavered. Were his eyelashes mattered wet? 'Why, you're my daughter, of course I wanted you to pass. But we're not the monsters under kiddies' beds who kill, and I have a duty to help you understand. Let's call it a C. Not a total fail but not strong enough to earn the Devil's Trident.'

'*Help, need you, not fair,*' Devil wailed from his entrapment underneath Lucifer's leather.

I shook my head, as my vampiric powers raged at the loss and fear...to have been cheated out of my birthright. Thick as tar, the black oozed behind my eyes, coated my nostrils in its scent, and weighed my tongue.

'*YOURS, YOURS, YOURS,*' Devil seethed, '*take me.*'

'Now, the Fallen who can't control killing...? They're the Pure.' Lucifer continued, turning his back, as if he hadn't sensed the rage building in me to tear him open, strip him to the bone to steal Devil for myself. 'Their leader, a Glory who lost her way a long time ago, risks everything I'm working on with the humans. So, I'm offering you another chance. Test Number Two: kill the leader of the Pure. You have permission to kill. Enjoy. Of course,' his shoulders slumped, 'you could just join them. What a dilemma: who do you choose?'

'*The Devil's Trident,*' I growled.

As I lunged for Lucifer's neck, however, he soared upwards in a shower of sparks; my fingers choked bone. I shrank back from the grinning skeleton, which stalked towards me, *Jason and the Argonauts* style, animated inside its ribcage by Lucifer's teeming lights.

The glowing skeleton swung for me. I ducked, but its skeletal fist caught the side of my head. Slamming into the wall in a cascade of white flashes, I gasped.

That bastard hurt.

It also knocked Devil's whining beneath the throbbing in my mind.

Why had I craved the trident like Rebel's blood...? What'd possessed me?

I dived under the skeleton's grasping hands.

Cheers and guffaws.

The FF lounged against the crypts, hooking their arms around Rebel and Ash to stop them joining in the fun.

I lunged at the bed of bones that I'd woken up on, snatching a femur and weighing it in my hand. I'd have preferred a baseball bat, but it'd do. I smashed the femur through the skeleton's rib cage. When the light's squealed, I jumped. Then they rushed out of the gaps, buzzing like indignant fairies around my head.

I rattled the femur. 'Bounce, bitches.'

With a final flounce, they hummed back to Lucifer, who welcomed them into his horns.

I wrenched my bone weapon out of the ribcage, smashing it down again into the skull, which shattered. The skeleton collapsed to nothing but inanimate bones again. Breathing harshly, I *swung and swung and swung*...until nothing was left but pulverised shards.

Tremors ran through me, as at last I hurled down the femur onto the remains. 'Nobody touches my blokes.'

'Splendid,' Lucifer drifted down from the roof, grinning. 'You can kill the leader of the Pure, Stephanie, just like that. Although — *eek* — all that messy rage. I blame the hormones, I truly do.'

I squared my shoulders. 'Stick it. I'm not an assassin. All this changing the game makes me wonder...do you want me to fail?'

Lucifer's grin faded. Unexpectedly, he looked vulnerable, and it wasn't a good look. 'You know who *wants* people to fail? *Glories*. They're cruel creatures who don't understand loyalty. All they want is your pain. Like you.' I took a step towards him, before looking away. My chest tightened. *I craved to prove him wrong.* 'You haven't opened yourself to me or this world and you haven't earnt my trust.'

So, that's what it was like to be bollocked by a parent.

What had my mum done to Lucifer as her Wing to make him Mr Paranoia?

'Perhaps it'll help you if I make this a test of loyalty alongside *my* pet?' Lucifer strode to the wall, spreading his palm on the smooth surface.

Then he yanked.

With a desperate gasp, Mischief tumbled out of the marble onto the floor like a landed fish.

Lucifer nudged him with his toe. 'You could hear, pet?'

Mischief nodded, his chest wildly rising and falling. *Hell, had he been frozen in the rock throughout my trial?* 'An inspired bonding session,' he gasped.

'Flatterer,' Lucifer fluttered his eyelashes.

Mischief glanced at me significantly. 'A worthy test of how well the future Queen of Chaos and I can fight together for you. Your daughter at your side, and me at your feet.'

'You've got to love an angel who knows their place.' Lucifer's high laugh rang through the Crypt.

Mischief cringed but met my gaze. 'I'm partial to not dying, and this test risks *both* our heads.'

Out with the stealthy; Mischief was branding his message across his forehead: **TAKE THE TEST**.

Despite what Mischief was urging, just as I hadn't become my mum's weapon, I wouldn't become my dad's hired killer. Even if the mark was Stephanie, who'd tried to execute me, stolen her followers' wings, and kept Anarchy as her pet.

I'd always thirsted for the moment you held someone's life, God-like, on a blade's knife-edge. I'd fought the addiction and I couldn't fall back into it.

Or else I'd devour the world.

'I'm a monster but I won't be your killer. So, stick it again.'

Sizzle — Lucifer's horns flared up, filling the Crypt behind him.

I threw my hand across my eyes to block out the painful light, trembling. A wave of heat hit my cheeks.

Then just as suddenly, Lucifer's Hulk-horns died down again, and he shrugged. 'Huh, like I thought.' He dragged Mischief into a tight one-armed hug; Mischief winced. 'Well, my wedding outfit is divine. You'll make a gorgeous bride.' His eyes mesmerised me with their infinite light. My mouth was dry. 'And your angel and Fallen are already almost trained...'

My limbs were too heavy; my eyelids drooped.

I could battle Lucifer's mesmerism act: I bastard could. 'I won't be your Champion in blood.'

'How the bones fall, that's your choice.' Lucifer twisted Mischief's head to the side. 'One question. Your sister? How do you think she'll taste?'

My eyes widened, as my heart thundered. I couldn't storm towards him, however, I couldn't move at all. *The bastard had enthralled me.* 'Don't...not my sister...please...'

'What I also love?' Lucifer's fangs shot out. He grazed them down Mischief's neck; Mischief whimpered. 'The taste of Shadows: their fear and shame. It's an aphrodisiac, it really is. They should bottle it. And with his magic, my pet will sparkle in delicious mouthfuls when I force him. After all, you don't want him...if you won't take the test?' Silent tears coursed down my face. I hadn't even known how much I didn't want Mischief hurt, until Lucifer's threat to Blood Bond him became so real. 'I'll instil worship, burning out love, even in our bond. Who needs sass, when I can have a slave?'

'Allow it,' I roared, battling against the pull of his gaze.

'I'm the king here, I have rights. Wings will find himself another Blood Lover. And your sister, well, she'll be fiery—'

'I'll do it.' I ripped my gaze away with a *snap* of light. I'd broken the spell, but Lucifer had broken me. I touched the pouch at my neck. 'I'll find a way to kill the leader of the Pure.'

Lucifer dragged Mischief round into a rough hug. *Was that relief?* 'The Bone Princess and long may she reign! Oh, wait, one more *teeny* detail: you have just one night.'

I caught Ash's gaze. I understood now why he'd betrayed me to save his sisters.

I'd risked freeing the beast inside to save mine.

I had one night to return to the haunt of the vampire fanatics, let out the monster, and then kill the worst vampire in England.

Or else she'd kill me.

16

There was an edge of smug swag to the way Mischief shoved me to my knees.

I hissed at the burn, like my skin had been set alight by matches, as I hit the rug. I kept my head down, however, even if I couldn't help easing my hands in the angel proof cuffs that shackled them behind my back.

Yeah, lap it up, Fallen Potter. I wasn't the one who had an eternity on my knees ahead of me.

Yet that thought didn't induce the counter smugness I'd expected. Instead, grief flooded me: at the loss of Mischief to my dad, his forced Blood Bond, at *anyone* being unwilling on their knees.

I edged closer, suddenly needing to feel Mischief: the heat of his thigh through his leather trousers. He flinched, before his long fingers settled on my head...just for a moment.

Then he stepped back, and it was a loss.

I was alone, on my knees in Conference Room D, Perfection Hotel.

The Pure's Headquarters.

We'd already paraded through hundreds of Pure soldiers, who'd been ranked in the halls, until we'd been hurled into the heart of their camp.

Mischief called out, 'I have a monstrous gift for whoever has the power to welcome in the Falling and save me from Lucifer's Light, as well as his wandering hands. Your thugs dragged us here, and it appears I'm to see both the organ grinder *and* her monkey.'

Only acting...this was our play... Hell, did he mean it...?

I struggled to control my whirling thoughts.

Mischief had plotted our operation in the rushed minutes before we'd soared through London to the hotel. He would be the unknown betrayer; I'd be bait.

Except, how had that turned out for Ash...?

I peeked from underneath my eyelashes; the conference room was an elegant Victorian confection in blue and white. A breeze through the French doors that looked out over the courtyard garden, blew the cloying scent of lilies from the bowl on the oak table across my cheeks.

Stephanie — *the organ grinder* — lounged against the table in a charcoal business suit and blouse, as tendrils of hair hung out of her blonde ponytail. She'd hiked up her skirt, like a sexy secretary, to rest her kitten heel on the quaking inner thigh of the *monkey*: Anarchy.

Anarchy was stretched, bent back over the table, in only a pair of tattered jeans. His chest was mottled with bruises, just like when we'd first been trapped together in this hotel. I'd escaped, but he'd been stuck here for months. And it didn't look like Stephanie took care of her pets.

Anarchy turned his head, his jet curls falling

over his elfin face. Then his gaze caught mine, and he stiffened. He tremored with such desperate despair at my *recapture* that I craved to let him know the truth: to trust him. But I had one night to assassinate Stephanie or I lost all my fam.

So, on with the show...

'*Princess*,' Anarchy breathed, before glaring at Mischief and baring his fangs. 'You're dead, wanker. I'll—'

Thwack — Stephanie kicked Anarchy's balls with the pointed toe of her shoe.

Anarchy squealed, doubling over, but Stephanie hauled him back over the table, holding him by the throat. 'Be quiet, sweetie. Do you want to give me a migraine?'

Anarchy shook his head. He breathed raggedly through his nose, whilst clamping shut his mouth.

Stephanie rewarded him with a lick, slow and sensuous, across the seam of his lips. 'My good little pet.' Then her gaze hardened, as she swept it over first me, then Mischief. 'Yet here is such a bad doggy and her owner.' Her assessing gaze appraised Mischief in a knowing way that made me shudder....*because she wasn't buying it*. 'Or is it just two bad bitches?'

Time to put on a real show, Violet-Mutt, unless you want the wizard's ass fried alongside your own.

If I take this offscript, how'd I know he'll play along?

His Highness of Mischief has improv down. Outside of Under World, he's not the prisoner, he's the bloke you're trusting at your side.

And should I? Trust him?

If you don't, you won't pass this test. Then it's hello, wedding night and Mrs Wild.

But should you trust him? That's a whole different question.

Why hasn't he flown back to the angels?

You think he'd be welcomed home with a glittery party? His nickname's *traitor* for a reason, and having been whore to Lucifer would lower him to the rank of toy.

The Fae Mage knows he's still watched by the vampires. This isn't freedom, only the illusion.

I sighed. Then growled, lunging for Stephanie. When my blunt teeth sank into her ankle, she squealed.

Whoosh — Stephanie's blood gurgled through me like rancid milk.

I gagged, letting go of her leg. 'I bite but I don't bark.'

'It can, however, be arranged on request.' Mischief slipped his hand over my mouth, prising open my lips.

Silver sparks prickled like tiny electric eels down my throat. I jolted, staring up at Mischief; his gaze was flat and unreadable.

I was the bitch who'd taken this into Improv Land. The plan had been for me to keep silent, whilst Mischief did the Big Sell.

Stephanie clutched her ankle, as if I'd slit her Achilles tendon, rather than taken a nibble.

I flinched, when Mischief patted me on the head. 'Good doggy. Speak.'

He wanted me to speak? Then I'd tell the disrespecting brat just where I'd bite *him* on his...

Yap, yap, yap.

I scrambled against the wall, breathing hard. I cleared my throat.

Yap, yap, yap.

Stephanie hooted with delighted laughter, and it twisted my heart the way Mischief joined in. 'That's the most divine thing I've heard in decades, darling.'

I flushed.

If Mischief had decided to make me bark like a dog, why couldn't it at least have been like a badass guard dog, rather than some yapping lapdog?

Humiliation, got it.

I tilted my chin: lapdog does death threat.

Yap, yap, yap?

Mischief blanched. Maybe he could understand my words through the spell?

I bastard hoped he could.

'Where are my manners, bringing in a dog without a collar and leash?' Mischief raised his eyebrow at me.

Were we caught in a freaky game of Chicken, where neither of us dared blink?

Either trust him or don't.

You're the only two in this whole hotel, however, who haven't yet been purified.

If you don't convince Stephanie that Mischief's an asshole who's selling you out to save his own skin, then you'll both be reduced to the ranks of the Pure too before the end of the night.

No risk there, J, even I think Mischief's a prick.

I shrank back, but metallic light swirled from the tips of Mischief's fingers, spinning in discs, before lashing out.

I gave a high-pitched *yap*, pushing my back

against the wall.

The strand of silver settled as softly as gossamer, however, around my neck, even though it looked as hard as steel. Mischief wound his end around his wrist.

Safe.

The word thrummed through the leash; I shivered with it.

Mischief's intense gaze met mine, before flicking away to Stephanie's. But I'd understood, just as I felt it, curling in my gut.

It wasn't a collar: it was a connection.

A bond.

Even though Mischief was playing the bastard, he was caressing me through his magic — sensual and *safe*.

Trust: Rebel had told me I could fly on it.

I took a deep breath. I guess it was time to test that.

Whining, I bowed my head: monster beaten.

I fought not to snap at Stephanie's fingers, as they carded through my hair. 'Impressive training techniques,' she simpered. Then she caressed a hand beneath Mischief's tunic, tweaking his nipples, before slipping her fingers lower. His smile became tighter. 'Oh, you have potential. I shall enjoy purifying you.'

'I only live to please.'

When she ran her hand over his wing, playing with the violet feathers that peeked between the grey, Mischief tensed. Stephanie examined them, entranced. 'Oh, you shall. Such pretty feathers. I've never purified the wings of one not yet Fallen.' *You mean chopped them off — stolen them — psycho vampire*. Stephanie rubbed her thumb along Mischief's wingtip, and he gasped. 'I shall wear them in an evening shawl. I'll be an envy of the

Pure.'

When I snarled, Mischief yanked on the leash, pulling me onto my face.

Anarchy leapt off the table, his battered body quivering. One dark curl fell over his eye. 'She's a *princess*...brave, loyal, and better than any of us, mate. If you want someone to crawl for you, I'll crawl. But not—'

Crack — Stephanie backhanded Anarchy, knocking him against the table.

Anarchy's hip hit the table's corner with a sickening *thump*. He gasped, but struggled to stand, bracing himself.

I swallowed, clenching my sweaty hands behind me in their cuffs.

Trust? It was time to jump from the nest.

When I raised my head, my face covered by my hair, Anarchy gave me a determined nod, but in turn *I winked*.

Anarchy startled, then fell to his knees.

He was another actor now in our play. The only one left out of the gag was Stephanie. Also, the one who could kill us all.

'I'm sorry,' Anarchy whispered, 'please...help me remember the light. Cleanse me.' He bent down, kissing Stephanie's foot.

Stephanie preened, leaning over to tangle her hand in Anarchy's curls. 'How adorable, of course I'll cleanse and guide you to the light. Don't I always? This one was a rebel, so hard to break and remake that he sometimes, even now, forgets himself. Although, he's a good enough boy to be my second-in-command. Would you like to play awhile?' She nipped at Mischief's lip, drawing blood.

Mischief gasped but nodded.

My vampiric and angelic sides both boiled and

raged that she'd tasted him, taking what was mine.

Mine?

Lucifer would kick my arse if his spies caught on to my *bonding* thoughts. But why was I...or my ancient powers...even having them?

Stephanie grasped Anarchy by the hair and Mischief by the wrist, tugging them over the conference table. I was forced to follow, yanked after them on my leash. My knees burned on the rug.

When Mischief shoved Anarchy facedown over the table, however, I almost stood up, plan or no plan.

There's method acting, then there's so deep undercover that you forget you're the good guy and not the villain.

I'll read you into a kennel and take your doggy ass to obedience training school. Whoever said you were the good guy?

What...?

You're *you*, Violet, and the leader you choose to become.

Right now?

You're the dog, and your lickable magic owner is in charge. Isn't that the true problem? The loss of control?

Get out of my head, bitch.

Hit a nerve, did I?

What he'll do to Anarchy... How can I let it happen to my fam?

Don't you see? Mischief is doing it for the mission, and Anarchy is letting it happen...for you.

How's it feel to be the fire the world dances around?

Like I'm being burned alive.

Anarchy whimpered, as Mischief brushed his

fingers reverentially over the cauterised stumps on his back, where his wings had once been. I realised he might never have seen a Pure's back up close before.

And I'd been there when Stephanie had swung the axe...

'They're still sensitive,' Stephanie whispered into Mischief's ear, 'as yours will be.' Mischief shuddered, as she ran her hand through his feathers, no doubt imagining her *shawl*. 'Perhaps I'll keep you both as my personal pets. Would you enjoy that?' She nudged Anarchy, but he only pulled his arms over his face to hide it. 'When I was busy, you could play with each other. The two of you together make the most delectable picture.'

Mischief mouthed over the stumps of Anarchy's wings, sucking deep bruises; Mischief arched over the table, held in place by Stephanie's elbow on the base of his back. At the same time, Mischief shot bursts of silver in electric shocks stinging across his shoulders, which were painted in the yellow and green of faded bruises.

Mischief wailed, caught between the pain of the shocks and the passion of the love bites.

Pain and pleasure: Mischief had either been taught the methods in Angel World, or watched them inflicted on someone else.

Why did I ache that a Glory might've done this to him? *Why did I tremble that he desired to do this to me?*

A *cry* from Anarchy, *sizzle* of sparks from Mischief, and clap of hands from Stephanie.

Mischief had promised Ash, before we'd started this charade, that we wouldn't harm Anarchy.

If we survived...? *Ash would kill Mischief.*

I gritted my teeth, as Anarchy panted, humping the table's edge. I craved to cut off Stephanie's hands for the way she soothed the hollow of his back, like she was edging him towards giving birth rather than humiliation.

Mischief kissed each stump, even as he shocked it.

I tensed to surge up, breaking our cover because I couldn't be the bitch who let this happen and not in my name, when I noticed Mischief's wince.

Although it was Anarchy who writhed beneath him, it was Mischief who held onto the lip of the table, white knuckled.

I was a wallad.

Mischief had been *sucking* out the pain, stealing it to suffer in silence, just as he'd left behind the pleasure for Anarchy. And Anarchy had played along, acting up the agony.

'Sweet as the two of you are together...' Stephanie gripped Mischief's chin, forcing his lips away from Anarchy and pressing them to her mouth instead. 'There's one thing that makes me even hornier than watching pets in training.'

'Do tell.'

'Putting down monstrous bitches.'

I almost rolled my eyes, but this psycho wasn't joking for dramatic effect.

I shrank back as far as I could on my leash.

Hiss.

Stephanie swung a staff from her belt in a single arc; it exploded into a blazing axe.

This time?

Anarchy's whimpers were real.

'Over the table. Next to pet.' Stephanie swished the axe, which burned with black flames. 'No need to make a display of the freak, like last time. Those that don't walk in the light of the Pure, will walk in

174

the dark of my axe.'

Yap, yap, yap.

Where was the big speech? The intricate plans for my decapitation? The *moment* we'd know to spring the assassination?
What was this *wham, bam, thank you monster?*

Yap, yap, yap.

Mischief yanked me by the leash, yapping wildly, to bend over the table next to Anarchy.
Oomph — the hard edge knocked the wind out of me.
Like the last time we'd both been bent over the executioner's block, Anarchy's fingers crept into mine.
'Your blokes don't give up; I've never forgotten,' Anarchy murmured.
His fierce gaze met mine under the harsh light of the conference room. He'd changed: hardened, become stronger, and a second-in-command, even if he was also a *pet.*
He'd suffered in the world of the Pure for months but he'd survived and he'd never forgotten that he was one of *my* blokes.
My fingers tightened around his.

Yap, yap, yap.

Tears tumbled down my cheeks because I couldn't even say a single word of that to him.
Bastard Mischief. Bastard magic.
Anarchy smiled, however, as if he'd understood at least the attitude behind my *woofing* and nodded.

Then he jolted at the same time as I did. My skin blistered, and I hissed. The air wavered with heat.

Stephanie's axe kissed against the back of both our necks, as if deciding who to snog first.

I was no assassin. This had been Mischief's plan. He'd been *the moment* bloke.

Had we missed it? Because as my skin seared under the axe, and I didn't dare move for the risk of Anarchy losing his head as well, I was pretty sure we had.

'Nothing to say?' Stephanie scoffed. *Every bastard's a comedian.* In defiance, I closed my eyes. 'No famous last words? How about: I was born a monster,' she shifted the axe to press against my neck alone. 'I die a monster.'

My skin blackened under the flames.

17

A roar of pain rushed through my head, branching down the nerves of my spine: scorching, white-hot, and blinding.

I juddered, as my ears buzzed, choking on my own body turned barbecue.

Was this death?

Had my head been lopped off, and only my heart still beat, whilst my body flopped on the table in Conference Room D in Perfection Hotel — heart of the Pure vampire fanatics — like a beheaded chicken running around the farmyard?

Two words, Violet-pup: nerves and spine. If your fabulousness is still attached to them, then you're not headless.

Plus, I'm still working my thing and I'd bet your sweet ass that I'm not welcome inside the Pearly Gates.

The dead don't talk...

Tune down the drama queen. You wanted *a moment*...?

This business suited skank is ruthlessness on a stick. Did you think you'd get one without being destroyed first?

So, now the bitch believes she can kill you. Pull on your assassin pants. Finally, you have a chance.

I could feel it: the seared line of the axe's cut across the back of my neck.

Mischief had simply stood and watched...? Had he even *tried* to stop Stephanie from decapitating me?

At last, sensation bled back: the hardness of the table underneath me, the cool draught through the window across my temple, and Anarchy's hand still squeezing mine.

When I could open my eyes again, I met Anarchy's anguished gaze. He was bent over the table next to me. His eyelashes were wet, and he was paler than me.

I forced myself to give him a shaky smile, even though the muscles of my face felt like they'd been electrocuted with a cattle prod.

The buzzing in my ears quietened enough to hear Mischief's low murmur to Stephanie, as they hovered behind us.

I smarted with shame then because I realised Mischief *had* saved me from execution. Although, I wished I could return to my fuzzed agony if it meant blissful ignorance of *how*.

'...The greatest service, my exquisite goddess...may I call you that?' A delighted simper from Stephanie at Mischief's suave act. 'Such a service that I'd, of course, repay undoubtedly in my willing bondage.' This time a moan, followed by the wet *smacking* of a snogging. I grimaced. 'I would have her watch, before she died, whilst I'm taken by a pure Fallen.'

I jolted at the cruelty in the jeer, even though I knew it was part of the test.

But hell, why did it still have to hurt?

Yap, yap, yap.

I booted at the table in frustration. My words were my weapon, and right now I was as kickass as a chihuahua.

'Afterwards, once we've slaughtered the monster...' Stephanie kicked the back of my knees, tumbling me to the floor; I tangled in the leash, which was attached to Mischief's wrist. I twisted, gasping as my handcuffed hands caught on the carpet. '...And you're liberated of your wings — a purified solider marching into the light — we'll make a feast of the humans, and they shall worship the shadows because they'll know to fear them.'

Stephanie smirked, patting me on the head.

I bared my teeth, pulling away. I could at least be a hellhound.

'Worship? Now, I love the sound of that.' I didn't like the way Mischief's eyes lit up. 'Do you know, I trapped the monster by seducing her. She's a simple thing.' Mischief stroked the backs of his fingers down Stephanie's arm; she shivered. He met my gaze, a twinkle hidden in his eyes. That bumped him to top of my List of Asses to Kick. 'You wouldn't believe her kinks,' he whispered, hunching his shoulders and batting his eyelashes in the picture of innocence, even as his lips quirked conspiratorially.

Nope, I was starting a whole new section with a points system just for him.

'Do tell,' Stephanie leaned in closer.

List of Asses to Kick: one point.

'She loves to *hurt* because she doesn't know how to feel.' *Two points.* 'She dreads losing control, so she controls you: bondage.' *Three points.* 'Then there's marking, tattoos, the whole *kneel before the great princess* thing...'

Three, four, five...

He sniffed. 'But what she loves best...? For you to pretend you don't know any of that and treat her like she's just a regular human with no ancient powers inside and all she needs is sweet romance.'

Bastard a million.

Yap, yap, yap.

'How sad, you've made your puppy cry,' Stephanie cooed. 'Now my pet is tamed, it's so much harder to truly make him weep.'

I was desperate to wipe away the tears, tugging at the cuffs behind my back.

For a moment, Mischief looked stricken, as if he hadn't meant to flay me to the bone in front of the bitch who wanted me dead.

Except, he had.

Just as fast, Mischief's mask was back in place. He wrapped his arms around Stephanie's waist, pulling her hard against his chest. 'Every sacrifice, however, has been worth it. Do you know how long I've dreamed of you, the Pure's leader, wrapped in the warmth of my feathers?'

He cocooned them both in his wings — the ones she intended to steal from him, and it was sick and twisted, and I wanted to look away but found that I couldn't — as he stroked his sensitive wingtips along her cheeks.

She shuddered, relaxing in his hold. Her eyes closed, and she licked her lips.

Now.

The word quivered through the silky leash, humming through the collar.

Now, urgent and insistent.

Mischief's signal: *the moment.*

Our gazes met over Stephanie's head. Mischief nodded; his mouth thinned.

He caressed Stephanie in his wings, as my leash silently snapped, before slinking back into Mischief.

My throat tingled, and although I couldn't test it, I was certain my voice had returned. My angel proof cuffs vanished because they'd never been more than an illusion.

I rose up to a crouch, reaching to pat Anarchy's shoulder. He glanced around, his eyes widening, before he hunkered, ready to attack.

Mischief waved his hand — although I knew that was just showing off for Anarchy because he could teleport with a thought — and Star materialised in my palm.

Its sudden weight was like a blessing.

'*Kill, kill, kill,*' Devil chanted, a lurking presence at the back of my mind, thrilled at the shank glinting in the light, the victim held ready for the blade, and my transformation from prey to executioner.

The trident stirred, hungry for death.

I was just as hungry as Devil. This kill was months overdue, and with it I claimed my throne.

I lunged, plunging the shank into Stephanie's throat.

Stephanie squawked, flapping her arms in shock, as scarlet flooded around the blade, slicking my hands and spraying across my face.

A red sea.

I blinked my eyes, which were coated in Stephanie's blood. She tried to push me back, but Mischief held her firmly in his wings: the ones she'd wanted to steal. Like the ones she'd taken from every other Pure and Anarchy...whose gaze was as hungry as mine.

'Nothing to say?' I spat. Stephanie hung in Mischief's hold, drowning in her own blood. Was this what it felt like to defeat a Big Bad? I struggled not to hurl. 'No famous last words?'

She gurgled, low in her throat. Her desperate stare swung to Anarchy, as if he'd spring forward and defend her.

Instead, Anarchy pushed himself up, leaning against the table with crossed arms and watched her death as calmly as she'd watched his torture.

He didn't look tamed now.

'How about: I was born a bitch,' I wrenched the shank out of Stephanie's neck. She jerked, her eyes rolling back. 'I die a bitch.'

I raised the shank to bring it down again, but Mischief hurled Stephanie to the side.

The ancient powers inside flamed with fury. The Devil's Trident howled at its feast being ripped away.

A rush of violet-fuelled psycho slashed the blade through the air...at Mischief.

But he was no longer there. Instead, glittering hooves knocked me back on my arse.

I stared, dazed, at a silver unicorn, the size of a Shetland pony. But his violet eyes glowed like a war horse.

I picked myself up and reached out, touching his mane with my scarlet fingers. For one mental moment, I craved to swing my leg over him and ride the wild bastard. Mischief was no longer a toy unicorn.

Then he threw himself forward, stamping on Stephanie, who was attempting to crawl towards the door. A flare of metallic light, like liquid mercury, shot from his twisted horn, slicing off Stephanie's head. It blasted out so rapidly that her feet still twitched.

This time, I did hurl.

The unicorn snorted, before rearing up on his hindlegs and neighing.

Bent over, covered in Stephanie's blood and my own puke, I *shushed* a killer unicorn to stop an army of vampire fanatics from kicking our arses.

My life was screwed-up.

Anarchy tentatively laid his hand on the unicorn's pink muzzle, before petting his nose. The unicorn gave a rumbling *nicker*, pushing his head against Anarchy's hand, before calming.

Why hadn't I thought of that?

Slowly, Mischief transformed back into his Sugar Plum self, panting and self-consciously pulling his cheek away from Anarchy's caress.

Anarchy gaped at him. 'Legendary, mate. Cheers for the rescue.'

'I'll start with a *what* and end with *the hell*?

Mischief glanced at me uneasily, pulling at the crimson strands in his hair, where I'd stroked his mane. 'I have a lot of repressed rage. I don't like...people making me hurt others. Or threatening to kill you. It's a thing.'

'And the killer unicorn God-out?'

'It's my go to when I'm stressed.'

I stared at my hands: red.

The blue-and-white room was sprayed in scarlet like we'd fallen into a slasher film. My face itched with Stephanie's blood; my hair was plastered with it.

Lucifer had wanted to learn if I'd become his assassin, and I'd jumped through that hoop. I'd stained myself with blood. Was that what it meant to be a Bone Princess amongst vampires?

Suddenly, two sets of arms were wrapped around me. Anarchy and Mischief, amidst the sour milk stench of Stephanie's blood, held me close, as I shook.

I'd killed before, but never as an assassin.

I hated it.

'I knew you'd never just forget me,' Anarchy pulled back, vibrating with joy. 'I survived every day, worked my way up to second-in-command even, thinking you and Ash would figure a clever way to save me and the rest of us. Because I trust you.'

New levels of guilt booted me because although I hadn't forgotten him, I hadn't come here to save Anarchy but to win a test and the trident.

I avoided his gaze, shrugging.

'You and your mate,' Anarchy glanced between Mischief and me, as if puzzling out how we fitted, 'you've freed us. It's not just me. Most of the other poor wankers here didn't want the whole *lose your wings package* either. I can't give them back their feathers but I can give them back themselves.'

'What about the whole *eating humans package*?' Mischief asked.

Anarchy pulled a face. 'The militants who get their jollies tearing out throats? They'll break away and form a new group. But the rest of us prefer Blood Lovers. Blood that's unwilling tastes...off.'

Bang, bang, bang.

The large door to the conference room shook to

the *thumping* on the other side.

I raised my eyebrow at Mischief.

He raised his own right back at me. 'I locked it, of course, as soon as we were so kindly shoved inside. The bitch was distracted, and I'm sneaky, or hadn't you noticed?'

Anarchy, however, had blanched. 'Stephanie's next meeting... Every bigwig in the Pure's bollocking army are out there waiting for her.'

'I have a hunch,' Mischief lounged against a chair, 'that she'll be missing it.'

I snatched up the axe that still blazed at the head of the table like an abandoned guest, slicing it over the cut on Stephanie's neck and decapitated head, struggling not to gag at the *sizzle*. Then I tossed the axe to Anarchy, who almost dropped it like I'd chucked acid at him. 'Your trophy. When you let in the bastards, you stand over her: the winner takes the prize, you get me?'

Anarchy nodded.

Mischief materialised a second knife, swiping it through the blood, before shoving it into Anarchy's other hand. 'Now you look like a real warrior. Not a pet. Ever. Again.'

Mischief leapt for the window, unlatching it and beckoning for me.

I hesitated. 'Your brother—'

Mischief sharply drew in his breath. 'One would suggest now is not the time.'

Bang, bang, bang.

Anarchy's gaze snapped to mine. 'What about Key?'

'Without you he was—'

'What good can come of telling *his brother*?' Mischief's gaze was hard. 'Or do you wish to shank him too? I had not realised we were here to assassinate them both.'

I recoiled.

Was I wrong to tell Anarchy? Since when had the truth become so much more dangerous than secrets and lies?

Anarchy's eyes glistened; he swallowed with difficulty. 'Tell me. Please...'

'The Bones. They put him in...'

Anarchy keened, falling to his knees. The knife fell from his hands.

Bang, bang, bang.

The knocking on the door had become more frantic now. Hollering had been added to the mix.

Mischief clenched his jaw. 'Two Pure slain in a single night. Quite the record.'

'Ash is looking out for him, feeding him, and...,' I stumbled over the words in my desperation to reassure Anarchy. *What the hell were the Bones that they terrified everyone?* 'Ash has—'

'Given enough. The wankers already hurt him. If he's also having to help...pay...for Key as well...?' When Anarchy looked up at me his cheeks were tear tracked, but he straightened his shoulders, pushing himself up again and glaring at the door.

Crash — the door trembled; the bastards were battering their way in.

'*Anarchy*, yeah? Like I understood where it'd lead.' Anarchy gave a small smile. 'When we rebelled, however, I was barely more than a kid... We never thought about the world we'd build afterwards. So, it became *Lucifer's* world because he'd been the Matriarch's Wing and the wanker claimed that made him *king*. He's a hard bloke to say *no* to. We were all half wallowing in despair at being thrown into the shadows, and half partying because we were free of Angel World. Welcome to the Bone Carnival, lose yourself in chaos! And now we're stuck in Lucifer's show.'

'I'll free your brother,' I breathed. 'Free all those in the Bones. I won't... I'll stop the Carnival and the chaos.'

Creak — the door splintered.

I laced my fingers through Anarchy's curls, touching our foreheads, even as he quivered.

'You'll bring the whole show tumbling down on your head. And the king will try to burn you to ash. Only a bastard would ask you to risk yourself like that, princess.' Anarchy took a deep breath, tears trembling on his lashes, as he whispered, '*Please* do it anyway. Help my little brother.'

I nodded, squeezing his shoulders with my bloodstained hands before I soared out through the window with Mischief into the night.

The one advantage we held over the Pure? By sacrificing their wings, they couldn't take to the heavens after us.

Yet I wasn't safe.

I'd promised to save a Pure's brother from the King of the Under World — my own dad.

Lucifer had said I suffered from conflicted loyalty. Yet he was wrong. My loyalty wasn't conflicted: it lay with the blokes who fought for me and had my back.

My true fam.

Yet even though I'd passed the test and killed the leader of the dangerous vampire fanatics, I was returning not to claim my throne but to overthrow Lucifer's.

18

There's nothing more dangerous than the shank
tongue of a traitor.

Or rebel.

When Ash smashed Mischief against the wall of
the bunker, I winced at the *bang*. Even the concrete
ceiling shuddered. I didn't look up, however, as I
bent over, washing my hands in the stainless-steel
sink: *rub, rub, rub.*

My skin stung, pink and raw underneath the
water. I scrubbed the bristles of the brush over my
knuckles like the blood still stuck to them, Lady
Macbeth style.

When you lose it? Always copy the greats.

Pull your head out of your pretty ass. The

Queen of the Pure's chopping days are over. The rebellion in *your* ranks, however, is only just starting.

I'm not a leader; I gave that up, along with Angel World.

You never stopped being a leader. The only question is whether you're a tyrant or a freedom fighter.

What if I'm both?

A struggle, hollers, sparks.

Smash.

Another *squeal* from Mischief, as Ash crushed him beneath a Viking hammer.

As soon as Ash had learnt the details of Stephanie's defeat, including Mischief's kinky playtime with Anarchy, I'd known Ash would go postal.

I rubbed my hands again: *blood, must get out the blood, red, red, red...*

Rebel caught my hands between his. His candy sweetness wrapped around us both, distracting me from the coppery stench that'd followed me from Perfection Hotel, whilst he gently reached over and turned off the tap. Then he pulled me round, drying off my hands on his t-shirt; his chest was solid and reassuring underneath. I shivered at the *safety* in it.

Tenderness and concern warmed me through the bond.

Stop it, I was desperate to scream, just as much as I wanted to order him to *hold me*. Yet I battled down both thoughts. After witnessing Stephanie's abuse of Anarchy — her reduction of blokes to nothing but pets — I could never force Rebel through the Blood Bond like that again.

I blinked, as the weirdest-arsed battle played

out in the bunker.

When Ash booted Mischief across a pile of collectibles, something *crunched*. Ash *squeaked* in a way I was certain he'd forever deny. 'What have I done? C-3PO...'

'You've just managed what an entire Empire couldn't,' Mischief sneered, although his hands shook as he ran them over his broken *Star Wars* droid like a funeral rite, before pouncing onto Ash and ramming him against the computer chair.

I started towards them, but Rebel grasped my hand, pulling me away to lounge against the wall next to him.

Tuning in for the Geek Bitch Fight...

Ash scrambled for a weapon, snatching up a mechanical device and cracking it across Mischief's nose. Whilst Mischief howled, cradling his swollen nose, Ash grinned, hefting the device in his palm. 'The Doctor's sonic screwdriver: useful.'

Mischief swirled in a fury of silver, magicking (and how much easier was it to think *that* since knowing the Fae Angel?), a sword with a decorative wolf on its hilt out of its display case on the wall and into his palm.

I glanced out of the corner of my eye at Rebel, but he only gave a small shake of his head.

Mischief prowled towards Ash, who threw down the sonic screwdriver and kicked at a tapered spear that was like an icicle, spinning it into his palm.

They eyed each other across the standoff.

Ash was the first to break. 'What? You'd battle me, angel, with *Jon Snow's* Longclaw?'

Mischief sniffed. 'Please never repeat that *Game of Throne's* impression; it was embarrassing for us both. And you'd battle me, Fallen, with a White Walker's ice blade? I hadn't realised you were truly amongst the undead.'

Ash sniggered.

Until I lunged from the wall, swinging the wooden hammer, which Ash had dropped earlier.

I spread out my wings; they flamed to glory before I held aloft the hammer. 'And I battle with Mjolnir, Thor's hammer, which means I'm worthy, bitches. Plus, Ash?' He shifted his feet sheepishly. 'You've officially fallen off the Don't Fight Wagon.' He pinked. And no, not feeling the guilty at his *crushed and addicted to the trident, please help me* look. Because I suffered too. 'Stop with the cosplay.'

Mischief and Ash eyed each other warily. Then they counted to three on their fingers, before chucking their swords to the side with a *clang*.

Hell, did they even realise they'd found in each other their kindred misfit double?

Ash hugged his arms around himself. 'You failed the test, Violet.' Ash glared at Mischief. '*He* made you fail.'

I laughed. This was about more than Anarchy? 'Maybe check with me next time before you decide to beat someone into a fine red mist. I *passed*. Ding, dong, the bitch is shanked.'

'But who melted her?'

I jolted. My mouth was suddenly too dry to form words.

I hadn't passed because although I'd shanked Stephanie, I hadn't killed her: *Mischief had.*

Yet had Mischief realised? Had that been what he'd intended all along?

Let it be a no...

'I warned you,' Mischief held up his head defiantly, but his voice was soft, 'that the king chooses his words as carefully as one would pick up a snake. You were to kill the leader of the Pure. Not wound or have killed. You were to assassinate her yourself. I'm afraid I stole that honour from you.'

'Why?' The word came out cracked and broken.

Mischief shrugged, dropping his gaze.

When I unsheathed Star, she was no prop but blazed with righteous violet like the ancient powers inside that raged to punish Mischief, as I knew Lucifer would punish me for failing the test.

When I shakily held the hissing blade to Mischief's throat, he didn't flinch. And this time, he didn't fight back. 'You want a killer? This is me. Killer. Now I know why they call you *traitor*.' Mischief flinched again, but he still allowed the shank to blister the skin of his neck. Rebel's hands were suddenly on my shoulders, although he didn't pull me away. Instead, they were steadying: supportive. I wasn't alone. 'Why'd you trick me? Was it...?' Hell, why was I grasping at *anything* to explain this away as a mistake? 'Does becoming that unicorn screw with your decision making or...?'

Mischief sighed. 'Shapeshifting naturally affects your instincts.' I let out a breath I hadn't known I'd been holding. Mischief raised his hand, however, in surrender. 'Yet I'd always planned to be the assassin in this gig. I'm sorry, did you believe that *you* were in control?'

I roared, primal. I jerked back Mischief's head, burning a deeper line along his throat; he whimpered.

'Feathers,' Rebel's grip tightened, 'mind yourself.'

Violet and black blazed, whilst Devil whispered: *burn, burn, burn...*

'Why...? You let me go through all... Why even let me take the test, just to fail it?'

Mischief's gaze was pitying, even through his pain. 'You're the one who accepted it. That Pure creature... I've never relished a death as much as hers.' Silver sparked in his eyes, as venom laced his words; I recoiled from his hatred. Then it was gone, and his expression softened. 'You are not the beast I believed when we first fought in the Cage. I've been misinformed about you, at least in some ways. Yet you walk a knife's edge.' He looked down; his lip trembled. 'Enough of this mawkishness. Slit my throat.'

I tightened my hold on Star, but Ash grasped my wrist, edging the flames away from Mischief.

'You couldn't allow her to become the killer the Devil's Trident wants?' Ash asked, assessing Mischief with a soldier's respect. *What the hell had I missed?* 'She was lost in its blood lust, so you took the kill?'

Mischief nodded, breathing hard, as he grasped his charred throat. 'I knew it imperative she didn't become the assassin the king wishes, or the beast she herself truly fears. And she would have.'

'Sweet Jesus, I'm after voting we can't any of us allow that.' Rebel let go of my shoulders, fussing instead at Mischief's neck like a mother hen.

'*She* is still in the room.' I waved my hand, but they ignored me, pushing Mischief into the computer chair.

Tyrant or freedom fighter?

A tyrant would've chopped off Mischief's head for disobeying. She'd kick her blokes' arses for disrespecting now.

A freedom fighter, however, would grin that her fam no longer cowered in fear. Although, was it completely messed up that I missed the cringing respect an *itty-bitty* bit...?

'I'm not packing much in the way of trust.' I sighed, slipping Star into her scabbard. 'Why not just tell me?'

'Because you'd have stopped me and taken the kill anyway,' Mischief linked his hands in his lap.

'Have you forgotten what losing the test will cost you?'

Bonding to Wild, my blokes belonging to the FF, *not possessing Devil...*

The back of my throat burned, as the world warped, tainted with violet. I lunged at Mischief, and he shrank back with an *eep*.

Then apple-scented wings enfolded me, and I was swept around into Harahel's arms. When I squirmed, slowly the violet bled away.

It was dangerous how lost we'd been in our feuding that we hadn't watched for the enemies outside our walls. What if it'd been Wild, Trick, or Wings breaking into our bunker rather than Harahel?

What if it'd been Lucifer...?

When my pulse thundered, Harahel drew his wings against mine in comfort, until he glanced at Mischief's neck. Then his eyes widened, before he held me at arm's length with a stern glare that wasn't entirely mock. 'Hey, did I train you to barbecue our allies?'

'I'll guess...no? But you can wipe off the disappointed teacher look because since when was Sassy Silver here your ally?'

'When wasn't he?' Harahel slouched to Mischief, ruffling his hair. To my gaping amazement, Mischief allowed it with only the slightest sneer. 'What do you think it was like shut away in that nightmare Ossuary? But Mischief helped.' Guilt warred with shock: Mischief had *helped* the other angels? Then why had Rebel acted like he hated him? 'Plus, every revolution needs a secret agent.'

'Is that a pretty way of saying spy?'

Bang — the Master of Misrule soared through the door, before slamming it shut behind him.

When Misrule *thwapped* his cane on the wall, Harahel flinched. 'Would you welcome in the king and his spies as easily? Shall we line up now in obedient rows and walk into Lucifer's Light rejoicing?'

'Open door, hung drawn and quartered time, point made.' Ash sprawled against the wall.

Misrule nodded, sauntering to Mischief, before examining his neck; Mischief arched into the touch.

Had the world gone mental or had I woken in an alternative dimension where Mischief was the princess and I was the reject?

Have you forgotten already, Feathery-pride, what it feels like to be the freak in the circus, rather than the princess on her throne?

I'm always the monster.

You're the Monster Princess, and we both know it's not the same thing.

That feeling, dark and festering? It's jealousy.

Why would I be jealous of his tiny wizard arse?

You tell me.

Misrule swung round, twirling his coat. He pointed the end of his cane at me like an accusing finger. 'You damaged the star of the show.'

'It was always a risk with her temper. After all, she has eighty-eight fangs on her necklace...and *my* feather.' Mischief shrugged.

What the bastard hell...?

The ancient powers inside roared to teach Mischief what happened to blokes who challenged the Champion. *I should've pulled the stuffing out of his unicorn belly when I'd had the chance.*

Instead, I forced down the flames, flushing. 'I'm not wearing any bastard necklace,' I muttered. 'I've been trying—'

'Princess,' Rebel caught my chin, ghosting his lips against mine. 'We've explained this all arseway, so we have. Harahel's my mate and legendary at planning battles,' *I'd forgotten how much of a Harahel fanboy Rebel was*, 'if he says Misrule can... Look, there's no plot. I mean, there *is* a plot but it's against the king, not you.'

'Wait, you all got together in a merry band and decided because I was the king's daughter...I couldn't be trusted? I'd choose my dad over you? I'd turn out to love the FF life-style?'

'Pick one.' Mischief rose out of his chair, silver sparking around him in sudden dark splendour.

How much of his power had he been hiding? And why?

I crumpled, clutching onto Harahel's arm to hold myself up because I wasn't going onto my knees before Mischief.

Harahel soothed his thumb over the back of my hand. 'Look, amongst the Fallen I can chat to you like we're mates and I'm not less because I sacrificed...' He lifted his arm with its missing hand. 'Yet there's also the Bloods, the Shadows, Bones...Seducers.' He glanced at Ash, who was staring pointedly at the wall. 'It blows my mind how they can punish the Children of the Dark merely because they're born here. Plus, how could I turn down the chance to light a fire under the King of the Under World?'

'I knew there was a reason I liked you, angel,' Ash smirked.

'Et tu, bastard?' I snarled.

Ash winced. 'Rebel told me the angels were planning something,' he muttered. 'My sisters are Bloods. I'd do anything to save them. And your eyes, Violet, on that first night...they had the king's spark in them.'

'Everything since has been playing me?' Hot bile burnt the back of my throat.

All of a sudden, my chest was too tight. When I swayed, Rebel caught one side of me, Ash the other, and between them and Harahel, they nested with me on the floor, cocooning me in their warmth, sweet aromas, and kisses.

I should've been safe. *But they'd betrayed me.*

Now caught between these Judases, I was unwittingly at the heart of a dangerous civil war against Lucifer. Yet by failing the test, turning to him would only mean pain.

In this anarchic Under World, there were only traitors and rebels.

19

The sweet scent of candied apples studded with cloves wove the lie that I was sheltered from the Under World: Lucifer, the civil war, *secrets*...

On the cold floor of Mischief's bunker, protected in the hot wings of angels and Fallen, I could make-believe that I was still leader of the gang of rebels.

I shuddered, as Ash kissed along my neck, Rebel's breath spectred across my cheek, and Harahel's curls tickled my shoulder. Yet I hadn't stepped-up and become the leader they'd needed: Mischief had. *And I'd been too blind to see it.*

I punched my fists against my thighs, welcoming the thudding pain.

Lost in the whirl of the Bone Carnival, I'd forgotten who I was. But the Bitch of Utopia was back and I'd become what my fam needed.

Finally, your feathery arse has joined the party!

But wearing what costume, J? Rebel Princess? Bone, Monster, or Vampire?

All of the above, or none. You're just you. When will you realise that's enough?

I shook myself loose from the blokes' embraces, refusing to meet Rebel's wounded gaze, as I backed against the computer chair. When I hit Mischief's legs, I glared; he simply raised his eyebrow. 'Why the big conspiracy?'

'The only conspiracy,' Harahel murmured, 'is against Lucifer and the FF. We don't even know how or what we're going to do yet, it's simply a bunch of folks swearing loyalty to the cause for when the time's right. Do you think I could leave *you* with Lucifer, any more than I can the Bloods? When the king was cruel to you in the Crypt, I was all for — BOOM! — taking him out there and—'

Misrule swung Harahel up, catching him close by his waist. 'Remember the fascinating discussion we had afterwards about tantrums?'

I stiffened.

Harahel pouted. 'That your mean spanking twin would pay a visit...? I hate that bully.'

Misrule adjusted his cravat with the tip of his cane, even as his other arm tightened around Harahel's waist. 'No respect....'

I launched myself up, sparks buzzing beneath my skin.

Misrule had forced Harahel into becoming his Blood Lover. In Angel World, I'd rescued Harahel from his brutal Glory, although I'd regretted allowing him to be claimed by her in the first place, but here I'd left him in Misrule's ownership.

Because I'd trusted.

'Sorry, *Master...*' Harahel looked down, blushing. Then he burst out laughing, twisting out of Misrule's grip with a smirk. 'How does anyone ever call you that without cracking up?'

I gawked at them: I'd never seen Harahel so unafraid. Or *equal.* Misrule was an important vampire, and Harahel was an angel prisoner, yet here he had more equality than he'd been allowed on Angel World. Maybe I was right to trust.

Even if they'd all lied to me.

Misrule swung his cane with a dark grin. 'Oh, because I can put them into the Cage if they don't.' *Way to kill a mood.* 'And Harahel?'

This time, Harahel forced himself to keep a straight face, whilst he nodded.

'I'll take a wild stab and say you revealed our secrets to the princess?'

Harahel squirmed, staring up at the ceiling. 'On the flip side, I revealed our secrets and now she can help, *like I've been saying she would.*'

'If you manipulated this on purpose, my sweetest angel, I shall—'

'Enough with the tedious lovers' tiff,' Mischief interrupted with such authority, I couldn't stop myself taking a step back. 'He told her in defence of me. It's done. She'll join, lead, or betray us.' He calmly checked off the options on his fingers.

I bristled. 'They aren't choices.'

Mischief tilted his head. 'Did I say choices or consequences?'

I growled. 'I'll lead you, and that's *my choice.*'

'Surely you can understand the reason we hid this from you, since you're under such scrutiny...?'

'You were protecting me?'

'This is all about you,' Mischief snarled, yanking

me closer by the elbow. 'Your dad is a tyrant, but you could be the worst dictator who has ever ruled. To save the Under World, we have been trying to save *you.*'

My vision blacked; I swayed in his hold.

Dictator?

'I'm not...that's not me, bro,' I whispered.

Mischief's expression gentled. 'I have come to believe not. But the Cage changes you. As does Lucifer's Light and the Devil's Trident. We have all — here — sworn to hold onto you. To keep you away from the flames.'

'Why? What do you care?' I regretted it as soon as I said it.

Mischief's eye twitched; his mouth set in a thin line. 'Isn't it enough that I do?'

I nodded. Then I flamed my wings behind me in a blazing arc, lighting the shadowy bunker in their glory.

Yeah, sometimes go for the dramatic classics.

'This is your new leader, bitches: no fighting between fam, or I'll make you all drop and give me twenty.'

Ash grinned. 'Don't turn all *Full Metal Jacket* on us.'

I smiled, eyeing Mischief. 'Where's your Che Guevara hat?'

At last, Mischief's shoulders relaxed. 'Did Guevara shag Lucifer too then?'

I sniggered before catching Rebel by his spiked collar. Startled, he still let himself be dragged into my arms; I smoothed over the chafed skin beneath the leather. 'What was all the Mischief hating back in the underground tunnels, if he'd helped you in the dark?'

Rebel's gaze was troubled. 'Here's the thing of it: this bunker isn't watched. But those git firefly spies of Lucifer's could always be watching elsewhere. We had to put on a show.'

What was real?

Had Lucifer watched everything I'd done as entertainment?

'And you have to put on a show now,' Misrule grinned but it was grim. 'You were always a savage joy in the Bone Carnival. Most of the Fallen won't join us until they *see* you're stronger than Lucifer or at least, as strong as him. *Your* light, it shines like it's going to burn out the eyes of the universe. As Queen of Chaos? You'll have the Fallen's loyalty, and we'll have our civil war.'

'Hold up the rebellion train,' I slammed my fist onto a pile of gadgets, cracking the crumpled head of the Star Wars droid — Mischief and Ash groaned in unison. 'Now you *want* me to win Devil?'

'Contrary bunch, aren't we?' Mischief met my gaze. 'You see, the trident *wants* you. It was essential you didn't claim it, until you'd decided to *take* it. Not the other way around.'

Devil's whispers... His demands for death... His hunger...

I'd been under the trident's thrall.

Yet how did I battle it? I steeled myself because if they could risk...*everything*...then I could fight Devil's temptation.

I nodded. 'I won't be the bitch. Got it.'

When Ash spun me away from Rebel, wrapping me in his wings, I tensed. Then I melted, lost in his quiet strength.

'First, we have to win the trident,' Ash murmured, not letting go. 'You didn't pass Lucifer's test: this, with a bloke whose idea of second chances is to red hot poker you for each mistake.' *How had I forgotten that?* 'When he calls for you tonight — and he will — remember you're our leader now. He'll hurt us to hurt you. But you're stronger than he is. You're the Protector, and we believe in you. Just...remember that.'

I held onto his shoulders, trembling.

Tonight, I faced Lucifer and the consequences of losing the test. Even if I was the Protector, my first job as leader was to let those I loved suffer.

I understood now that truly was my hell.

I choked, holding the back of my hand across my mouth. The sulphurous stench rose in a haze of heat off the stagnant pools, which blazed with flames, as if they were coated with oil. I ducked, slinking through the shadows.

Ash paced along the banks of a subterranean river that curled through the tunnels: The Fire Catacombs, Mischief had told me they were called.

Nocturnal, since I'd been dragged to the Under World, I'd become used to sleeping away the days in my carriage cell, exhausted from the Cage fights.

I'd woken an hour ago blissed in a pile of feathers, fur, and inked tattoos: *fam*.

I hadn't remembered inviting Mischief into the mix, but his slim arm had been slung around my neck, and his head had nestled on my shoulder. Rebel had been studying him, almost as perplexed as me.

Because that had been Ash's spot.

I'd bolted upright, knocking off Mischief.

What had happened to Ash?

Last night...that couldn't have been Ash's way of saying *goodbye*...?

Not again...

Mischief had lain on his back, as I'd shaken him. 'What've you done with our Brigadier?'

Mischief had blinked up at me, sleepily. 'Your

beloved whore is missing, so you think I...? Why not rather believe him with the Blood Lovers? They are intimate, after all.'

'Or with Lucifer,' Rebel had added.

I'd winced, but what if they'd been right? What if Ash, who'd already betrayed me once, had done it again?

Yet even as I'd thought it, I hadn't believed it. What I'd feared...?

That Ash had already sacrificed himself. And I'd never see him again.

When I'd lunged for the door, Mischief had called out, 'Do you think I wouldn't have slipped another tracker onto the Fallen, after we lost him the last time? It's almost like you don't know me at all.'

So, I'd tracked Ash here to the Fire Catacombs.

Ash hunkered down, holding his arms over his head. Across the tongue of the black river, an island of garbage mushroomed out of the blood-tainted waters, which led to an archway that flickers of light licked around.

Lucifer's Light.

Which was better...betrayed or sacrificed?

I held my breath as I crept closer.

Hiss — a jet of fire exploded beneath my foot.

I rolled to the side, as the catacombs gave birth to a hundred baby fountains of flames. My elbow seared, and my ankle bruised, as I kicked away. My latex top started to melt.

I screamed.

Then Ash was rolling me, hissing himself at the burns, before ducking me into the stinking waters. I swallowed slimy mouthfuls before wishing I hadn't and chucking up; it burned my nostrils.

Hell, the filth...

There was a hand at my neck, and I was being

dragged backwards onto the edge of Volcano Land before my wet clothes and weapons were ripped off.

I shivered, staring up at Ash, whilst I coughed.

Ash's eyes were red-rimmed, and his face was worn in a way I'd never seen. He avoided my gaze as he slipped off his black shirt and slid it over my shoulders; at least it wasn't one of his shiny hustler tops.

'You haven't slept a wink, bro?'

He sighed. 'I'm sorry. I meant to be back before you woke up and discovered Mischief drooling on your shoulder.'

When he eased my wings through the slashes of his shirt, it hung down like a dress. I'd never worn a bloke's clothes before, and his warmth and scent next to my skin shuddered through me.

Yet Ash was shivering for a different reason, and it made me want to nuke from orbit whatever had made him look so *weary*.

I reached out to touch his cheek, but he flinched back. 'Don't...I'm not clean.'

'No one talks about my blokes like that. Even you.'

We sat eyeing each other, as the fire flared in firework displays behind us, and the river gurgled by.

'This is where he...Lucifer...made me a Seducer,' Ash finally admitted. '*Why* he made me one. He'd already lost my loyalty...love...to my babe.' He glanced underneath his eyelashes at me, as if daring me to threaten him with a new form of death.

The vampiric powers inside seethed to hold him over the fire pools until he roasted, as I had inside, to hear him talk about his *other* love.

Were they still alive? Did he *still* love them?

I wanted to be the freedom fighter, however, not the tyrant. The psycho powers wouldn't rule me: I'd rule them. Even if it meant denying the crushing waves of *mine, mine, mine* every time I smelled the clove scent of Ash on his shirt around my shoulders.

I clenched my jaw to stop myself spewing out venomous words.

'No hating on the *babe*?' Ash ventured.

'You're not calling *me* it. So, knock yourself out and call your skank *monkey muffins*.'

I didn't expect the huff of laughter. 'She'd cut off my head, phoenix resurrect me, and cut it off again if I did that.'

I tensed, before shoving Ash's shirt off my shoulders. 'Keep it for her. I'd rather strut my stuff back naked.'

Ash caught my wrists, easing the shirt back on me. 'There's nobody but you, m*onkey muffins*.'

'I'm not following.'

Ash's fangs shot out, and I juddered, as he grazed them along my neck. Yet it was like being *home*, the same as the first time I'd met him in Hackney Cemetery. 'I love you, Violet, only you. I needed time here to remind myself why I'm fighting...suffering...and why I gave up Devil.' His pupils were blown, his gaze desperate. 'He whispers to me, begging me to take him back.'

Devil had been running to daddy, using us *both*.

I had to salute the manipulative trident. Now I was onto his tricks, however, he wouldn't come out as top boy. The weapon might've played these games in a supernatural arena for centuries, but I'd learnt them from J and fought them in Hackney. There was no contest.

I'd win.

'I know you don't want my protection,' Ash kissed my neck; his large hands stroked up my spine. 'All hail the Champion. But just once...*pretend*. I'm not a hero but I could be—'

'I don't need to pretend.'

I caressed Ash's bare chest, and his wings fluttered. When my fingers moved towards the waistband of his jeans, however, his breath hitched.

'How can you touch me?' He rested his head on my shoulder. I hated the way the self-loathing spun him as fragile as glass. 'When you know what I am?'

'You're mine.' *Those words were halleluiahs.* If Lucifer killed us tonight, at least we died claimed and together. 'Fam. And the *Brigadier*. No bastard can take that away.'

I'd show Ash just how much I craved to touch...

I pushed open the button on his jeans, and although his breathing became harsh, as he clung around my neck, he didn't stop me this time.

I slid my hand lower again.

Suddenly, long steel nails burst out of my hands. I shrieked, as I skewered Ash through the guts with my claws.

20

I've never had my claws inside a bloke before.

Maybe <u>in</u> a bloke...

Not a foot of violet gleaming steel skewering in one side and out the other, whilst a trickle of scarlet gurgled out of the corner of his mouth.

Yeah, I knew how to romance.

First, snuggle next to sulphurous pools that farted fire into the catacombs, which ran with a sewage river and its island of garbage, then run your lover boy through.

Violet nails, J, violet nails.

I can see them, Feathery-muffin, both in and out of your brave solider.

This is a freak out: I'm labelling it. Big arsed

freak out. Take them away. No claws for this bitch.

Hold on one hell fire minute, hooker, you earned those babies. I told you, you're the Vampire Princess. Down here in the Under World? Those nails are *pride*. Haven't your hidden behind your shame long enough?

Ash had raised his head from my shoulder. He stared with shock and wonder at my nails that had almost unmanned him.

Shuddering, my body tremored, as I wrenched at the nails.

Squelch — my claws were caught on Ash's innards.

When Ash winced, I hunched. 'Ehm, sorry?'

Ash grinned, licking at the blood around his lips. 'That is...hot. Well, without the kebabbing me part.'

I glared at him. 'I thought you weren't a kinky bastard like Rebel?'

Ash rolled his eyes. 'You came into your claws, and they're gorgeous. Thinking about someone...*something*...sexy, were you?' He bucked his hips, then groaned at the *rip*, as my nails slid even deeper. 'Can we finish this with less of the Wolverine?'

I blushed. 'They just...pop out...when I'm getting a happy?'

'Or in throat slashing mode. You were tingling good, not tingling bad?' Ash smirked. 'Relax. Imagine drawing them in.' I tugged, shaking with frustration, and Ash yelped. 'Ninja-like, as if you're slipping a blade up your sleeve.'

'How'd you know? You don't even have this mod.'

Way to emasculate a bloke, almost literally.

Ash stilled; he couldn't hide the pain fast enough before he forced a smile. '*Ouch*, and that only hurt two on a scale out of ten. Your dad managed the full ten out of ten when he ripped out my claws right here in these catacombs, and unlike fangs, they don't grow back.'

That killed all happy tingles.

My claws shot back into my nails, just like Ash had said.

Shanks had become part of me. Or I'd become a shank.

I'd always loved the feel of the blade in my hand, slicing through skin. I'd fled from that truth, but I *was* the weapon.

Ash hollered, falling onto his back. 'Now you've made it up to a solid three.'

I leaned over him, pushing his sable mane away from his forehead. 'Why come here? Why did Lucifer make you a Seducer? Why did he steal your claws?'

'Disobeyed,' Ash whispered, shaking, yet his charcoal gaze never left mine. 'Rebelled. Fought the Light.' He glanced across at the flickering archway. 'Every empire makes examples: don't misbehave or you'll become nothing but a whore like the dark Brigadier. Who'll stand up after they witness...?'

'The Bitch of Utopia will,' I flared my wings behind me, forcing his gaze back to mine. 'And what did I say about disrespecting my blokes?' My fingers cramped with the desperation to touch, but Ash had been used enough, and this time I craved his permission. 'Trick says a Seducer is only there to bring pleasure to others. I say: *screw the bastard.* Let me bring pleasure just to you.'

Ash wet his lips, before nodding.

'Words would help, bro.'

'Please...'

I'd take that.

I kissed Ash softly, trailing my fingers down his

neck, across his fluttering pulse. He jolted, as if expecting roughness, yet twined his tongue with mine, when all I did was circle his nipples. He quivered with hypersensitivity, still on edge. This time, however, I didn't tease. I'd only started touching him, yet already he arched beneath me. I pressed closer, ignoring the winding coils tingling through my wings, gums, and deep inside.

This wasn't for me.

Ash had been transformed into a creature of pleasure, but that pleasure had been turned against him to torment. How long had it been since he'd been touched out of *love*?

I almost paused in my caresses at the revelation.

Hell, that's what this was: *love*.

When I stretched out his wings, Ash closed his eyes. I sucked the tips of each feather between my lips, mouthing along the line of Ash's right wing, whilst he moaned, fisting his hands in my shirt — *his* shirt.

I trembled at the intimacy.

Just release, I swore mantra-like, *a wank mate helping to release...*

But it was more than that. A reclaiming of identity. Self. Manhood.

Love.

I kissed Ash's pulsing wingtip. He bucked, his eyes flying open. His fingers tore at my shoulders, as if he was drowning. Then he slumped back, blacked out.

I smiled, settling my wings over him like a blanket.

Then fireflies blazed, bobbing across the pools: *Lucifer's Lights.*

I froze.

Being discovered half naked with my dad's

favourite whipping boy — in the fiery catacomb where he first took his whip to him — didn't scream loyalty.

To a paranoid despot like Lucifer? It'd sing gunpowder, treason, and plot.

And, of course, the bastard would be right.

I cringed in the gloom, shielding Ash's still body, as the flames died in my wings. But if the fire pools behind us exploded again? We'd be lit up like shadow puppets.

I slowed my breathing, ducking my head over my wings, as the lights wove closer, questing.

Closer, closer, and closer...

I struggled back to the skills I'd honed in Angel World, throwing up mental walls in my mind to shield us both. Yet unlike when I'd protected Rebel and me from discovery by the Mage, I couldn't reach through a bond to pull Ash behind my wall because Ash wasn't my Marked Wing and I hadn't Bonded with him.

Why did that make me feel so isolated from Ash my chest ached?

At last, the lights veered away across the river, hovering around the archway.

I risked peeking through the damp strands of hair that stuck to my cheeks.

A giant bat soared along the roof of the catacomb. In the dark, all I could see were grey wings and chocolate body.

I shuddered.

It circled, high above, before plummeting down, as if guided by the lights. Except, it wasn't a bat: it was *Wild*.

Wild clutched a boy to his chest: an inked Blood who was crimson in tattoos.

Beautiful.

Yet the Blood trembled, weeping. When they

landed, the only thing holding the boy on his feet were Wild's arms around him, like a dad supporting his son. Yet it was less paternalistic and more punishing.

'Rejoice, the king has ordered your sacrifice. Today, you walk into Lucifer's Light. Thank him in your bones and blood for the honour.' They didn't sound like Wild's words. They were stilted as a ritual, as if he'd said them enough times to become bored of the routine.

He didn't even react when the boy wailed.

Still the Blood didn't say a word.

And that's what did it: I didn't know what freaky *sacrifice* went down in these catacombs but it wasn't happening today. Because the kid wasn't even allowed to speak in his defence. I was his Protector, however, and I bastard would.

When I tried to shove myself up, however, snatching Flight who hummed approvingly from my pile of sodden clothes, Ash's hand shot out, dragging me down by the wrist.

His eyes snapped open, sparking with rage and misery. 'You wanted to know why Lucifer punished me?'

'Not a good time.'

'*This* is why.' Ash yanked mc back onto him. 'I defied his order to burn the dissenters.'

My heart lurched.

Burn? No way in hell I was letting that happen to the inked kid.

Wild shoved the Blood, and he stumbled, catching himself against the rock archway. His bare feet sank into the garbage.

'And now I'm going to defy the bastard as well.' I pulled my wrist free.

Ash wrapped his wings around me, however, tumbling me around, knocking Flight out of my hand, and pinning me beneath him.

Hell, he was strong when he wanted to be.

'You're not,' Ash barked in the commanding tone of the Brigadier freed again, 'you'll listen to me. This boy's execution is on *Lucifer's* order. There's no way to stop it. If you try and save even one, then *ten* will die in their place.'

The flickering lights dimmed, as the Blood stepped hesitantly through the archway into the crevice beyond.

I almost murdered ten kids. I could've...

You almost did nothing. Your daddy set up this nightmare carnival, and you've been caught in the show.

Cold choked me. I clasped at Ash's wings, my throat tight. 'How...?'

'I tried...' Ash's gaze was empty. 'When Lucifer first started *cleansing* our ranks. I won't ever forget the deaths I caused because I tried to save triplets...'

Tears dripped from his eyes, yet still he only stared with that blank, broken stare.

I shook him. 'You *tried*. You lost your claws, trident, right to be anything but a Seducer because you tried to stop Lucifer.'

'But I lost.'

'You didn't have me. Now you do.'

Ash scrutinised me in a way I couldn't understand, although anything was better than the lost look he'd had going on before. 'Good to know I have the Protector this time.'

He linked our hands.

Clank — a steel door smashed down, shutting in the kid.

There was a clear viewing panel through into the light chamber, like this was just another Cage fight. Somehow, however, I didn't think a Champion would be stepping away free.

'We can try—'

'Ten kids, Violet, in place of one. We can't fight the entire FF, Under World, and Lucifer. Not yet...and not before those kids would die.'

'What happens next?' I tightened my fingers around Ash's, my pulse pounding.

The powers inside howled to jump up and battle for the kid, even as I knew that'd kill ten more.

How could I judge to allow one to die to save a theoretical ten? Ash had been presented with the same choice, and he knew the consequences. I allowed him to hold me back, even as part of me hated him for it.

Hated myself.

Yet I hated Lucifer more.

Ash shook his head, holding me closer. 'Don't watch. Don't ever watch. Like I had to.'

I shivered, caught beneath Ash, wrapped in his warmth, and I burnt with the power of the trident.

'*Yours, take me, always*', Devil wheedled, '*Queen, mighty, kill them all.*'

Tonight, I'd meet Lucifer, and he'd make us suffer for the failure of the second test. Yet now I knew the truth of the Fire Catacombs...? Every part of me was singing in unison — vampiric, angelic, and Protector — to take the bastard down. To do that, however, I had to let the monster inside play with Devil, which would make me more dangerous than the Light-bringer. And I didn't know if I could control either once they were free.

I screwed closed my eyes, shuddering at the Blood's screams.

21

When I was a freaky eyed kid in the school yard, I'd invent stories about my dad. Dragon tamer, computer tycoon, or heroic firefighter, he always played the hero.

It didn't matter though because nobody believed me: not even myself. I needed an imaginary dad, however, to light the shadow one that followed me every day since my abandonment.

I'd called out to the angels to save me because no one had answered when I'd called out *dad*. And maybe I *was* a bitch, but you had to step up to survive.

Alone.

But I wasn't alone anymore. Now I had my dad,

and he wasn't a dragon tamer, he was the bastard dragon whose fire wouldn't save me. Instead, it'd burn hotter than the sun.

Lucifer's light blazed like judgement in the pitch-black. Blinding, scarring, and immolating.

His spy fireflies buzzed along the roof.

I huddled in the warmth of Rebel's arms against the chalky stench that chilled the deep-level air raid shelter that mouldered, abandoned after World War Two, with its low ceiling and the rumble of Tube trains above.

The Bones.

Why the hell had Lucifer demanded we meet him here? Alone? And why did it terrify the vampires into obeying?

I took a deep breath of my shirt's collar: citrus cloves.

When Ash and I had stumbled back to my carriage room — the kid's *screams* still echoing in accusation — I'd slipped into my leather trousers and latex, but I'd pulled Ash's shirt on over the top again. I hadn't been able to abandon our new closeness.

Ash would have to wrestle me for the shirt if he wanted it back. And wouldn't Misrule get off on placing bets on that...?

Ash paced at the back of the shelter, in front of a colossal vampire who'd been hooked by a harness to a mechanical wheel, which rusted in flaking copper: A Roman slave at a waterwheel.

But what nightmare did the wheel pull...or open?

The Roman Vampire's skin shone silvery white, Gollumesque, as he sagged against the wall.

Lucifer's wings flared. He looked even taller

than last time; he was kitted out in full leather outfit, blazing horns and all. A cape, which flowed around him like oil, had been added to his Big Bad costume.

Yet even through the surging flames, Lucifer's mouth was tighter, and dark shadows bruised underneath his eyes. For the first time, I saw the cost of his power, played out on his flesh.

Because of me.

Our hunt in his bedroom — no flames, horns, cape, or *trident* — suddenly appeared an innocent memory.

Mischief knelt in front of Lucifer but he didn't bow his head; he held his back straight and his chin lifted. His haughty gaze met mine, shining through the dark, as Lucifer possessively petted his hair.

The proud consort.

I fisted my hands to stop myself storming over and wrenching Lucifer away to stop him touching *my* Fae Angel. Just as the forces inside raged to punish Mischief for *allowing* it, even though I knew he was risking himself undercover.

The illusion of submission.

The warring powers were as hard to fight as Devil. His pull, tugging on me, adrenaline-shot me with power.

Lucifer had the trident on him.

I wriggled free of Rebel, stepping forward.

Clank, clank.

Surprised, I peered down at the metal beneath my feet, before tapping my boot — *clank, clank* — on the sheet of steel that covered the rest of the shelter's floor.

Lucifer chuckled. 'Wow, that's quite the tap dance of joy to see me. And there I was thinking you'd be an itty bit...I don't know...naughty girl sorry to have made daddy cross?'

I snorted. 'First, shove the daddy kink, and second...? What's with the hollow floor?'

Clank — I booted the metal.

Horror: it flashed across Mischief's face before he could smother it.

My chest tightened.

'Don't stand there, Violet,' Ash's command was threaded with anguish, as if I was standing on *his* dad's grave.

I took a cautious step back. Time to deal the Bluff Card. 'OK, pay up. Two wings and unpurified: I chose your team. That means I passed the test. Three prongs make a trident in my hand.'

I held my breath. I'd never expected both angels and vampires to be better liars than me.

Lucifer cocked his head, before smiling. 'You want Devil?'

I nodded.

This time, Devil materialised in the air before me, as Mischief had in the Bone Palace, every twisted bone inch of him *glowing* in glory.

'*Yours, yours, yours,*' Devil chanted, '*take me, take me, take...*'

'There's just this *eensy* last thing,' Lucifer mused, his hand tightening in Mischief's hair. 'Devil has been aching for a kill all day. You know, champ, this is exciting. You're my assassin now, after all. Who will it be? Addict, Seducer, or pet?'

Lucifer booted Mischief between his shoulders, sprawling him over the metal between us. Mischief landed with a startled *oomph*.

Rebel took a wary step away from me towards Ash, and that hurt the most.

'*Kill,*' Devil's light coiled around my hands, dragging my fingers to the shaft, '*kill, kill...*'

Its hunger to feast on death...devour my love...drag me into its whirling darkness...shuddered through me. I panted, throwing back my head, then howled.

'*Queen,*' Devil purred, '*my Queen. Anarchy, chaos, light.*'

I tried to yank away my hands, but coils of light held them lashed to the bone.

Devil swung me round, pointing first at Mischief, then at Rebel, and finally at Ash.

'*Choose,*' Devil ordered.

If I wasn't a bitch to Lucifer, then I wouldn't be a bitch to a pointy stick.

I shook the trident and was certain I heard it *yelp*. 'Shove it, Mr Poseidon. I'm the top boy here. I make the call on who we kill, and we don't kill fam. You either follow me like a good little fork or you're *not* mine.'

Devil blazed, hot enough to sear, as he thundered. I gasped but held on. At last, the fire died down, and Devil shrank, still grumbling. '*Yours,*' he muttered, '*good fork.*'

No bastard way he'd ever been *good*.

I shivered as I slipped him into the pocket of my trousers. I'd conquered Devil and I had the weapon we needed to fight the revolution.

I jumped, startled by the sudden touch to my cheek. Lucifer was studying me.

How had he moved so fast? Or had I been truly so lost in the battle with Devil that I hadn't even noticed him?

'Huh, you didn't kill.' Lucifer smiled sadly.

'You wanted me to?'

He shook his head. 'I think you missed my meaning: you *didn't* kill. You *aren't* an assassin. And my pet is better at taking off the heads of the Pure than my disobedient daughter.'

I dragged Ash's shirt more closely around myself; my skin tingled.

And that's how you call a Bluff Card.

'Then why give me the kickass weapon?'

Lucifer ducked his head, like he'd been the one caught out. 'Because here's what I'm learning with kids: their failures make *you* look bad. I have this whole...*thing*...planned, you know, party hats and cake for your coronation as Queen of Chaos.' His horns flared in sympathetic outrage. 'I gave you two chances. *Two!* Have a guess how many I give everyone else if they fail?'

'I'd go with trick question. You don't give bastard chances.'

Lucifer giggled. 'She truly is my daughter, I knew it.' He patted my head. 'On my blood, we'll share this final test in private: lucky number three. Then the Feathered can't bleat about my love for you being a *weakness*, and the dissenters can't spin it to tear down everything I've sacrificed to build here.'

A third test? Yet that was fair. I'd failed, after all.

And I flushed because *I* was one of those dissenters. It hadn't been difficult to rise up against my mum in Angel World. She'd barely pretended to offer me love. My dad, on the other hand, had offered me a throne, power, and a parent... And in return I was plotting to destroy everything *he'd* ever loved and fought for.

Remember the Fire Catacombs...the kid Blood...the screams...

I nodded, shakily.

'Good, good. This one's the simplest of them all: sacrifice. Cue the drum roll... What will you sacrifice to the Bones for me? *Who?*'

Bastard, no...

I twirled to Ash, but he was already striding towards me, catching me in his arms, dark Brigadier again. 'Step back.'

Clank, rattle, clank.

The walls shook, as Roman Vampire groaned and strained forwards, pulling the chains on the wheel.

'Sweet Mary,' Rebel gasped.

A section of metal floor trembled open like a mouth, before drawing to a *clanking* stop.

What lay beneath us?

'Show her the heart of pain, Seducer,' Lucifer flashed an arc of light towards the tomb beneath the Bones: a ghostly rainbow. 'The reason you sacrifice.'

Ash clasped my hand, edging us together towards the dark. Then he nodded grimly downwards, and I kneeled on the metal. 'Never feel guilt for how you won in the Cage. Your prize blood keeps Key alive.'

Anarchy's brother.

In the roasting heat beneath the air raid shelter, a kid who looked like he should be in the year below Jade at college, had been bound in barb wire and trapped in the dark. The wire had been jammed between his lips in a brutal muzzle.

Key stared up at me, squinting against the weak light with too large eyes in a gaunt face, hidden behind midnight curls. His skeletal frame was lost in his single item of clothing: bloody denim jeans.

He reminded me so much of Anarchy it booted me in the gut.

How much had seeing Key like this hurt Ash each time he'd fed him? And how many others were trapped beneath here — starving to nothing but bones? I'd been walking on top of them, as they'd been buried alive.

I didn't miss that there was one more space in the tomb. *Sacrifice*: I got it now.

I swallowed, digging my nails through my trousers. I *needed* it to hurt more. My claws shot out, slashing the leather. I hissed, as it sliced through skin.

'For the love of Christ, would you stop that, woman.' Rebel swooped down, yanking my claws away from my knees. 'You grew into your claws then? They're...'

'Different,' I whispered, shying away.

Rebel stroked across my knuckles. 'We're all after being different.' He raised the tips of my claws to his lips, kissing each one in turn. I juddered, as each light touch of his lips jolted me through my claws all the way to my throbbing wingtips. 'Beautiful,' he murmured. 'I was a muppet if I ever made you feel like you had to hide this side of yourself. You're the Fallen's princess too. But you'll never Fall. You'll rise above us lifted on our wings.'

When Lucifer swung his cloak around my eyes, a snaking blackness blindfolded me; I screamed.

'Time out, kiddies. I'm touched by your Fallen coming out moment, I truly am. But there's a timer *tick tick ticking* here: can you hear that? One minute, counting down. This is me, patience officially worn out.' Lucifer's teasing tone darkened. 'I've been daddy indulgence, haven't I? Three tests? Now, sacrifice.'

He swept away the cloak, and I coughed, clutching Rebel's arms. Grey spots danced in front of my eyes.

Hell, I couldn't bear being lost in that endless darkness again...a taste of what Key suffered in the Bones.

What I'd condemn whoever I chose as sacrifice to suffer.

Key's gaze swivelled between us, his tongue gargling words behind his wire gag; scarlet dribbled down his chin.

Rebel dangled his legs over the lip of the Bones into the gloom. He bowed his head; his eyelashes curved onto his cheek. 'I'm a bad angel but I can do something good. Look, I bicker with the Brigadier, but you need him because this is his world. Here, I'm nothing but wally of a captured angel...'

'You're not *nothing*...'

'Princess, please, I'm not awful good with sappy goodbyes and nonsense but—'

'I promised you'd never go back into the dark. I *promised*.'

I wiped my hand across my eyes: I wouldn't give Lucifer the show he wanted. To let him see what his *test* was costing me.

Rebel had suffered for forty years in a birdcage prison in the dark. When he'd been returned to it in Angel World, it'd broken him.

How could I watch it happen again? Was any bargain worth that?

I reached for Rebel, but he shrank back.

'I knelt for you, willingly.' He bit his lower lip, tearing at the tender flesh with his teeth; I craved to free it and kiss the cut until I tasted his sweet blood. 'And this is me, submitting to you. By all the saints, let me show you what that means.'

'Sorry to interrupt the *Casablanca* moment,' Ash hauled Rebel away from the edge; Rebel writhed in his hold. 'Wait, nope, not sorry at all.' Ash hurled Rebel across the shelter, staring down at me with regimental steeliness, before his expression softened, as he glanced at Key. 'I was the one who...saw what the dark did to our retro angel.

He's not returning to it.' I recognised the possessive protectiveness towards Rebel because it surged through me too, just like his blood. 'I remember equal kneeling duties. So, Ash: ready for sacrificing. Note the total lack of enthusiasm.'

I swallowed thickly. Both my blokes had offered themselves to this torment. To save me and to save the Under World.

'That's time up,' Lucifer frowned at Mischief. 'Why didn't you throw your hat into the Bones ring, pet?'

Mischief glanced up, startled. Then he peeked at me, before wetting his lips. 'I'm not a fan of barb wire gags, Your Majesty. Let other fools walk into the fire for her; I didn't kneel.'

Even though I knew...*hoped*...Mischief was playing his role, I still winced.

Lucifer laughed, his eyes twinkling. 'That's why I love you, my selfish scheming pet. You can't be taken under the spark. I need someone like you close to me. It's...refreshing.'

Ash closed his eyes, shuffling to perch on the edge of the Bones, but I stopped him from pushing himself down into the shadows.

'There's nothing in your test says I can't sacrifice *myself*.' Panting, I edged closer to the Bones' lip. Key's eyes widened, as my legs swung down. I smiled at him reassuringly. 'I'm done with others martyring themselves because of me. You want to know what I learnt from my mother? A queen shouldn't hide away, letting others get ganked for her. She should lead, even if that means being locked underneath the floor in some psycho's wet dream.'

Silence — so tense it smarted.

Lucifer assessed me. 'How can I have a carnival without its queen?'

Lucifer's fairy lights roared to pumpkin size, buzzing furiously. They shot towards me, catching me up in their midge haze.

I wailed, seared and suspended between them, hauled like a naughty kid due a spanking before her dad. Except, no dad had ever worn a cape of infinite night, flaming wings, and burning horns. I trembled, squirming between their stinging hold.

Lucifer leant in, whispering hot against my ear, 'Do I have to explain every detail of statesmanship to you? This is the Land of the Wild and Free. How do you think I manage to rule? What about the Children of the Dark, who've never even seen the light? How would you stop them tearing through the human world or converting to become the Pure?'

I shook my head because I didn't know.

Lucifer had been thrown down into this twilight punishment and had created a world from nothing. He'd saved the rest of the vampires from becoming like the Pure and the humans from being slaughtered. Despite everything, how couldn't I admire that?

Yet...*the screams in the Fire Catacombs... Key with barbwire in his mouth... Ash reduced to plaything for the FF...*

And Ash's sisters — *the Bloods* — who stood next to Ash, huddled and sniffling...

When the hell had they been brought here?

I glanced back at Lucifer, and his grin flipped my guts in a way that told me everything I didn't want to know. 'I need my queen by my side, not trapped beneath my feet.'

Why did I squirm with desperate pride at his words, even as I shook at what they'd mean? Because I couldn't offer him the unconditional loyalty he wanted. I wouldn't obey a dictator.

I yelped, as the lights dropped me, catching myself in a crouch. 'No kid is taking my place in that torture chamber.'

Yet when I turned, Ash was shuffling forward, his arms around his sisters' shoulders. Lucifer didn't look away from the bloke who'd once saved him from my mother; I realised that this was as much about Ash as it was about me.

'You told me that I was the only one who hadn't sacrificed,' Ash said, not lowering his gaze from Lucifer's. 'You lost Jade. Rebel lost Haman. So, now I lose my sisters.'

Lucifer's smile was too close to a bloke trying to look sombre when he wanted to dance the victory jig. How much of all this...the tests...had been about destroying Ash? And doing it in front of me?

When Ash loosened his hold on his sisters, they whimpered.

'Enough.' My wings arced behind me in violet flares. 'I won't make this choice. I've already made it wrong — twice — before. I've jumped through your blood and bone hoops but I won't sacrifice children just to prove you can trust me.' I faltered, and my voice was smaller than I'd intended, 'You said you loved me.'

'I *do*.' Lucifer gripped my shoulders. When his lip trembled, he looked young again and as lost as I felt. *Were those fire tears real?* 'But I warned you that I'd put my people first. All I wanted...' His distress drove the breath from me. 'I didn't ask for your love, only your loyalty. But you kill humans. Don't kill my enemy. And now? Refuse to obey me.'

Suddenly, Lucifer grew, until he towered above me. Light, the same as the living whirlwind that'd reduced the angels to ash swirled around him, as his wings beat, gusting against my cheeks. His eyes burnt in mesmerising stars. He was a creature of fire and death.

I cowered before him. I'd flown too close to the sun, and now my wings would be melted.

22

Lucifer's light spun twister-like around his giant shoulders: cold and cruel.

I choked on the bonfire ash that hovered in the musty air of the Bones, as I stared up at ballooned Big Bad that my dad had become. When the metal floor *clinked* and *rattled* from the passing of a train above, and the walls pulsed, I jumped, gritting my teeth.

Lucifer peered down at me. 'I am your king,' he bellowed. I shrank back, even as my palm itched for Flight. 'The Bloods will be your sacrifice.'

'*Fam, fam, fam,*' the Bloods whispered, as if it was a spell that could save them, in tiny voices raspy from disuse but formed enough that they must secretly talk when they were alone. They scampered to my side, hiding under the shelter of my wings. '*Protector.*'

I didn't understand Ash's gasp or the way he fell to his knees in front of Lucifer.

Why was he kneeling for Lucifer, instead of me?

'Forgive me.' *Why was Ash weeping?* 'Please... When will I have...? What will be enough? I bet... A bargain. *Anything.*'

'Na-ah, you have nothing left to bargain with that I can't simply *take*. You're worthless, Seducer.' Ash flinched through his tremors. 'And soon, you'll also be alone.'

'Don't...please...'

'Pop quiz. Who taught the little ones to speak?'

I stiffened, flushing.

Mischief's glance at me was equal parts sad and disappointed. When Ash turned to look at me, however, betrayal crawled in his stare.

I crushed the Bloods closer to my chest. 'No one told me your psycho rules.'

'Yet you still broke them. Bloods are silenced until they prove themselves more than pictures of our story. Come here, little ones, to your king.' The Bloods stared up at me with wide eyes. Yet Lucifer's power seared, illuminating the Bones: a twisting light that coiled around him, as we knelt in his shadow.

If I fought Lucifer, we'd all be reduced to ash, and I wouldn't have saved the Under World as I'd promised.

Hell, why was it so hard to be a leader? To *sacrifice*...? But Ash had done it. *Was* doing it now with his own sisters.

Could I with Jade?

I forced myself to push the Bloods away from the shelter of my arms towards Lucifer.

Lucifer encircled the Bloods with his cape, like they'd been slicked in oil. 'Rejoice.' His smile was sickly sweet, but his words sounded rote, just like Wild's had in the Fire Catacombs. 'Today you'll walk in Lucifer's Light.'

My stomach lurched, and I swayed; Rebel caught me. Ash keened, bowing down and covering his head with his wings.

I'd been arrogant, too steeped in humanity to understand the ways of the Under World. By teaching the Bloods to call me *fam* and look to me for protection, I'd condemned them to die.

I'd sacrificed them, after all.

'P-please,' I stammered. 'I'll obey you.'

'You'll watch,' Lucifer stroked over the Bloods' tattooed heads. 'And you'll never forget. Then we'll see if you'll obey. Even if...you can't love.'

Fire tears fell onto the inked heads of the Bloods. Just as tears streaked down my cheeks and Ash's. Trapped together in our hurt, to pass the test two little girls would die sacrificial in the flames.

Lucifer's Light — the flickers inside the archway on the garbage island — cast a stench, like leather being tanned over flames, which stuck in my throat.

I gagged on the scent of death.

Alone with Ash, I couldn't meet his gaze. He stared out over the river at the dragon breaths across the Fire Catacomb's ponds.

Except, we weren't alone.

Lucifer's fairy spies wove between us. I shoved my hands into the pockets of my trousers to stop myself swatting them. Because with them watching — Lucifer's eyes — I couldn't talk to Ash about our rebellion or why we were standing here, waiting for his sisters to be delivered to their fiery deaths.

Tell me there's a way to save these kids, J, don't make me do this.

No one's making you do anything, Violet-heart.

This is your choice.

How? It's the king's order and Ash's sacrifice.

Are you a leader or a pussy?

One day, every carnival has to stop. Anarchy has a price, but so does freedom.

Light the revolution. Then stand back and watch the fireworks.

But what will I have to watch first?

'Tell me to stick it,' I glanced sideways at Ash. 'All of it.'

The lights hummed, hovering closer.

Ash didn't look round at me, but I knew he understood the unspoken: my sacrifice to Lucifer, our escape, the rebellion...anything to stop his sisters' execution.

He hugged his arms across his bare chest. 'You don't mean it.'

Hell, that hurt.

I caught his arm, swinging him round, as if I had the right to touch him — force him to look at me — after I'd condemned his sisters to die by teaching them to call out to me.

Just like *I'd* called out to the angels.

My boots caught in the rubbish; rotting cartons skittered down the sides.

'I bastard do,' I trembled, desperate for him to believe in me. *Trust me*, like he always had. 'I'll take on the whole Under World to save your sisters.'

His gaze was hollow, as if he'd been burnt out from the inside. 'So, it goes rescue them, escape...then what? Go where? Lucifer is the only one who lights the way out of the Under World, and his routes are guarded. My sisters would die just the same, and we'd have condemned ten more kids.'

'You can't simply accept this.'

Ash tore himself from my grasp. 'Accept my sisters being put to death because you developed a god complex?' He shook with cold despair. 'You want to come over with a Spielberg moment? I fought the angels for centuries. And when that bastard...' The lights whined, nipping at Ash, whilst he bared his fangs. '...reduced me to Seducer, I fought it too. But look,' he raised his arms, 'still a Fallen whore. *What has fighting ever got me*?'

'Me,' I murmured, cupping his cheek. At last, he met my gaze, and something flickered: more life than the emptiness that'd made my heart clench before. 'I'm a newbie to bastard hope. I never had it before, but certain angels and vampires showed me that I could have fam and they could have my back. There's nothing Spielberg about our type of hope: it's dark, dirty, and tainted. But we can still fly on it.'

I remembered the boy Blood's terror as he'd wailed, stumbling towards the archway.

My choices were terrible, but maybe I could offer *hope*, saving Ash's sisters in the only way I could.

Wild's bat-like shadow soared through the gloom.

Ash and I stiffened, on instinct drawing closer to each other.

'Where's the Light-bringer himself?' I whispered.

Ash clasped my hand so tightly I winced, but I didn't draw back. I understood and I was glad that at least he wasn't alone for this, like he had been last time. Or that *I* wasn't because what I was about to do would slash me to ribbons.

'He doesn't need to be here,' Ash growled,

'because he's already got what he wanted.'

How long had Lucifer been planning this?

Wild landed, pulling one Blood off his shoulders like a backpack, and the other off his waist. They clung to him, however, in spider monkey mode, trembling.

They knew what lay behind that archway.

Taking a deep breath, I forced a smile on my face, even though it felt as fake as a clown's. I sauntered to Wild, who scrutinised me like I'd gone mental under the strain.

'Come on, wench, it's no use making a fuss.' Wild inched his hand towards the leather strap at his waist, as if all I needed was a belting to keep me in line. 'Go and play up your end, whilst I deal with the king's orders.'

'Back off, fascist-lite,' I snarled.

To my surprise, Wild raised his hands and stepped back. 'Throw a wobbly if you like. This will still end the same way.'

I curled the edges of my mouth back into a smile, before ducking down in front of the Bloods. They quivered, clutching my shoulders.

'First,' *don't cry,* I mentally slapped myself, as I announced brightly, 'I'm proud you called me *fam*.' Ash gasped behind him, and I willed him not to storm closer. 'I'll always be your Protector, and you're special because you spoke to me. You know what that means?' They shook their heads, but they'd stopped trembling and were studying me. 'I'm inked on you, yeah? Part of you? So, when you walk into Lucifer's Light...afterwards...when you wake up...you'll be in the *true* light.' Hell, their eyes were shining with awe and excitement now...and desperate hope. I swallowed, holding them tighter. 'It'll be legendary. You'll be the bitches in charge because you're the Protector's fam: full Fallen, not

Bloods. You'll be flying on epic wings and...' I wet my lips. '*You'll be free.*'

I gently disentangled Ash's sisters from around my neck, and they held hands.

They smiled, and my smile this time was real, although my eyes gleamed with tears.

Ones I didn't let fall.

I stood, as the Bloods strolled hand in hand towards the fire through the archway. Like it led to paradise, not hell.

'Rejoice, your king has ordered your sacrifice. Today, you walk into Lucifer's Light. Thank him in your bones and blood for the honour,' Wild intoned.

Ash dragged his sisters into a final hug. For a moment, I didn't think he'd let them go. It was *them*, however, pulling away from him and slipping into the crevice beyond the archway, whilst the fires dimmed.

Clank — the steel door crashed down.

I jumped, backing away.

Hell, this couldn't happen.

'*Fight, chaos, war,*' Devil raged, burning in my pocket.

My fingers inched towards him...

Then Ash caught me by the elbow, yanking me to the viewing panel. 'Watch,' he hissed. 'You don't get to not watch. Neither do I.'

The Bloods raised their tiny fingers to their side of the panel. Ash and I raised our fingers to touch the ghost of theirs; Ash's hand brushed mine.

Tears matted my eyelashes, as I struggled to match the soft smiles of the Bloods. 'I'm sorry—'

'Don't you dare cry,' Ash's voice was broken; thick with swallowed tears. 'Not until...' his voice hitched, '...only after...'

Fierce light blasted through the furnace: it

burnt the back of my retinas, spectred it with dancing ghosts. But I didn't look away or shield my eyes.

Because I deserved to see. To witness. And never forget.

Whilst Ash's sisters were burnt alive, their hands still reached out to ours, and they never screamed.

Because they'd believed they'd been freed.

Afterwards, I collapsed against the door, finally allowing the hot tears to scold my cheeks. 'I lied,' I howled. 'I'm just like my dad. I sent them walking into the fire on my lies.'

To hell with the firefly spies spitting in their fury. My dad was a dictator and if he wanted to buy my loyalty through sacrifice? He'd discover that he'd just bought my undying loyalty to the freedom fighters.

Ash sagged next to me; the tears on his cheeks mingled with mine. 'You gave them hope: dark, dirty, and tainted. But for the first time in their lives they *flew*. And let me...' He choked on a sob. '...Imagine a bit longer that they're still flying.'

Ash closed his eyes, still pressed against the door, as his sisters' ash settled.

I seethed, flushing hot and cold through my grief. Violet and black raged with a single screamed thought: *depose the king*.

Yet I shrank from its danger because just as insidious underneath rippled the whispered: *then take up the crown yourself as Queen of Chaos*.

Lucifer had freed a monster, and I shuddered because it also flew on hope.

The pulsing scarlet block hung between us in Mischief's bunker.

Grrrrrr.

The slab snarled, bucking bad-temperedly. Mischief bopped the stone thorn that stuck out of its middle, as if it was the block's nose.

Harrumph.

The Gateway — magical books that Harahel had used to train me, whilst I'd been in Angel World — rippled like it was shrugging its shoulders. It quietened.

'I will not be witness to another such travesty, kneeling as nothing more than the king's puppy.' Mischief pursed his lips.

'With you, bro. But why are we here together, whispering in corners? I need to be with... Ash shouldn't be alone.'

'How droll you believe only *you* cast a shadow in the world. He's not alone: he's with an angel who knows far more of comfort and loss than you.' When I flinched, Mischief grazed the back of his hand against mine. 'Allow others their talents and the Brigadier the respect to fall apart without you as audience.'

I swallowed. 'Rage: it's holding him together.'

Mischief's laugh was low. 'Isn't that true for us all, beast?'

My palms sparked at Mischief's *beast* disrespect.

'I'm trying...'

Mischief's smile was all teeth: he could feel the static crackling between our joined hands. 'Don't get me wrong, I love mayhem and *mischief* but...' The look he levelled at me was shrewd. 'The king whirls with orgiastic chaos in a crazy carnival where you play or burn. Instead, I spy. Misrule plots. And...what do you do again...?'

I dragged my hand out of Mischief's, shoving him back.

The Gateway rumbled, jumping up and down between us.

'I save your ungrateful arse.' I gripped Devil in my pocket; his power thrummed through me, dark and enticing. 'I stand beside my dad, the *puppet* you need to convince the Under World to rise up. Weren't three tests enough? Isn't stabbing my own dad in the back rating high enough on the Trust-O-Metre?'

Mischief grasped my arm, swinging me around the block and close to his side, before murmuring, 'Yet you don't even know why the Queen of Chaos has been summoned. What do you believe your true role to be?'

His breath against my skin tingled; I shivered.

'That's why you brought out the freaky book? I thought these were only in Angel World?' I peeked up at his intent gaze.

Mischief gave me a cool look, before turning me to face the Gateway. 'Harahel would spank me, even in my sweetest unicorn disguise, if he discovered I stole his books. Yet my secret library, which my magic unlocks, is why I'm never alone. I assure you, however, I can share.'

Mischief grabbed my hand, ramming it onto the stone thorn in the centre of the slab.

My blood dripped onto the stone, melding with the Gateway, whilst it roared.

I wailed, writhing, but I was already caught in the pull *into* the block.

Electric currents juddered through me.

Torn into a million itty pieces — and hell was it screwed sideways that the sensation of being ripped up like tissue paper was becoming familiar — I screamed.

Then the Gateway devoured me.

23

I soared over a metallic rainbow into Mischief's secret Gateway.

Globules showered me in silver rain, even whilst they jolted me electric. Star particles zinged grainy on my tongue. I lurched, battling to control my fall into the void.

Down below was the supernatural world's database: an interactive book. And I was the hacker.

What am I searching for, J?

Trapped in this freaky book, I only get one chance. I was almost dinosaur whomped the last time I wasn't careful.

So, what do I ask?

It seems to me, Feather-princess, there's only one thing. And we both know you've been asking it every day since you were brought to the Under World.

I somersaulted lower into the abyss. 'Why does my dad want me?' I howled. 'What's the Bone Princess?'

Silence.

A gust, like ghostly fingers, brushed against my foot. I jerked away.

Then a twister burst up beneath me, twirling me round in a stinging cloud of dust.

I squealed, but my arms were pinned to my side by the whirling air, which dragged me *down...down...and...*dashed me onto the valley of bones from my visions. In front of me rose the mountain of feathers, except now they were grey as well as violet.

The wind died.

I struggled to my knees. My mouth tasted of ash. The bones pulsed violet in time with the pounding of my head. Then my jeans' pocket burst into flames and my skin seared. I flailed at it with my palms, but the Devil's Trident burst out, growing larger in front of my startled gaze. White flames flared along its shaft and prongs.

'*Judgement,*' Devil rumbled. As his light blazed brighter, so the light in the world dimmed, blotted out. '*Reckoning.*' I shrank back into the darkness; the trident remained the single flaming point. '*Destroyer.*'

Death. The End. Destroyer.

Was that my answer? I wasn't simply a weapon, instead I'd...

I shook my head because if I didn't think it, then maybe it wouldn't come true.

Please, don't let it any of it be true.

My dad wanted me because I...

A *roar*.

Lucifer burst from the feathers in the same terrifying glory that he'd disguised himself with in the Bones. He beat his wings, and I was caught in his burning scent. His cape billowed behind him, and light danced around his skin, even as it'd been sucked from the rest of the world.

A world that suddenly shifted with life.

I smelled it: *humanity*.

I recoiled at the sight of the bowed backs prostrating themselves throughout the valley before Lucifer and the Devil's Trident.

Humans worshipping us as gods.

I'd cast them into darkness, and Lucifer had brought the light.

I couldn't hold the thought back any longer. My dad had fought to reclaim me to stand next to him, whilst he ruled the humans, as well as the vampires.

And I'd kick off the *Apocalypse*.

I'd expected the first time I'd smelled my dad's sizzling flesh to be at the tip of Flight's blade.

Even for me, that was hardcore badass.

Not whilst he thrust his hand into his own ball of light and shook, his skin peeling and blistering.

I'd been summoned by Lucifer to what Wild had called the Bat Cave, without even an ironic lift of his eyebrow.

When I'd swaggered into the disused service station, which was bare like the twisted insides of a metal caterpillar, I'd realised they weren't kidding.

Bats.

The furry brown bodies had exploded from their

roosts amongst the crystals that grew from the ceiling...straight at me.

A *scolding chattering*.

Leathery wings had beat against my cheeks, and I'd squealed, backing against the wall, as they'd shrouded me in their alien burbling...and darkness.
I hadn't been able to breathe.
What a way for a bitch to go: smothered to death by horse-shoe faced freaks.
A gasp, and I'd clutched my hand to my side.
Some bastard had harpooned me through the gut.
I'd twisted, but the bone harpoon had only burrowed deeper, until its feather line had winched backwards, dragging me out of the cloud of bats. And I'd come nose to nose with Lucifer.

Crackle.

Lucifer's fingers twisted as they charred.
I winced. 'I get it, you're a psycho who doesn't feel pain. But this bitch does, so let me go.'
To his official scare the subjects getup, Lucifer had added an obsidian belt, complete with bone buckle harpoon that'd pulled me in, trapping me at his side.
Pain lanced, throbbing from where it connected us, in sympathy with Lucifer's burning hand.
Sweat trembled on Lucifer's lower lip; he swiped it off with his tongue. 'Your mother loved just how much I *felt* pain. How I screamed for her.' He quivered. 'By the shadows, pain's not a weakness: it's joy. I *claim* it.' His charred hand forced itself into a shaking fist. *Hell, the Matriarch had done a number on the bloke*. 'Don't you

welcome the pain to forge yourself for your own coronation? The tests...the sacrifices...the Bones... The Fallen *need* pain. A thanks is customary, you know.'

Yet he was shaking, his gaze lost somewhere back in Angel World kneeling for the Matriarch.

I reached out, pulling Lucifer's hand from his own light. He whimpered, and I stroked his wing, even as the fire scorched my palm.

Lucifer's distress ached through me because I'd witnessed the abuse of the Wings in Angel World.

Lucifer purred, closing his eyes.

I hated the bastard, didn't I? Here he was, however, clutching his burnt hand to his chest and purring.

Find a bloke's weakness and shank him sharp.

Yet my heart had never clenched so hard, and the words had never stuck in my throat so badly because my dad wasn't simply the enemy: he thought himself the saviour who'd rescued the vampires from the Matriarch and made them powerful through pain. 'Somebody didn't get enough hugs as a kid.' I kept stroking, but Lucifer stopped purring and flinched. 'Pain is all you can hope for? That's dark. You've taken Ash apart piece by piece because that's how you were punished for disobedience, yeah? A rebel doesn't copy the top boy who bullied them, but you've been hurt for so long, you've created a whole world of it.'

'Wow, heartrending moment. Can't a guy harpoon his family to keep them close? Safe?' Lucifer smirked, but tears trembled on his eyelashes.

'Shove it. I'm not Moby Dick, so set me free.'

Lucifer stared down at where we were joined. Then he *tsked*. 'Why wouldn't my favourite...OK, you got me, *only*...daughter not want to be joined on the day she's crowned?' Suddenly his eyes lit up. 'I have so much to show you.'

'Your tiara collection, Mr Mood Swing?'

'Oh, and you don't think I have one? But that'll have to wait for later.' He lifted his undamaged hand to his mouth and let out a shrill whistle.

I shrieked, as an Aladdin's carpet of bats scooped us up on their wings.

I fell on my back, shuddering at the rippling living rug beneath us, which lifted us higher into the tunnel.

Lucifer fell on top of me, vanishing the flames in his armour. At least he didn't mean to incinerate me.

He grinned down. 'Meet Demon.' *And how much didn't I want to know the harpoon in my gut's name?*' 'Devil's wilder brother. He also has the power of prophecy.' He nudged me, like we were kids at a party, not would be conquerors. 'Aw, cheer up, I'm going to share with the class.' I panted, as Demon yanked out of me. Before I could press my own hand over the wound, Lucifer had pressed his; the unexpected intimacy of his small fingers was enough to prick my eyes with tears. He cocked his head. 'Daddy make it all better.'

Light threaded worm-like between his finger-tips and my wound, knitting the skin.

Its warmth arched through me. I juddered, flying on the light.

Spark.

It was addictive.

At last, Lucifer edged back, flopping onto his stomach. 'Now for the show.'

I hollered, as the bats swung us round.

The harpoon on its string of feathers burst out into the cavern's wall, and scenes I'd witnessed in the Gateway...the blotting out of the sun by the trident...Lucifer above the valley of bones...and the humans worshipping him, played movie-like.

This time, however, I acted my part too right next to Lucifer atop the mountain of feathers.

If I hadn't been ending the world, I'd have looked hot.

I put on my shocked mask, whilst Lucifer wrapped his arms around my shoulders. '*My* Queen of Chaos. Can't you taste it? Feeding off the savage dark? Calling to death?'

I shrugged him off, pushing myself onto my knees and balancing myself with a flap of my wings. 'You're hitting all the genocidal dictator notes: turning your enemies into ash with your light and destroying the world with your tamed monster.'

Lucifer blinked. 'Duh, you're not the brightest little spark are you? What I'm seeking is simply to have the right not to hide in the shadows. *You're* the dark that steals the humans' light. Then we all dance together.'

'You're still giving off a Thanos vibe, bitch.'

Lucifer lazily flipped onto his back with a grin. 'You mean, he gives off *my* vibe?'

Violet and black spiralled through me, as I roared, rising up from the bat sea. They *burbled*, flitting across the cave and tumbling Lucifer onto the rock below.

'Kick each other's arses over who's better at destroying the universe...or has the bigger prick...later. You're still all about the Apocalypse,' I snarled, beating my wings.

Lucifer scowled at me as he hauled himself up. His helmet and wings exploded into flame. 'Technically,' he spread his hands, 'it's *an* apocalypse. And...wait, whilst I hold together my shredded heart...did you think I meant to use my light *on* your beloved humans? How...obvious. You must believe me such a naughty boy.' He marched to the end of the tunnel, before twirling round; the bats flitted around him like a winged audience. 'I intend to create a new world. End of the world, pah! This is the beginning. Rebirth. And we're the saviours.'

I jolted.

How could Lucifer know those words? The ones that'd stalked me in my poisoned and power fuelled visions?

'What the hell did you just say?'

'Us, together, a team. First will come the darkness because that's how it goes. Then the light: mine. And I'll only shine it on the worthy, who'll become our Blood Lovers.'

A world of Jades, transformed — *bred* — to belong to the vampires. Where light had become a privilege to be earned.

Just like freedom.

Rage prickled underneath my skin. 'And ding, ding, let me guess who's choosing?'

Lucifer swept a bow, but his expression was lost again, fragile. 'We won't be the cast out anymore. The *shamed* Fallen. We'll be gods.'

'Sorry to burst your ego bubble, bro, but gods don't exist.'

Lucifer's bark of laughter was bitter. 'Aw, missy, you have no idea what truly exists. We're just one part of the story.'

I shivered. There were *more* supernaturals in this world?

I landed close to Lucifer. His fire imps hovered around him, buzzing angrily at the bats and zapping them if they flew too close.

'When you rule over the humans, no one will ever *dare* notice your differences again. You'll have the power to make them fear or love you,' Lucifer murmured.

I arched my brow. 'And in the Over-identify Corner...'

I didn't care that Lucifer paled. *I bastard didn't.*

'I should've known you'd be a brat and just when I've worked so hard on your party.' Lucifer waved his blackened hand; he hadn't healed himself, as he had me. Did he need the pain, or could he only heal others? The fiery lights rose in the air, poised between us. 'Tonight, you'll become the Queen of Chaos, and I'll announce you're bringing down the sun.'

I nodded, shakily.

'Three tests to prove your loyalty...? I have to say, it's not inspiring. You'll forgive me for, well...' Lucifer brought down his hand, and the fire imps attacked.

I stumbled backwards, sweeping at them with my wings, but they banded around my throat. I choked; my pulse pounded.

He meant to burn off my head.

The lights cooled, however, settling around my seared neck into a throbbing — *spying* — collar.

Lucifer avoided my eye. 'Only until after the Under World sees my daughter at my side. Until then, be a good girl because those darlings can get hot at a thought.'

How could we plan the uprising now?

I was Lucifer's eyes. Even if I could save my fam, the rest of Under World, and the humans, my neck would still be flamed by Lucifer's collar: there was no escape.

24

Magic: it sparked through the kiss, teasing, pain-laced, and welcoming like it knew me down to the bones.

My eyes fluttered closed, as I was held spellbound; my tongue thrust, whilst flames crackled — violet meeting silver — where our lips met.

For once, I didn't fear scorching my lover; Mischief's power danced with my own. I'd known Mischief was a spell caster, but not that he'd taste like this, awakening the forces inside.

I wrapped my arms tighter around him in the shadows of the empty Cage, whilst it swung: no baying crowd, calls for bets, or Bone Carnival. Just us, together on the eve of an apocalypse, losing ourselves in love.

I shuddered, stroking between Mischief's wings. I craved to *consume* him.

Pop — my ears burst like the pressure had dropped.

And I was bastard me again.

I clenched my jaw, forcing my lips to mouth up and down against Mischief's in the charade of snogging, even if I nibbled too hard.

Mischief let out a muffled yelp.

'*One, two, three...*' Mischief's counting slithered telepathically into my mind.

I stiffened, as his fingers slid around my neck, stroking over my fairy light collar: the one that could burn off my head.

Snap.

The magic ricocheted between us, before settling with an electric hum.

I disentangled myself from Mischief, stepping away from him. Weapons — crossbows, swords, and shanks — from the last fight *clinked* and *skittered* across the swaying floor.

Mischief watched me, warily.

My boots *clanked* across the metal, the stink of oil and tar assaulted my nostrils, and adrenaline flooded me from being caged again. The Under World was busy preparing for my legendary coronation. This was the one place, and I didn't miss the irony, that we'd have privacy.

Mischief scuffed his foot through a puddle of blood, avoiding my gaze.

Champion of almost ninety fights...this bitch could face the Awkward Moment After the Kiss.

Even if it *had* all been pretend.

'I'm not going to fry then?' I waggled my fingers at my still glowing throat.

Mischief arched his eyebrow. 'The king will only witness, until the coronation, our wild passion. Do you think he'll spank me for it or ask to join in next time?'

My eyes narrowed. 'How wild?'

Mischief coyly twirled a strand of hair between his fingers. 'Simply the highlights of my desires spun out for his viewing pleasure. Why? How wild would *you* wish them?'

'Wild enough to save my head.'

'They're nothing but a glamour. Yet as I lose my violet feathers, so I lose my magic.' He clutched his arms across his middle, flushing. His sudden shame reminded me of Rebel's when he was Falling. Why did that call to me so deeply? 'The Mage always taught in the Legion that they were *mental powers*, but it's always spun within me...*alive*...and I call it magic. But without the light, it's dying. Only the Light-bringer has ever held onto his magic.' Mischief ducked his head; his hair covered his face. 'He is so very much more powerful than me.'

'He's also a narcissistic paranoid control freak.' When Mischief sniggered, it tugged my own lips into a smile. 'So, this ultimate shock collar around my neck: am I screwed?'

'Not if we rebel tonight.' Mischief sauntered to the corner of the cage, resting against the bars. 'This seems rather a small war council. I know you're new to the whole *leader* concept, but you tend to need a gang...'

'I won't be a gang's top boy.' I marched after Mischief, pinning him against the bars. He huffed, pushing my shoulders, but I caught his wrists, trapping them between us. 'Vampires and angels have been playing turf war too long. I won't be your puppet to spark a civil war, leading you into massacre. I won't be that type of leader. I won't be...my dad.'

Mischief's lip curled. 'Then what use are you? You'll take the trident and stand *with* your dad? I should've known a taste of power and you'd—'

I shoved him back, silencing him with a kiss.

He let out a startled protest. When sparks sizzled between our mouths, however, he pushed closer, demanding more.

Our wings wrapped around each other, and he purred.

When I drew back, I studied Mischief. 'I've tasted power, and it's nothing but ash. I'll lead, but only if I can be the *Protector*. That means knowing the Bones and Bloods have somewhere to escape. I won't pull down the Under World on the kids. Not after witnessing what happened to Ash's sisters. I have to know we can win this. I won't bury us all alive.'

Mischief's brow furrowed. Then he rubbed his nose against mine. And hell, if that didn't feel more intimate than when my tongue had tangled with his. 'If I told you I knew a way out...*theoretically*...that I could light with my own magic...*theoretically*...and could show Harahel...*theoretically*...which I hid because I wanted to keep you here to help...*theoretically*...would that warrant a beating?'

I gazed at him levelly. 'Depends. Would this *theoretical* knowledge of yours include how to defeat Lucifer's magic?'

'The Legion may know...'

I backed away from him.

The same bastards as the Mage? Drake? The cult who tried to kill me, sliced off slaves' wings, and promised genocide on the vampires?

'The Discipliners?' I spat.

Mischief didn't hide his hurt expression fast enough. 'Do you need soap to wash the filth from your mouth?' He snorted. 'I was the one being disciplined; it's my brother who leads such an exclusive club. Why...?'

'If we want to survive tonight, it'll take more than rebelling from within. We also need bastards from outside. So, the Legion...?'

I closed my eyes, reaching into my mind for my connection with Drake.

I knew Mischief couldn't teleport through Lucifer's magics, but the link through minds was different: it couldn't be controlled by Lucifer.

I latched onto Drake's trembling strand of violet, yanking it towards me.

When has calling out to the angels ever done anything but bite you in the booty?

To fight the devil, sometimes you have to make a deal with the devil's enemy. Even if that enemy...is the true devil.

If you ask me, that's a whole lot of devils you're shaking your thing at.

If you ask a favour of the Legion, they'll want something in return. Don't you remember what they wanted last time?

You.

I hauled out the quivering thread, which writhed in my hold, before tumbling Drake to my feet.

Rushing on the thrill, I grinned.

Commander Drake groaned. Then he stared around in panic and confusion, tugging up his silk harem trousers that'd slipped down his hips, baring his creamy thighs.

Mischief was breathing raggedly, but he still gave Drake a droll wave.

Bastard mistake.

Drake roared, slamming Mischief against the Cage's floor.

'Why,' Mischief batted his eyelashes, 'I hadn't realised you'd missed me.'

'Be silent, traitor,' Drake's voice was low. He wound his fingers around Mischief's throat as he met my gaze. Had this already *bitten me in the booty*? Was I wrong to trust Drake because he was an angel? 'Why do you bring me here? You save me once, only to entrap me now?'

'Get over yourself, Genie Boy,' I growled. Drake blushed. 'We're after saving the world. My dad wants to take out the sun, and I want to save the poor bastards who need my help, like we did in Angel World. But I'm searching for someone with enough magic to take on Lucifer and free the Under World. Are you applying?'

'Your...*dad*?' Drake's eyes widened.

I'd forgotten the fact my dad was Lucifer was a secret in Angel World.

'I thought you'd already Sherlock deduced who my dad was?'

Drake gave a tight nod. 'Congratulations to me then. I assumed it with good reason.' His fingers tightened around Mischief's neck. I gasped at Mischief's *choke*. 'I apologise, princess, allow me to explain: the only angel who can contain the Lightbringer is the Matriarch. You see, he was once not simply her Wing but Marked.'

My stomach lurched. The Matriarch had Marked my dad as bed slave like she had Drake...? *As she'd tempted me to Mark Rebel?*

Had she played the same sadistic games, as I'd played by her side on Drake?

Drake's expression shuttered with lofty dignity. 'I suffer because she practised her sessions on

Lucifer. *All* Wings are brutally subjugated, since her tamed Wing fought back, burning away the Mark and leading the rebellion that broke our world.' He cocked his head; his curls fell over his eyes. 'It's extraordinary that you'd ask my help to break *another* world.' I clenched my fists. *Why had I hoped he'd trust me?* 'What's freedom worth, if it leads to slavery? You're better than that, princess.'

I lunged at Drake, dragging him off Mischief by the scruff of the neck. Frankincense wound round me, rich and familiar.

Hell, I'd missed every cold predatory inch of him.

I also missed the sword he'd snatched from the floor of the Cage, until its tip kissed at my kidneys.

'Barakiel...?' Drake whispered, urgent with hope. 'He's alive?'

Barakiel: The Lightning Angel that Drake had demanded we save when we escaped Angel World. Why was he so important?

Violet screamed in jealous rage that Drake would think of another angel before me. Yet I quietened the dominant Glory inside because Drake wasn't mine. He belonged to my mother.

What right did I have to claim anyone as belonging to me, as the Matriarch had with Lucifer?

'He's safe with the Blood Angels,' I murmured. 'Not here, bro.'

Drake nodded, sagging. 'Thank you, princess.' He smiled, grimly. 'I understand that Glories may *say* they love. But they can't because it's poisoned.' He trembled, even as he pressed harder. 'I am still your lamb, am I not?'

I hissed at the worming pain of the steel slicing my back. 'I'm not the same. I won't sacrifice you.'

'Lie.'

'Then *you* choose.' Drake's questing gaze met

mine; I lifted my eyebrow. 'This isn't Angel World, and I'm not wearing the Dictator Hat. Who apart from the Matriarch can take down Devil Daddy?'

Drake's brow furrowed. 'You'd hand me the power?'

Mischief raised his hand like the naughty school kid at the back of the class. 'Sorry, did I miss the vote where we all lost our minds?'

'Hush, now, Zophia, or I shall make you lose far more than your mind.' *Zophia?* Note to self to take the piss out of Fae Angel about his girlie angel name. Drake gave a curt nod. 'My father, Mage Drake. He shall exact a price, but if it means your escape from the Under World...?' He shuddered. 'I'll ask him, and whatever he demands, I'll give.' His smile was sad, although his gaze had softened. 'See? I make an honourable sacrifice.'

Clatter — the sword hit the floor.

Drake had vanished back to Angel World to ask the most powerful Mage, my enemy, to join our rebellion and stop Lucifer taking the light.

Tonight, I became Queen of Chaos, and I either saved the world, or by my trident, it was ended.

25

When Sleeping Beauty woke up, she didn't marry Prince Charming and live Happily Ever After. Instead, the kiss awoke the monster inside.

Next, came bloody vengeance and the pulling down of the world.

That's your bedtime fairy tale, Bone Princess style.

I strutted into the giant chamber where we'd battled with the angels — the charred walls still stank of ash — on the night of my coronation.

My eyes widened.

When Lucifer had promised a party, he hadn't

meant he'd hired clowns.

Vampires soared, sprawled, and even rocked out: bare arsed. Except for their tattoos, piercings, and body paint: they'd graffitied the words of their rebellion across themselves.

FREEDOM. SEX. MAYHEM.

Cages swung from chains as entertainment; captive angels and Shadows were crammed into them as if they were strippers but instead of dancing they were forced to fight, as the bars heated.

Vampires called out bets, amongst the laughter and jeers at the angels' wails.

Misrule, with Harahel tucked under his arm, twirled his cane — true Master of the celebration — spinning the madness into a tightrope that he walked.

When I swaggered in, with an angel on one arm, a Shadow on the other, and a naked Seducer leading the way like *he* was the queen...

Awkward.

I smirked. 'When in Rome...join the orgy.'

Rebel clasped his arms around me, whilst Mischief rested his head on my shoulder.

Ash sighed, although his lips quirked. 'One cuddle. No touching. Keep it above the waist.'

Mischief sniggered.

Ash's large wings encircled us all, then he swayed us to the alienated goth-punk angst of My Chemical Romance's "Vampires Will Never Hurt You".

'What muppet chose the music?' Rebel muttered.

Mischief grinned. 'This is Lucifer's playlist. He's a killer but one with an astounding sense of irony.'

I pulled at the twisting bone that ran like Egyptian bracelets from my shoulders to my wrists. 'Don't forget the flare for the dramatic.'

The deadly lights around my neck glowed like a Pharaoh's collar necklace: here came Nefertiti resurrected. And this time, she didn't worship the sun, she ruled it.

Rebel had pulled on each piece of my coronation outfit in the quiet of my carriage room, as if he'd been my squire arming me for war: twisting strips of bone in my Mistress bodice and black leather panels floating out into a satin skirt in a Dark Queen's ball dress.

When he'd drawn on the bone bracelets, he'd kissed the sensitive skin beneath: inner wrist, elbow, and shoulder.

I'd drawn in my breath, as I'd tingled down to the tips of my feathers.

'Sweet Jesus, you're after being *my* queen,' Rebel had whispered. 'You always were. The whole shebang could go up in flames tonight, and I'd walk into them for you.'

I'd caught his lips between mine, shaking at even the thought of him trapped in Lucifer's Light.

The screams...

My dad had told me I manipulated others with the same *spark* as him.

Has anything been real? Does Rebel love me? Or has my power whammied him?

You've no broomstick, Feathery-poppet, and no love potion either. It's all genuine Irish loving.

Like the bond, Mark, Blood Lover?

That's a different type of power. You're the bitch who chose to force control. Whether you use it over him...? That depends if you decide to work your

extravaganza as a Puppet Mistress over *all* **your fam.**

What the hell have I done? Are any of my fam free?

I'd gasped, clinging to Rebel's arms.

'Princess...?' He'd swung me round to Ash.

Ash had stripped on Lucifer's order, whilst I'd dressed, only buckling his holster back around his waist. I'd bitten my lip not to tell him how hot the *naked with only his shooter* stripper look had been.

Sprawled over my foam bed, Mischief had crouched over Ash, whilst he'd worked on piercing Ash's nipples with bone shards. Silver had shot from Mischief's fingertips like a needle, and Ash had hissed.

'Concentrating...' Mischief had pierced Ash's second nipple; Ash had whimpered. I'd been surprised at Mischief's tender stroke of his cheek. 'I've been a monumental brat, but the king's never ordered bone shoved through my delicate bits.'

Ash had smiled crookedly. 'Now I feel all special inside.'

Rebel had waved his hand in the air. 'Excuse me, gits, banjaxed princess here.'

'Are you...?' I'd looked down. 'Is all of this...your sacrifices, fam, love...because you're under *my* light?'

Three pairs of eyes had blinked at me.

Then Ash had burst out laughing.

Yeah, not the way I'd expected it to go.

Ash had pushed himself up from the foam, flinching at the pull on his red nubs. 'You're a Queen of Chaos but a newbie when it comes to blokes.' I'd flushed. 'Read me.'

He'd spread out his arms in all his naked glory, spinning slowly as if it'd been a striptease.

I'd arched a brow but studied him; he'd daubed

words over himself in purple body paint: *names.*

REBEL, ANARCHY, KEY, BLAZE, SPARK, MISCHIEF, HARAHEL, MISRULE...

And over his heart?

VIOLET.

Ash had covered himself in his fam. How could that only be an illusion?

I hadn't recognised two smaller names, which had been under mine.

Ash had hurriedly crossed his arms over them, however, before I'd been able to read them. 'My sisters,' his voice had been as hard as steel. 'Lucifer's Light is cold. It's like the Devil's Trident: dark. There's no love. But you, Violet? You're the opposite, even if you can't see it yet. *That's* why we follow you.'

At an insistent tugging on the violet strands in my mind, I'd pulled back, dragging out Drake at my feet.

Or his charred body.

The singed scent of feathers had wafted through my bedroom.

I'd peered down at Drake, who'd groaned, forcing open his swollen eyes.

Why had I been so desperate for Mischief to heal Drake by taking his pain? Or at least to crouch down myself and stroke his curls?

Instead, I'd forced myself to balance on my bone tiara. 'Your chat with the Mage went well then?'

Drake had spat a globule of blood onto my boot. 'Hush,' he'd rasped like he'd been screaming ever since his return to Angel World. *Maybe he had.*

'The deal is simple. The Mage shall offer his assistance at a time you shall not miss. In return for a bargain.'

'Watch how shocked I'm not.'

The corners of Drake's mouth had twitched into a smile before he'd smothered it. 'Afterwards, you'll return with me to the Legion and train as an Apprentice in the Brotherhood of the Phoenix.'

'Not a chance,' Rebel had hunkered by Drake, pushing back his curls, just as I'd itched to. 'Those brutal bad bastards—'

'As you wish,' Drake had slumped, closing his eyes.

Wait...Drake had given up?

What had been so terrifying about the Legion that even Drake hadn't wanted me trained by them? Yet something had shivered through him — a despairing acceptance — at Rebel's refusal.

Your collared punk has it right. The Brotherhood of Assholes is no Hogwarts. Remember, the Mage is all about making you star of the genocide show *against* the vampires.

It's like when you unleash an even bigger mutant to bring down Godzilla. I can't risk letting out my monster or Devil. If the Mage is the only bastard who can stop Lucifer—

You abandoned Rebel's brother to escape the Mage's influence. Was Haman's sacrifice for nothing?

I'd flushed as I'd finally allowed myself to crouch next to Drake. 'What'll happen to you if I tell the Mage to stick his offer?'

'Nothing that concerns you.'

'You are my concern.'

Drake's smile had been soft. 'A lie. But a kind one.' He'd hesitated. 'I cannot return if you do not accompany me.'

Rebel had whirled to his feet. 'The great idiot can't do that to his own son. With you being the Commander and the Matriarch's Marked...the Feathered will get off on hurting you. Not to mention how Lucifer will burn —'

'I am aware,' Drake had replied, drily.

I'd grasped Drake's blistered fingers between mine. It'd been time for me to step-up and become the lamb. 'I've been taking bets and bargains from the moment I became the Bone Princess.' I'd squeezed his fingers. 'Deal.' Then I'd stood, straightening my dress. 'Now let's go party like it's the end of the world.'

At my own coronation, I breathed in the sweet scent of my blokes — not owned by me, Poly-wings, like they'd have been in Angel World — but fam fighting by my side.

A boy Blood, inked in battle scenes like a human comic, knelt at my side, holding up a skull goblet. Other Bloods were darting between the dancing or shagging couples: kid butlers.

I wrinkled my nose at the coppery richness, but Ash knelt, tipping the goblet to the Blood's lips. The boy jerked back, even daring to shake his head. At the same time, he swallowed the blood convulsively like he hadn't been fed in months.

I bet he hadn't.

We were being watched: vampires swooped closer, pulled out of their hedonistic daze to snarl at Ash's insolence.

Black eyes, beating wings, sneering lips.

Mischief lifted his head from my shoulder. 'Oh look, what a Master Spy your whore *isn't.*' He hooked me closer, as if for a kiss. Instead, he mouthed against my lips, 'Punish him, before you appear weak, and we appear dead.'

Ash was feeding the boy with such tenderness, his gaze distant. This was Ash's first true moment of calm since...*hell, I couldn't even think it*...and I had to break it.

A gang of vampires circled closer to the scream of distorted guitars.

I steeled myself.

Then I booted Ash in the thigh, startling him tumbling onto his side. He gasped, the goblet soaring in an arc, before clattering down and spilling its precious life in a red sea.

The Blood cowered.

I hated that blokes were back to cowering before me.

Cheers and whistles.

That was another life ambition checked off: giving the happies to a bunch of brutal vampires.

Crash — the vampires at the far side of the chamber chucked their goblets at the walls, making a game of Hit the Slave.

The Bloods ducked, spluttered under sprays of crimson, or were smacked in the face.

And nope, imitation wasn't flattery.

When a thug with more piercings than skin held a Blood's head underneath a fountain that spewed blood champagne, like bullying jocks everywhere, Ash snarled, jumping up.

Until Mischief rested his hand on his shoulder with an authority that shocked me. 'Steady, soldier. Beaten dogs need to learn to bite their own masters, and we're teaching them that trick.'

When Ash glanced back at him, I nodded.

Just a little longer...

Except, then it was *my* sister who threatened the rebellion. Because she was *here*, along with the other Blood Lovers, soaring above our heads.

The vampires held their partners in their arms, dancing through the air, like an epically twisted Cinderella's ball. They fed from their necks, in between kisses, as if they were only sucking love bites. As my sister's over bright gaze met mine across the room, I had to admit that I could see it now: the *connection*.

Love: dark and self-destructive. But then, who was I to talk about love? I wished I could feel...*anything*...as purely as those Blood Lovers.

Even if they were idiots.

I still shook because if I did this now, I'd be risking Jade's life, not protecting her. I'd be shattering her fairy tale, whilst she watched.

Could I shatter her world, as well as my dad's?

Rebel linked our pinkies, twisting me to face him. I blinked up at him, as he murmured, 'Everybody thought my da a fine fellah and a good angel. But he wasn't. He was the type to break a slave's neck just to teach me a lesson, belt me, and do such things...' He bit his lip. 'But I still wept when Drake killed him.' He looked at me through his thick eyelashes. 'See, the others may not understand, but I do. It doesn't matter what he's done: the git's still your da.'

I shivered. Full points and bonus round to my punk angel.

Twenty-one years without family and now I'd discovered my dad at last? And he wanted me? Loved me?

Yet I had to betray him.

Suddenly, the lights dimmed. An explosion of raging guitar riffs and...

Hold onto your scaredy-cat pants, the ride's about to get real.

Lucifer: ethereal and transcendent. Hovering

with slow wingbeats above the party, he wore nothing but his own light, which spun around him in an ever-moving beauty, revealing glimpses of his skin. The branded **FIRE** stood out starkly on his chest. He commanded the attention of every partygoer on charisma alone. Yet all *his* attention focused on me, as he held out his hand. Tingles spread down my shoulder blades *to no longer be the misfit outcast*.

Jade had sold herself for acceptance; I bastard got it.

I let my pinkie slip out of Rebel's and swooped up towards Lucifer. I was the one picked for once. *Special.* I hugged the moment, even whilst it burnt me.

'*Yours, need, now.*' Devil writhed. I'd tucked him into my bodice, and I hissed, as he pricked my tit. '*Hungry, hungry, hungry.*'

'Greedy,' I muttered, edging him out.

Devil sprang into full length, twisting his prongs as if stretching. His dark power flooded through me, and I thrilled, caught in its merciless tide.

I could taste the brutal joy of death and I craved *more, more, more...*

Lucifer's fingers drew circles on my wing, and I blinked back to his concerned gaze.

Why the hell did his *care* have to be genuine, when mine wasn't? Why couldn't he get with the Bad Guy script?

'Welcome to the coronation of my daughter, Children of the Light!' Lucifer's feathers flared, as he grinned.

I scrutinised the vampires soaring around us or shifting down in the shadows: the sideways glances and clenched fists.

This was a powder keg of a divided world. And I was the match.

Yet Lucifer who was so desperate for loyalty, announced with an obliviousness that made me wonder whether *my* power had enthralled him, 'On my fangs, the princess has passed the tests. Yay for me, I birthed a Champion. And yay for the Under World, we now have a Queen of Chaos to sing in the dying of the sun and the dawn of Lucifer's Light.' The Devil's Trident jumped in my hand. 'You know, being together with my daughter, after missing her all these years...' His smile was soft and fragile. 'Huh, I didn't know joy or pride *hurt*. But what's the cost matter, when we have our queen, and I have my daughter?'

I quailed; my chest tight with a desperate ache.

Stop tempting me with everything I've always longed for...

I squeezed my sweaty hand around Devil's shaft.

He squirmed, whining. '*Death, death, death.*'

'Now I'm queen, you can take off the Kill Collar,' I lifted my chin, baring my neck. And held my breath.

Lucifer shrugged. 'Why not? I mean, yikes, I only witnessed the kinkiest smut. You are a naughty thing, aren't you?'

Sniggers.

I blushed. *Bastard Mischief.*

Lucifer waved his hand, however, and the imp lights around my neck broke away. I sagged, as they swayed back to their master, settling around his feet.

I was free.

I clasped Devil tighter.

'*Death, death, death.*' Devil shook.

Devil wanted death? Hell, I couldn't control it:

the savage appetite.

Desire.

Lucifer raised his arm. 'To the Queen of Chaos!'

Cheers, beating of wings, and stamping of feet.

Lucifer grinned. 'Now, let the Anarchy commen—'

I stabbed the Devil's Trident through Lucifer's throat.

Then I wrenched out the prongs, thrumming with Devil's high at the kill, shaking to shadow the world, even as deep inside I wailed at the betrayal.

'*Kill, kill, kill,*' Devil screeched in blood-thirsty delight. '*Delicious.*'

At first, Lucifer stared at me, his eyes widening. His lights fizzed, flickering like their power was failing. Then they faded, and he was naked and exposed before the Under World.

Sniggers.

I wanted to turn Devil on every one of the bastards who laughed at Lucifer's fall.

He deserved a lot, but not that.

Lucifer never said a word and he never looked away from me, unbelieving, then devastated.

Finally, his eyes rolled back, his wings stopped beating, and he crashed down.

That's when the world exploded into chaos, and the angelic army attacked.

26

You can fight for your king — or rebel against him. Stand up for your family, freedom, or love. But when everything's said and done, every bastard needs the courage to fight for themselves.

An arc of flame blasted me against the wall. I twisted to the side, shielding my singed wing, whilst fire burned down Armageddon-like from the Glories storming my party. There were no angel kid soldiers this time, just Amazonian war bitches in gleaming armour and they weren't here to dance.

Drake had said I'd know the *time*.

He hadn't been kidding.

Screams, feathers, and fangs. Violet met grey in a crimson parade. A coronation transformed to slaughter.

The vampires had no armour or swords and were bare arsed...

Guilt clawed at me. Where were the FF? The vampire army? Why had they abandoned their civilians?

I flinched. I couldn't betray a whole world to the Glories: that hadn't been the deal. The angels hadn't arrived as liberators but *conquerors*.

Misrule, who should've been leading a simple coup right now, slipped between the cages, letting out the Shadows and captive angels who cast him disbelieving glances before throwing themselves gleefully into the fight. Only then did I notice that vampires were battling vampires in snarling gangs. The civil war had been sparked, just when the bastards needed to unite.

I truly was the Queen of Chaos.

I spun Devil between my hands, and he hummed approvingly. His power surged through me; my eyes flared with fire.

'*Pain,*' Devil howled, '*devour pain.*'

'You want pain? Time for din dins.' I swooped into the bedlam. 'The angels,' I hollered at my blokes, who'd been pinned on one side by vampires, and the other by angels, 'stop the angels.'

Ash nodded, shoving back the vampire gang and taking effortless command in a way that shocked them into good little tin soldiers.

Rebel unsheathed Eclipse — because I hadn't allowed him to come to this shindig defenceless — and bounced up and down on the balls of his feet as he swung it, before signalling the nearest Glory with the universal gesture for *come on then, wanker.* A hunter, the battle electrified Rebel as much as it did me.

I dived into the ranks of the violet-winged

Glories, ramming the prongs through one, then shoving the sharp end of the shaft back into another. Laughing, high on the shadowed power of the trident, all was a blur of glorious death. One name rang out, however, clearer than anything since I'd been mired in the Under World: *Protector*.

Angel or vampire...did it matter what side I chose in this supernatural world, if I protected those who needed me?

I span and fought, until nothing stood alive. At last, my gaze refocused, and I choked, stepping back with a wet *squelch* onto an outstretched hand.

I stood atop a mound of feathered corpses.

When Devil cackled, my hands shook. *How had I lost myself like that?*

'Back in your box.' I shook Devil.

Devil burnt my palm in protest but shrank down. I hid him in my bodice, before picking my way over the bodies.

I'd promised Anarchy and Ash that I'd save the Bloods and I bastard would.

Whish — crack.

I stumbled backwards into the maelstrom.

Mischief crackled with energy, which snapped across his flowing hair, transforming him into Gandalf leading an army, and his magic ranks were the *Bloods*. Their tattoos glowed, snaking out in whips.

Whish — crack.

A scream, as a tattoo whip burst through the chest of the pierced vampire who'd tormented the Blood by holding his head beneath the fountain. Another gurgled scream, and a second whip exploded through his eye socket.

What had Mischief said about beaten dogs needing to learn to bite their masters?

Yeah, they'd got that trick down.

Mischief had planned this. But had he intended the brutal beauty of this uprising?

Then I caught my sister's gaze across the chamber. She fought with the Blood Lovers right next to their vampire partners — *next to Wings* — blasting the angels flying with her power. She wasn't human anymore, just as I wasn't, and the deadly glare she shot me told me that we'd landed on opposite sides of the war. To her? I'd been offered my dad's love, the Crown, and dominion over the world, and instead I'd turned traitor and murdered Lucifer.

I was the big bad wolf. *And she was the huntress*.

I touched the pouch around my neck, which held her necklace.

The sister I'd known was dead. I'd been clinging to a fairy tale, the same as Jade. She was no damsel; she was a fully-grown bitch, and hard as it was, I had to trust her to make her own choices, despite the fact I ached to storm over and drag her by the hair onto *my* side. Yet my friend Gizem had rejected me, as firmly as Jade had rejected her angel necklace, the moment she'd known I'd lost my humanity. I couldn't do that to Jade. She'd always be my sister, even if I was nothing to her.

The Bones couldn't choose or fight for themselves, however, and unlike the Bloods, they needed rescuing before they could be taught to bite.

I nodded at Ash over the mayhem. He fell back, spinning sidekicks through the angels.

I still hadn't spied where Lucifer fell. I cast a final anxious glance over my shoulder because if I *hadn't* killed him...? Then this battle had only been the sideshow before the finale that was coming next with warnings for violence and character death.

My wings flared in the pitch-black of the shelter, catching flickering glimpses of the curved ceiling. Above, thundered the human trains. Below, the Bones lay in ghostly quiet.

I buried my nose in Ash's wing to hide from the chalky mustiness. Ash smiled, grabbing me around the waist and turning me into his kiss. It was tender, trembling with everything we'd witnessed.

We shared Devil's darkness: the whispered temptation to *kill*.

Ash must've made one hell of a dark soldier.

When Ash drew back, his gaze was alive in a way it hadn't been since his sisters' deaths. 'You're even hotter with the trident than me.'

I sniggered, tracing over the names Ash had painted onto his skin, hesitating at the letters over his heart: **VIOLET.**

As well as the two smaller names beneath...

Ash caught my hand. 'Free the Bones. Win the civil war. Elect Misrule. This first part...? It's for Anarchy: the best mate a bloke ever had. And I'll deny that, even under threat of death by butter knife.'

I swaggered towards Roman Vampire, who was harnessed to the mechanical wheel that opened the floor. He studied me balefully.

I tapped my tiara. 'Queen of Chaos here, so *open sesame*.'

Roman Vampire merely hunched his shoulders, slumping against the wall.

I stiffened. The fighting above grew louder...*closer*.

How long did we have to rescue the captives before either vampires or angels discovered us?

Why's it not working?

You think wearing that tiara makes you a Queen? A leader?

This Not So Friendly Giant has been trapped in your dad's nightmare for longer than you've been *Violet Feathers*. Why should he trust your bony pussy just because you say so?

Incentivise the bitch, I get you.

I unsheathed Star, surging with Devil's shadowed ectasy in carnage. Then I leapt at Roman Vampire, holding the tip of the shank to his throat.

Ash gasped.

'I said, open it,' I repeated, pressing the blade just hard enough to slice his silvery skin.

Then I was being dragged back by my shoulders, struggling like a wild-cat. I stared with wild, dilated eyes at Ash, who smoothed my hair, even as I held Star to his gut.

When I fell from the high, I sheathed Star, horrified. 'I don't know... I didn't mean...'

Why the hell had I attacked? Why had I listened to J?

That was a bitch move.

I gave you the steps, but you're the one who danced.

Why do you reach for a blade, instead of words? If you want to have freedom, then you need to make your own choices and control the monster.

Ash gentled me down from my spiralling panic with circling caresses on my arms. 'The trident's a drug; the hit's powerful if you're not used to it. Devil's still in your system. How about I try out my charm?'

I nodded.

Ash slunk to Roman Vampire, lounging on the wall next to him. 'Lucifer's a tyrant who deserves nothing less than execution for what he's done to you.' Roman Vampire's flat gaze flared with sudden terror. He writhed as if he could escape Ash's treasonous words. Ash shrugged. 'The bastard's dead. Probably.' Roman Vampire reared back. 'I gave *everything* to fight him and free you because if you help us rescue the Bones, then they'll save you as well. Deal?'

Roman Vampire cleared his throat, and I wondered how long it'd been since he'd been allowed to speak; his gaze darted around the shadows, like he'd find the answer there.

At last, he gave a curt nod, before straightening his shoulders and pushing. As he strained, pulling on the chains, the metal floor *clanked* open.

'One at a time,' Ash warned. 'We'll have to take off the wire...'

Clank, clank, clank.

I stepped to the lip of the tomb, before kneeling down next to Ash. A wave of roasting heat shimmered across my cheeks.

Key squinted up at us through his curls, shaking.

Hell, that barbed wire muzzle stretching his lips...

I nodded at Ash, and we bent down, pulling Key out of the hole.

Key howled, as his limbs cramped after being held still for so long, and the sharp barbs of the wire dug into his skeletal frame.

I winced; my palms had shallow cuts just from moving him.

How could we free him?

'Vampire proof?' I asked.

'When you're starved of blood, you're weaker than Sarah Connor, and I'm talking *The Terminator*, not her kickass transformation in *Judgement Day*. It doesn't need to be that strong to punish.'

'No one's punishing the Bones again.' I eased behind Key's head, unwinding the wire from his hair, which was stiff with matted blood.

Key whimpered, as I unmuzzled him. I hurled the wire into the black, before unwrapping the remainder from the rest of his body like stripping open a thorny parcel. I bit my lip not to let out a gasp; my palms were slick with my own blood. I was suffering for a moment. How long had Key been trapped in this agony?

Then soft fingers stroked my hair, and I glanced up at the whispered, 'Thank you.' Key's voice was hoarse, like his throat had been sandpapered. He coughed, trying again. 'Anarchy...?'

And how much was I *not* having that conversation about his brother when Key had only just been dragged from hell?

'You're bro's safe.' It wasn't a total lie: Anarchy was safer than he'd been as Stephanie's pet. 'Plus, we're going to free every single vampire trapped in the Bones. Then the bloke who's helped plan this, Harahel, is waiting in the Bat Cave to keep you safe until the war's over. He's an angel, but you'll have to trust him, just like you need to trust me. This is the big hope moment.'

Words, not weapons.

Key studied me, thoughtfully. Then he smiled, even though it split open the gashes on his lips. 'Saviour.'

I flew on the word: not Champion, beast, or

destroyer. I couldn't save everyone, but I could bring the whole world tumbling down, like I'd promised Anarchy. And if that saved one person's little brother from torment...? Then it was worth more than every fang or feather I'd earned on my leather necklace, the Devil's Trident, or my Crown.

I'd made my choice and I'd controlled the monster: *I soared.*

Finally, Key twisted to Ash, falling into his arms with a sob.

Ash held him close, stroking the back of his neck. 'Key,' he murmured, 'you're OK, mate. I said I'd take care of you and wouldn't forget you. I'm sorry...'

They rocked in each other's arms.

Anarchy was like Ash's little brother, he'd once said. No wonder Lucifer had tortured him through Key. I hadn't been able to save Ash's sisters, but I'd stopped Lucifer taking the last of his family.

'Open the next tomb,' I called out to Roman Vampire. 'I'm busting this gaol wide open.'

'Wrong, wench.' I startled at Wild's bellow, jumping up and fizzing violet across my skin.

Wild loomed in the doorway to the shelter, flanked by the FF. Unlike the vampires at the party, they were dressed and armed.

What had happened to the rebellion? Why were the FF hunting me?

When Wild swaggered closer, Ash crouched in front of Key. He pulled out his shooter, balancing it on his knee, as he pointed it at Wild's balls.

Wild chuckled. 'Still defiant? Are you throwing a wobbly because your riot has been crushed?'

I dropped my gaze, paling.

The bastard was lying. He *had* to be lying...

My heart shrank, but I forced on a smile. 'Not much left for you to fight for when the king's *dead*.'

Wild stilled: fury and distress flickered across his face. His eyes shone.

Wild was under Lucifer's spark. The Feathered were caught in his fervour.

The original and most loyal were also the most enthralled.

'Wrong again.' Wild stalked closer, sweat dripping from his muscled arms. 'And he's right mad about being betrayed. You'll be begging me to save you, bab. He won't just take your head, he'll *burn* you.'

I shuddered: *screams, blinding light, charred flesh...*

Yet I knew it wouldn't be that *easy*. When Ash had been disloyal, Lucifer had taken his weapons, rank, and identity, and then had hurt or killed everybody he loved in front of him.

He'd burned him inside and out.

I was the leader, however, and that meant no more running away. If there were consequences, I was the one who'd face them.

'*Yours, use, fight,*' Devil wheedled, shifting in excited anticipation.

My hands lifted puppet-like towards my bodice...and the trident. I stilled them, however, because I couldn't risk another monster in the yard. I'd let one out to take down Lucifer; I couldn't let it out again.

I trembled; fire flicked on and off my fingertips.

'Enough of the Moriarty,' Ash snarled, 'more of the *bang, bang.*'

Wild growled, before the Feathered swarmed into the Bones, surrounding us with flames.

I hollered, shooting a fireball. It sputtered out, weakened by my confused righteousness, or after my taste of Devil, *lack of it.* I hissed, backing up.

Bang, bang.

Wild clutched at his crimson guts.
Direct shot.
At last, the Feathered howled as they attacked.

27

Once, I'd stood up to the top boy in my class. In the teen equivalent of pulling my pigtails to get into my pants, he'd tormented me for weeks, until I'd snapped, holding a shank to his face behind the science lab, whilst he'd pissed himself.

Only, the next time he'd cornered me, he'd had a gang at his back, whilst they'd pinned me to the floor, and he'd shown me just why blokes were bastards.

Me? I'd been alone.

'You going to tell your mummy? Daddy?' He'd sneered.

Because everyone had known I was the orphan from the children's home. What they hadn't known...? I'd stopped calling for my parents a long time ago.

There'd been nobody to save me but myself.

I'd spent the next school year taking apart those bastards stealthily one at a time, without them even knowing I'd become the devil haunting them.

There was danger in a gang. But power in shadowed tricks.

My nose *crunched*, and I whined. Blood flooded the back of my throat, until I choked.

Clank — my face cracked against the metal floor of the Bones again.

Wild wound his hand more tightly in my hair, pressing his foot onto my back. He licked a hot stripe down my neck, and I jerked, struggling.

'So much for *never striking* me,' I snarled.

'You hadn't tried to commit regicide then,' Wild shrugged.

He had a point.

I peered into the gloom, which was lighted in feathered sweeps by the ranks of FF.

Key had been dragged to his knees amongst them. His thin arms clutched over his chest, as he panted for breath, his eyes bleak with fear. I tried to smile comfortingly, but through the blood dripping from my nose and staining my teeth like I'd savaged someone's throat, I don't think I pulled it off.

I blinked against the pain.

Trick had slung his arm around Ash's shoulders, as if he wasn't holding Ash up because Ash's knee had been shattered. Trick's hold was tight enough to force Ash's mouth into a grim line and possessive enough to make me crave to burn off his hands.

Ash's shooter was now tucked into Trick's waistband.

Wild shifted, laying his weight against me to show me how much this was turning him on. 'You thought to run our world? You'll be tamed, and we'll be Bonded. Then you'll learn your place.'

'Not happening in a world of freaky misogynists. And my place? My boot, your balls.'

Clank — my face, meet floor again.

I swallowed coppery blood.

'Violet, this would be a Plan B situation,' Ash warned, 'not a piss off the enemy one.'

'New bargain. Your pet Seducer will be kept by General Trick who knows how to keep him in line.' Wild nibbled my ear. I glanced up at Trick, who'd cupped his hand over Ash's prick through his jeans: *message received*. Ash refused to meet my eye. 'You Blood Bond and obey, or your punishment will be taken out by Trick on the Seducer. Maybe Trick will give him to the Feathered ranks. They deserve a reward for their loyalty.'

'Don't...' I bucked, threaded with violet and black despair.

Wild groaned, clutching his guts that bled from the gunshot wound.

What had happened to Rebel? Mischief? Misrule and Harehel? Had they been defeated?

Killed...?

I choked, as my muscles cramped on the panic.

Screw on your queenly head and bring the Bitch of Utopia to the party.

I tried, but what if—

What if the universe is balanced on your peachy ass? What if the sky rains gods? What if you die and live and die and...

What ifs **are for pussies. You have the power: choice, decision, and control.**

But how do I know...?

You want to stop the carnival and take

down Lucifer? Then remember how to trust. You're not just a vampire queen, but an angel princess as well.

Have you already forgotten how you chose the loyal Irish punk?

Rebel: in the vampire Under World, it wasn't always easy to remember my connection with an angel.

I reached out through our bond, desperate to feel Rebel alive, flooded with a relieved warmth at the union. An *exhilarated righteousness* buzzed through me in a rush. I'd tasted that before in the thrill of my own kills; I sighed with relief. If Rebel was still battling, I called bollocks on Wild's *riot crushed* speech.

Had Wild also lied about my dad?

I had to escape, find Lucifer, and if he was alive...destroy him for real this time. Because there was one truth amidst Wild's lies: Lucifer would burn me and my fam if I didn't.

First I had a gang of FF to take down, however, and weakened as I was, I still had *shadowed tricks*. The angels would call it dishonourable. But when had there ever been an honourable monster?

'Bet,' I hissed at Ash.

Ash finally met my gaze. 'Now...?'

'You. Make a bet. Now.'

His expression cleared, and he grinned, even though Trick was still palming him through his jeans. 'General Wild,' he barked out, one solider to another — *perfect*, 'bet that when we fight, right now, I won't kill you.'

Wild stilled his grinding against my arse, only to rumble with laughter. 'You? Kill me?'

'If I lose...then Violet accepts your bargain and...I'm given as a pet to your FF army.' I blanched: Ash was playing for high stakes. This was his world, however, and for once, I had to trust a bloke. 'But if *you* lose.' He held up his hand, listing each consequence with a smirk. 'You're dead. Trick and the Feathered let us go. We free the Bones and whoever else we like. And no one tries to recapture the Bones, Bloods, or Shadows.' The cocky bastard waggled his thumb, 'I can't think of a fifth demand, so I'll let that go.'

Wild hurled me down, prowling towards Ash like he hadn't even been shot.

Ash tried to straighten, tilting his chin, but Trick suddenly let go of him, and he yelped: warrior reduced to captive on his knees.

Wild toed him. 'You can't even stand.'

'Scared to take a bet?' Ash gasped.

Titters.

The FF gawked at their leader.

Turning down a bet from another vampire in the Under World: *big fat no no.*

Yet why had Ash chosen a bet he couldn't win? He had to crawl with his shattered leg dragging behind him, just to haul himself closer to me. My skin crawled with what I'd done. I opened my mouth to say...*something*...but Ash hurriedly shook his head at me, instead slipping his hand down my bodice.

What the actual hell...?

Then Ash's fingers clasped around Devil, and I understood. His expression transformed from something broken to something *terrible*. Shaking from the power fizzing through him, he still managed to stare at me imploringly.

To ask my permission for the return of his own weapon.

I nodded.

'It's right rude of you to imply I'd turn down a bet.' Wild scooped up the barbwire muzzle, wrapping it around his knuckles. 'I just want to up the stakes. The kid you rescued...' Key shrank back, his eyes gleaming with tears. 'He could share your Seducer workload once he's trained up.'

Key whimpered, 'Please...'

Ash stiffened, his breathing harsh.

'Don't start bawling, after all, the Seducer could win this bet,' Wild mocked. 'Here, I'll even help him stand.'

Wild snatched Ash by the collar, hauling him onto his bad leg. Ash's wail was cut off by Wild's clout to his mouth. Warm crimson rained down on my cheek from Ash's lips, which were as split open now as Key's, from the barbed wire around Wild's knuckles.

'You'd better *hope* Ash kills you,' I growled. 'Or I'll dedicate my life to making yours hell.'

Wild laughed as he pulled back his arm again; my stomach lurched at the scarlet glistening on the metal. 'No time limit on the fight, babby?'

'I won't need one.' Ash spat blood into Wild's eyes.

When Wild reached up to smear away the scarlet, Ash swung the Devil's Trident, which he'd hidden in the palm of his hand. His eyes sparked with silver, and his face suddenly shuttered to a blankness like he was nothing but a vessel for Devil's darkness. He thrust the trident in a flaring white arc, more beautiful than any move I'd seen, as if Devil was part of him. He howled to the music of Wild's scream, as he skewered Wild through the throat.

Wild hung, staring at the tamed Seducer turned dark solider, his eyes still widened with shock, before slumping.

Silence.

My pulse raced, as I howled too, buzzing with the kill that stung like Devil was inside me, even though I hadn't been the one to deliver the blow.

We were free.

Ash retracted the trident, stumbling even though his eyes still sparked, as he turned to the stunned ranks of the FF.

Then I realised: once these men would've respected the Brigadier and taken orders from him in battle. Ash might not have been an FF, but he'd been Lucifer's righthand man. *Lucifer had humiliated Ash in front of those who knew him.*

Let the bastards call him traitor, they'd never call him *pet* again. *Or whore.*

I glowed, leaping up; the ancient powers rode the glinting waves of joy.

Triumph.

This was Ash's chance to reclaim what had been stolen, and I quivered with pride that he *chose* to be mine.

Trick recoiled, fanning his hands along the wall, as if he could disappear through it, as Ash stalked towards him, plucking his shooter from Trick's waistband.

'You remember who I am now?' Ash's smile was deadly. 'Before you unmade me? Built me again with your games?'

Trick nodded.

Ash leaned closer. 'I'm the Brigadier, and there was a bet. You'll honour it, or you'll also get close and personal with Devil.'

Trick swallowed. 'By the blood and bones, you always were insufferable. You have my word. But nothing changes what you are, nor you, Bone Princess. I said you'd devour the world in dark anarchy, did I not?'

Oomph — Ash kneed Trick in the balls.

Trick doubled over with a groan.

Ash grinned. 'And it was just as satisfying as in all my daydreams.' He stared longingly at Devil, before closing his eyes and holding him out to me on his palm. 'I don't want this to be *Lord of the Rings* dramatic but take the fiend before he tempts me to run off and hide in a cave.'

I closed Ash's fingers around the trident. 'He's yours. Rebel once told me every angel has an ancient weapon. Devil's a bratty psycho, but you fight like a god together. I shouldn't become...what he makes me. I'm monster enough already.'

Ash fidgeted, slipping Devil into his holster along with his shooter, but the elation in his gaze as he smiled, tingled such relief through me that my wings ached to *soar*.

And I would, once Rebel was safe by my side.

Yet now, once we'd freed the Bones, this monster had a king to kill, even if it was my own dad. It didn't matter that I'd injured him, he was the most powerful vampire in the Under World, and I'd betrayed him.

If I didn't kill him first, I'd burn.

Pulsing light seeped from the wounds at Lucifer's neck: a sun slowly dying.

And I was the star-slaughterer.

I shuffled my feet, trying not to notice how *small* my dad looked shrunk back to nothing but his leather shorts and shirt. He panted, slumped across his bed; his spiky hair stuck out in sweaty points.

Ash limped round one side of the bed, Rebel prowled round the other in a pincer movement.

Lucifer raised his chin, but the hand that lifted to the gashes at his neck trembled.

I clenched my hands, my nose still throbbing and broken.

Why did this have to be somewhere so intimate?

We'd stormed the Crypt, whilst Mischief had his own mission to protect and collect the Blood Familiars, expecting to find Lucifer in his Bone Palace, psyched for a slamdown.

Instead, a weak light had glimmered from his bedroom because like a wounded animal, Lucifer had crept into his nest to die.

When Ash drew his pistol, pressing it to Lucifer's forehead, and Rebel held Lucifer down by the shoulder, I flinched.

Wasn't this what I'd plotted? To be the saviour of the humans and Under World?

To kill my own dad...?

I froze. Why wasn't Lucifer fighting back? Why was he forcing me to execute him?

Ash glanced at me, even now asking for permission to shoot the bloke who'd murdered his sisters.

When I hesitated, Lucifer smiled. 'My, so many Judases for little old me.' He cocked his head, his breathing ragged. 'And how many worshippers crawl at the feet of the Queen of Chaos, even sacrificing family...?'

Ash growled, pistol whipping Lucifer. I jumped, and Lucifer gasped, blinking rapidly. His fractured cheek swelled, hot and tender.

Shut up...just bastard shut up...

Words were weapons, however, and Lucifer was battling even now.

'Boo-hoo, did I make the whore sad?' Lucifer pouted. 'Wow, when you think about it, champ, it only took you a couple of months to incite rebellion.' He grinned, even though it must've been agonising through the pain of his cheek. 'Hooray to the power of my sperm, I couldn't have hoped for a better display of your inherited *spark*.'

Rebel shoved Lucifer lower on the bed, and he coughed, gagging on his own light. 'Just shoot the git.'

'Wait...' I dived to the bed, hovering over Lucifer, smarting with desperate hope. 'You're *proud* of me for...?'

'What daughter of mine wouldn't rebel?' Lucifer smirked. 'I warned you that I had to wear my official face for the sake of my people. Yet you held them under your sway, until sensing the angels...' He cut off, catching my hunted expression. 'Huh, you *didn't* sense the angels...?' Doubt and grief shone in his tear brightened eyes. 'You truly wished...to kill me?'

I'd burned Lucifer, just as he'd burned Ash. And if I'd ever expected it to be a moment of purifying vengeance, then I'd been wrong because I was caught in the flames as well.

If my dad hadn't loved me, I wouldn't have been able to hurt him. He'd transformed me into a assassin, after all.

I narrowed my lips, forcing myself to remember everything we'd suffered, lost, the *Apocalypse*...

Nope, it still wasn't any easier. But then, that's why it was called a *sacrifice*.

I trembled violet onto my fingertips. Passing Devil back to Ash, who he truly belonged to, had reignited my fire. 'I'm the Protector.' I gazed at Lucifer, pleading and desperate. I needed him to understand. 'Love's not enough. Not for a leader.'

His expression crumpled, as finally a tear slipped down his purpled cheek. He turned his head away on the pillow, closing his eyes.

I shook my head at Ash, and he lifted the

shooter, backing away. I gently held my hand to Lucifer's pulsing throat. My violet wove with his white light, and he hissed at the burn.

I shook, tightening my hand around Lucifer's neck. Then his eyes snapped open: blazing infinite stars.

I gasped, juddering with the spellbinding depths of his power.

Lucifer had been *allowing* us to threaten and hurt him. Deceiving us to work out how far our disloyalty lay...whether I'd truly do...*that*...to him.

And now he bastard knew.

Lucifer roared, and light exploded.

28

For the first time since I'd been abandoned...or snatched by my mother...as a baby, I was at last truly held by my dad. Yet it wasn't in his arms, rather in his cold white light: it bound me, helpless, in the air.

Connected.

The light shone from Lucifer on the bed, linking Rebel, Ash, and me to him in fairyland tentacles. The femurs and ribs sticking out of the walls glowed in throbbing sympathy between the graffiti.

I closed my eyes, whilst the light explored me: prickles like frost. Lost to the closeness — a glimpse inside my dad, as if his hand was curled in mine — I almost missed his anguished howl.

Lucifer curled over on the bed, his face pressed to the silk, trying to muffle his despair and grief at my rejection.

His light wept with it.

The prickles turned into nips; my fingers and nose became numb with the cold. Rebel gasped, and Ash writhed.

I twisted, but the undulating tentacle arm simply smashed me against the floor.

Crack — I shrieked, as my elbow fractured.

I'd saved the Bones, stopped an apocalypse in the human world, and pulled off a rebellion headed by Misrule and Harahel... If I died in Lucifer's Light now, then better a dead rebel, than a living tyrant. Yet with this power, Lucifer could recapture the Bones, overturn the revolution, and plot *another* apocalypse...and I'd be just another slain monster.

'B-bastard s-s-stop,' I chattered through frozen lips.

Lucifer didn't even raise his head, only covering it with his arms.

'I believe the princess requested you to stop.' Drake sauntered between the snaking lights that trapped us, even though I could see beneath the swag to his stumbling step and tight-lipped expression; his seared chest and blackened wings must've been agonising. His gaze met mine, questioning and concerned, before it snapped to Lucifer and became as cold as the light around me. 'Enough of this tantrum. Calm yourself.'

I snorted. *Drake had some balls*. Then I realised: he wasn't talking to Lucifer as if he was a king but as one Marked Wing to another.

Why did that chill me, even worse than the shivers that wracked me?

Finally, Lucifer raised his face from the pillows; he blinked, confused.

The light warmed, and I shuddered at the tingling rush of blood to my limbs.

'You...?' Lucifer suddenly looked young...lost, like me. 'You know, I'm not open for meetings with cute angel boys today; I'm...busy.' He tried for a leer, but it didn't hide the hitch at the end of the sentence.

'Withdraw your light from the princess and her...' Drake hesitated, '...family, and I promise you shan't suffer in your capture.'

Lucifer laughed but it was only to cover the sob. 'And afterwards? You know better than any, don't you *Marked*, why I have to say *catch me!*'

I hollered, as Lucifer spun the light towards himself, like a spider pulling in its thread. Ash and Rebel whirled towards him at the same time as me, until we tumbled on top of Lucifer like a shield.

I stared down into my dad's eyes and could pretend...just for a moment...that he wasn't a genocidal psycho who I'd betrayed.

And that he hadn't just spared our lives.

Lucifer pressed his hand to my cheek. His light slipped back into his body, and I breathed out, as my fingers and toes heated.

'As you like. Of course, I shan't be able to *catch* you,' Drake's cool voice called. 'I believe, however, that my father shall.'

Lucifer paled, his lips twisting with fear. He clutched my shoulders, as if I was *his* Protector.

I hadn't expected Drake's smug *my dad could fight your dad*. Or my own desire to snarl back: *oh yeah, him and whose army?*

The Mage already had an angelic army, however, that's what happened when you made deals with your enemy.

The Mage swooped through the archway into the Crypt; his wings flamed in majesty. He scrutinized Lucifer, crackling with candyfloss power. An invisible wave ebbed like heat around his harem trousers and emerald shirt. When he tilted his head, his silver threaded golden curls fell across his eyes.

Then he raised his hands.

And this was *the moment:* the one Drake had promised I wouldn't miss.

Why did I wish I could hide under the sheets and make the monsters vanish? Why were my hands trembling?

Rebel and Ash dived over the side of the bed. Rebel's hand around my ankle jerked me after him to the floor. I hollered, landing on my elbow, before bottom shuffling against the wall.

The Mage shot an invisible blast at Lucifer, who pushed himself to his knees, catching the attack with his crossed forearms. When the Mage had tried that on me in the Legions' chambers in Angel World, I'd been paralysed. Lucifer only grimaced, however, shooting out a flare of his own light and shoving back.

The Mage soared closer, blasting again.

Stalemate.

Lucifer quivered, whilst he kept up his stream of light, which arced as it met the Mage's in a deadly rainbow. 'You always hated me, Rahab. With all my sweet spies, don't you think I know how you whispered in the Matriarch's ear? You *wish* you'd been born a Glory, so you play at it with your boys. Aw, did I hurt your feelings? At least I offered the Wings a choice to Fall. You're just a cog in a wheel that crushes them.'

'Hush, little king.' The Mage hovered over Lucifer, like an eagle over a sparrow. I stiffened. 'I should fry your tongue for speaking of my boys. And only one of us is the King of Spies.' The Mage's voice lowered. 'I shall tear apart your mind before I steal your light. Aw, did I hurt *your* feelings...?'

'You steal my kingdom, daughter...' Lucifer's light flickered, as he glanced at me. '...and now you'd dare threaten...?'

I couldn't bastard take it.

Shoving myself up, violet swirled through me: not righteousness to revenge, but to save Lucifer from the Mage's torment. I wasn't an assassin, and Rebel had taught me as a huntress to go for the quick kill. If Lucifer was to die, I wouldn't let him be played with first, even if it shanked my heart to bolt flames that skittered down my arms and from my palms at Lucifer's head.

Lucifer screamed, bucking. Hit by the twin lights, he fought to divide his light but taken by surprise, his light faded, and he fell back amongst the silk.

Paralysed.

The Mage flicked his wrist at me, knocking my fire exploding against the wall, whilst his blasts still shot through Lucifer's motionless body.

I shuddered at Lucifer's wails.

'Allow it,' I growled at the Mage. 'Finish it, or we're Geneva Conventioning from now on.'

The Mage arched a pale eyebrow. 'Have you forgotten the power I hold over every prideful angel? I believe it now includes you...?'

I swallowed. *The bastard had me.*

The shimmering wave that had been torturing Lucifer, however, disappeared. Lucifer remained still; his chest rapidly rose and fell.

The gaze he shot me floored me with the depth of its sorrow. 'Yay for you: you've trapped me and stolen my daughter's love.' Lucifer carefully didn't look at me this time. 'So, that's everything. All out of *owie* places to be knifed. This is as good a time as any to decapitate me.'

The Mage landed on the bed, straddling

Lucifer. He stroked Lucifer's sweaty hair back from his forehead. 'I haven't taken everything from you yet, little king. I have only begun your chastisement. Don't you remember what happens next?'

Lucifer's eyes widened. 'Uh-uh... Y-y-ou can't... S-she's not...'

Terror.

So, that's what it looked like.

Why was I flooded with the feeling I'd invited in the wrong devil?

All of a sudden, the bones glowed shocking violet.

Boom.

An echoing rumble rocked the chamber. Ash caught me, holding me upright in his wings.

Please, no, it couldn't bastard be...

That wasn't the deal. She hadn't been invited to the party...

Regal in a pearl-like dress with a train that slithered behind her in iridescent perfection, my mother stood in the archway in frosty silence.

I'd forgotten how tall the Matriarch was, and how much of an Ice Bitch, casting me a haughty glance, before tossing her ash-blonde hair, which cascaded to the floor with grey feathers woven into the strands.

Blood-tipped feathers.

How had I forgotten the savagery of the angels?

I backed away, only flickers of violet still curling on my skin.

Ash edged in front of me, drawing his shooter, just as Rebel flamed alive Eclipse.

I'd belonged to the Matriarch, like a precious weapon, and I'd turned on her, freeing her Broken slaves, abandoning her offer of the world and escaping instead. The bitch had to want her vengeance moment, and here I was: elbow and nose shattered, half-frozen, and cornered, whilst she had the Mage and Drake in her corner.

Yeah, no more bargains with devils for me.

'Haman,' Rebel breathed, 'my brother... Please, take me instead...'

The Matriarch ignored him. After all, he was a Marked Wing, an Addict, Imperfect, and a Son of the Fallen in her warped view. What right had Rebel to talk to a Glory and a queen?

An *Angel Princess* on the other hand...?

'You stole Haman, bitch, and we want him back,' I growled.

The Matriarch's mouth twitched at one corner, before she cast me a steely glare. 'You miss him as your Poly-Wing? Return with me to Angel World then. The toy's agony has been delectable.'

Rebel let out a sob, Eclipse shaking in his hand. I didn't miss either Drake or the Mage's flinch either: Haman had been a servant to the Legion, shielded and indulged even if still enslaved. But not a Glory's *toy*.

Clack, clack, clack.

The Matriarch's diamond stilettos *rapped* against the floor, like she was trying to crack the skulls or break Lucifer's balls from the way she was giving him the death stare.

Unable to draw back, Lucifer's breaths became so shallow and fast, he trembled on the edge of panic attack.

And I knew how that felt.

The Mage lounged back onto the end of the bed, resting up on his elbow, as if they were lovers.

I clenched my fists because there was no way to doubt Lucifer's version — kidnapped, forced, child stolen from him — when faced by the Matriarch's predatory prowl around the bed and slink in her satins across him.

Or how she spoke about Haman.

The Matriarch circled one finger over the back of Lucifer's neck, where his Mark would've been before he burnt it off. Where she could've inflicted pain or unwilling pleasure without even touching, just as I'd seen her punish Drake.

Drake looked away, refusing to meet my eye.

Trapped underneath the queen's finery, Lucifer looked so much smaller.

'I am not y-yours anymore,' Lucifer's eyes glistened with tears. I hated to hear him stammer. 'You d-don't own me.'

'I d-don't?' The Matriarch mocked. 'By my feathers, you'll become mine again, and we shall have such dark amusements. Your fear is a sweet treat, my star. And your pain soars on the wings of corrupted love.' Her tongue flicked out, as if tasting the air. When she twisted to me, my stomach lurched. 'So, you fly in my shadow after all, baby bird? You rule with love and force your slaves to drink its poison.'

I blanched. 'I'll never be a slaveowner, bitch.'

The Matriarch shifted her hips against Lucifer's, sliding her fingers along his wing tips. 'How do you imagine you defeated this naughty boy?'

Snap — she twisted Lucifer's sensitive wingtips.

Lucifer yowled, but she swallowed it in a kiss, forcing her tongue between his lips, as he lay bound by the Mage and unable to struggle.

Is this how she'd forced him last time?

'Enough gross mum and dad kinkiness before I have to bleach my eyeballs.' When I booted the bed, the Matriarch broke the kiss. 'I didn't go running to you for help, so you can just take your arse back to Angel World.'

The Matriarch's eyes sparked. 'Soon, my daughter, you'll receive the firm hand you're begging for to learn to fly true. Yet now I have a monster's wings to clip.'

She drew out a golden vial that swung at her belt; a Merlin falcon was engraved on the front.

Lucifer's eyes widened impossibly larger. 'Please... Mark, beat, brand me...but don't take away my light.'

Brand?

The Matriarch traced over the **FIRE** that had been branded from one nipple to the other on Lucifer's chest. Hell, had that been *punishment*? Not a declaration of freedom, but her control? And what kind of magic...and how much pain...did it take to brand an angel?

No wonder the bastards had rebelled.

The Matriarch wrenched back Lucifer's head, forcing open his mouth. Then she opened the bottle and tipped out a single sapphire drop.

When Lucifer gagged, his eyes rolling back, his sweet aroma of ash and bonfires was put out, replaced by the Matriarch's rich myrrh. A chill blue crept through his veins; his breath ghosted in icy puffs.

I guessed by the agonised panting that the sapphire poison wasn't a fun day at the carnival.

The Matriarch tied the vial back onto her belt, before bending over Lucifer. His blue tinge had faded. 'No more fire, my star,' she whispered.

I shuddered. Why did it bother me that Lucifer's flames had been taken from him? Did she have a toxin that could steal *my* fire? I tried to catch Drake's eye, but he bowed his head, refusing to watch.

Whatever Lucifer suffered, Drake would be suffering it right alongside him.

'When I Mark you,' the Matriarch bit down on Lucifer's throat, sucking bruises, 'I'll make such use of you, boy, that you'll *wish* I was the harsh Glory you believed me before. You'll put on delicious shows and learn that a Wing's place is on his knees.'

'Let me introduce you: this is King of the Underworld. And I rather think he's neither one of your Wings, nor the kneeling type.' Mischief soared into the chamber, landing next to Lucifer's bedside.

A guttural *gekkering*, and Blaze and Spark burst into the chamber, winding around Mischief's ankles in red blurs as if *he* was their Keeper.

'Mischief, my darling pet, *run*,' Lucifer hissed. 'I'm in the middle of being...stabbed in the back...poisoned...kidnapped...all the fun party games.'

Like he believed Mischief was the only one who hadn't betrayed him.

Lucifer's gaze softened as it met Mischief's, shining with...*love*.

Despite the hunts, threats, and naming him *pet*, Lucifer had truly intended to Blood Bond willingly with Mischief: A Shadow.

How much of Lucifer's cruelty had been his *official face*? Why hadn't I guessed the truth behind the carnival masks? Because despite betraying the king, Mischief was walking into the fire now to save him from the Matriarch; he couldn't see *that* happen to him.

To anyone.

At last, righteousness sparked, spiralling through me. I nodded at Mischief, and he smiled.

'Lucifer's a king. He belongs in the Under World, so he can be put on trial.' I grimaced because the Fire Catacombs seemed the most likely bet for vampire justice, rather than picking up litter by the roadside. 'Their prisoner, their sentence.'

The Matriarch cradled Lucifer in her arms possessively like a child. 'By my wing, you'll be glorious, ruling and destroying worlds. But you shan't take what's mine.'

When Mischief hollered, it changed into a *whinny*, as he transformed into a killer unicorn. He snorted, stamping his hooves at the Matriarch. Blaze and Spark leapt onto the bed, snapping for her throat, just as Mischief lowered his horn.

When the Mage raised his hands, I shot a firebolt towards him, but Drake jumped in front of it. The flames caught his shoulders, and he screamed, writhing on the floor, as his back blistered.

The Mage continued to spin his spell to vanish the Matriarch with Lucifer clutched to her chest...*just as Mischief had sensed.*

I stared at the empty space where my parents had been. Then I howled, shooting out another sizzling arc.

The Mage, however, grabbed Mischief by the horn and shrank him toy size. The unicorn swung from his hand, mewling.

I stilled, allowing the violet to die down.

What was the point of fighting? Lucifer was gone. *We'd won.* So, why did it bastard feel like we'd also lost?

Smack — the Mage whacked Mischief across his rump.

Mischief's eyes screwed up in pain, and his hooves kicked the air.

'I hope my boy entertained you,' the Mage shook the unicorn, throwing off the illusion, and Mischief transformed back into an angel, held by the scruff of the neck; I winced. 'He can be charming, if he has a mind to be.'

I nodded to Ash and Rebel, who finally put away their weapons, although they looked almost as shaken as me.

'Congratulations, you may return home.' The Mage studied his son, as Drake pulled himself shakily to his knees...*as if he hadn't just saved the Mage from my flames*. 'Your fondness for the princess will make for an interesting training tool. The Matriarch has allowed me to borrow you, whilst the princess is an Apprentice.' Drake shot a glance at me, startled. 'In fact, I'm intrigued by the use I may make of all those who adore her.' He glanced around the chamber at my fam. *Hell, no...* 'You'll be welcome in the Brotherhood of the Phoenix.'

I stormed up to the Mage. 'The deal was for one Queen of Chaos.'

'Be silent. Do I look like a Fallen, driven by base desires for bargains and bets? Once, I offered *you* the chance to join me willingly. Now?' His grin was feral; his eyes narrowed. 'I take it all.'

The air thickened throughout the room in candyfloss waves, until I choked. Finally, everything dwindled to white.

29

My human life of gamers, shanks, and sister had burnt on my twenty-first birthday, when my powers had arisen phoenix-like. Tricked into the harem and feathered Angel World, *I'd* torched the corrupted court and my role as Angel Princess.

And now?

I'd stolen the light from the Under World.

Was I truly nothing more than death, the End, destroyer? What had I become?

Queen of Chaos? Saviour? Protector?

Or a corrupter of love and loyalty like my parents?

White light distorted and distended; I hurtled between the shards of shattered mirrors, endlessly reflecting *black and violet, black and violet...*

I tumbled onto the rock, catching myself before my brains were dashed out on the boulders.

Oomph — the wind was knocked out of me.

I groaned, hugging my aching arm closer.

Three dazed blokes (and two blinking fox familiars), sprawled on top of me, like we'd been roughhousing, rather than pulled by the Mage's mental powers from the Under World to...

Where the hell were we?

A stone castle, battle weary and rugged, loomed above us: Winterfell met the grimmest of Grimm. Precarious, on three sides it perched on crumbling cliffs. The fourth, where we lay under the eye of a smiling Mage, was nothing but a strip of coral rocks, leading to a gatehouse.

Because this was a bastard island in the middle of an ocean.

'Balls,' Rebel muttered, pulling Ash up next to him, before grudgingly offering Mischief his hand as well.

Mischief studied Rebel, before clasping his hand and allowing himself to be swung to his feet. Then he turned and ducked to help me up. Grey no longer dappled Mischief's wings; they shone with a glittering violet, which was pale enough to shade to silver on their tips.

Mischief noticed my stare and blushed.

Blaze and Spark whined. They tottered, sniffing at the air.

I swayed, as the salt breeze flayed my cheeks. I'd been...teleported...to a freaky arsed magical island, leaving behind Jade and the other Hackney kids. I gasped, clasping at the pouch that held Jade's necklace. Yet they weren't kids anymore, they were Blood Lovers. And I had to trust Jade, just like I trusted Misrule and Harahel to lead the Under World that we'd liberated.

I was apprenticed to the Mage, but the world was safe. Key and the vampires — my followers — were *free*.

I couldn't help the grin.

Mischief sought out my gaze with a sudden earnestness. I didn't understand what he meant, except I could read his apology.

What the hell did he have to be sorry for?

Drake hung behind the Mage, his head bowed. Why hadn't he arrived, caught in a tangle of limbs with me? Had he chosen a side...and it wasn't mine?

My grin faltered. I tore my nails into my swollen elbow because that pain was less than the thought that I'd lost Drake. When I'd left Drake behind in Angel World, he'd still been *mine*.

Yet what if he never had been? What if he'd only saved us to rescue the Lightning Angel from the cells?

I forced myself to swagger towards the Mage. 'You want a *dragon* apprenticed with your knights...? Then let's lay siege to your castle. Because I'm no damsel.'

The Mage gave a deep laugh, catching me in his wings. Creamy sandalwood enveloped me. 'What would I do with a damsel? And I already have my boys to enjoy.' His lips quirked. 'It's the monster I crave.'

'Everybody has their kinks'

Drake hissed, 'Princess, be silent.'

'I'm a queen now. This bitch has a crown.'

The Mage, however, only waved a lazy hand. 'Naïve, little apprentice, you'll learn. You have exceptional powers, but your rage and lust control them. Aren't you intrigued to discover the mental strength I could unlock?'

'I've had enough of being used as a weapon. I'm not some magic bomb.'

The Mage shoved me away with a pat on the head. 'You believe I'm a bad father, like Lucifer?' I winced. 'Of course I shan't use you. I'll set you free.'

I stared at him in shock, but he'd already whirled to Drake.

'Take these...creatures...' The Mage's gaze cooled, as he pointed at each of my fam in turn like they were a line-up of schoolkids waiting in front of the headmaster for a caning. 'Seducer, Addict, and Blood Familiars—'

'Fam,' I hopped onto a boulder, staring across at the hulking castle. 'And they're mine.'

'They're the Legion's, and in case you were unclear, so are you.'

'Please, *queen*, obey,' Drake begged.

I hadn't noticed the tremors through Drake's wings before, or his anxious glances between the Mage and me.

The Mage's long finger finally pointed at Mischief, before crooking at him. Mischief shuffled closer, his expression schooled to blankness.

'Is the *deserter*, *traitor*, and *whore* family too?' The Mage asked.

Why couldn't I read Mischief's expression? I knew a loaded question when I heard it.

'He's one of yours, yeah?' I shrugged.

The Mage backhanded Mischief hard enough to knock him to his knees and split his lip.

Wrong answer.

Blaze growled, and Spark nudged his head against Mischief's hand.

Mischief's hair hung over his face, his shoulders slumped, and he didn't look up.

I wished I could tell Mischief that I'd only been trying to cover for him. *Did he believe I meant it?*

'Take her *family* to the barracks,' the Mage wiped his hand down his shirt, as if disgusted to have been tainted with Mischief's blood.

Drake nodded, still not meeting my gaze.

'Seducer,' Ash whispered, waggling his eyebrows and throwing a mocking glance over his shoulder at the Mage. Then he snogged me, and I was caught in his aromatic embrace...*safety*.

When Ash followed Drake down the pebbled path, Rebel dragged me close, touching our foreheads. 'Addict,' he smirked.

Then he patted his thigh, and the familiars chased after him, pausing to rub their heads against my ankles, gazing up at me and winking.

I laughed. If we'd been alone, I knew they'd have been saying *Blood Familiars*.

That was why I loved them all: funny, brave...misfits like me and they *owned* it. I forced myself to look away...and not think about what would happen to them at the *barracks*.

The Mage rapped his fingers against his palm, deep in concentration. 'Now you're joining the Legion, you should know I reward with the truth.'

Mischief's head shot up. He stared frantically between us. 'Mage Drake, I'll be useless if—'

'More useless than you already are?' The Mage enquired. Mischief flushed. 'I punish, as well as reward. This is your chastisement, Zophia, for defying me. This boy, little apprentice, is a—'

'*Spy*,' Mischief burst out, his fists clenched on his lap, and his eyes blazing with a burning mix of defiance and shame. 'After all, am I not *useless*? Good for nothing but being invisible, as I always have been?' He breathed hard through his nostrils, calming himself. I shivered, crossing my arms to trap my hands under my armpits and stop the violet from bursting out and burning him. How could I crave to hurt and hold him at the same time? 'When you were in Angel World and the first vampires attacked, secretly to the rest of the Legion, the Mage decided to sacrifice me by allowing Lucifer to make me his captive. The others believe I played traitor.'

The Ossuary and Charnel House... The cruelty of the FF to the angels, and Lucifer's play with Mischief...

The Mage had ordered that because of me...?

I leapt off the boulder, prowling closer. 'Why the hell...?'

'So you'd have an ally if *you* were taken.' He peered from underneath his eyelashes at me. 'Who could then rescue you, tricking you into the hands of the Mage...' His voice dropped to a whisper. 'Even if that meant staging a rebellion.'

My legs buckled. I fell to my knees next to Mischief.

The Mage chuckled, but I didn't care about him. I couldn't look away from Mischief's bruised face.

Because nothing had been real.

'Architect and hero of the Bone Revolution,' I sneered.

Mischief's gaze was level. 'An illusion. I *warned* you.' I flinched. 'You were never in control, but then, neither was I.'

When I reached up to touch Mischief's bleeding...*lying*...lip, he winced. 'If you were whoring yourself out to the enemy for info and spying on me, why are you returning the whipped dog?'

Mischief's tongue swiped across my finger, as if for comfort. 'What high standards you hold others to. The Mage told me I'd be trapping a brutal beast.

Yet when I discovered you were...something else...'
His cheeks pinked. 'Let us simply say that I went offscript. The revolution became real, and I swapped loyalties. Spies are rewarded, deserters become the whipped.'

'Why did you desert?'

He met my gaze. 'And I imagined you cleverer than a beast.'

My heart thundered, and my fingers shook as they stroked his cheek.

The powers inside raged to spit out their fury at his betrayal and beat him, just like the Mage had. Yet I'd learnt in the Under World to control Devil's whispers and the call of my vampiric side. I might not always win the struggle, but I was bastard trying.

Instead, I sucked on Mischief's lip, as he bucked in surprise. His blood zinged through me, sparking with desire and magic.

When I drew back, his eyes were wide, and he was panting.

My claws slid out, raking down his chest, and he hissed. 'A beast has claws.'

'Excited, are we? Such big talons you have. One could almost think you were showing off.'

'If you ever trick me with illusions again...?' I rested my steel nails over the fluttering pulse in his neck; he didn't pull away. 'I'll behead you, traitor, with these *talons*.' When Mischief cringed on the *traitor*, a claw nicked his skin. When I bent to lick up the blood, he shuddered. 'But you chose to stand by my side, and I won't forget that.'

The Mage snorted, snatching Mischief by the hair and dragging him to a boulder on the edge of the path, before pressing him over it. 'Stay. The *queen* may choose not to punish you, but you'll be contemplating your behaviour in the Lower Vault for betraying me.' Mischief struggled, but the Mage pinned him. He cast a glance over his shoulder at me. 'We shall have a good while without the Matriarch's interference; she'll be too busy playing with her favourite Wing now she has him finally.'

I stared at the Mage in shock.

Had everything...from the moment I'd been taken to Angel World, to when I'd been snatched to the Brotherhood of the Phoenix...been a plan by my mother *to steal back my dad*?

To force him to conceive another child like me?

I shook, pulling in my claws, before pressing my knuckles across my mouth.

The Mage thrust his thumb into the base of Mischief's neck, and Mischief howled, convulsing across the rock. 'Never play games with those who've been weaving webs for centuries, little apprentice. Lucifer was paying for...unbalancing...the status quo. His punishment was darkness, yet he thirsted for the light. And love. He had no right to either.' The Mage cocked his head, at last lifting his hand from Mischief's neck as he assessed me. 'Your tears are fruitless. Why weep for a Fallen monster?' Surprised I swiped at my cheeks. *Wet.* I turned away my head. 'Lucifer wished to turn you into an assassin: a devil to win the Devil's Trident. Tell me, was it worth it? Or are you ready to turn to the Legion?'

Everything had been an illusion?

Despite that, Misrule's rebellion had saved the Bones, Shadows, and Bloods. He now ruled in place of Lucifer.

So, I was stuck here, apprentice to a fascist spell caster. But who said it had to be as a prisoner? The Mage was the power behind the Matriarch and Angel World. He'd taken out Lucifer with a single spy and our power combined. There'd be no true freedom, whilst the Mage reigned: the shadow with the magic. And now he'd invited me in. Mischief wasn't the only one who could play the Mata Hari.

Time to fake it with the best of them.

I strutted to Mischief, brushing past the Mage. Then I hauled Mischief up by his tunic. 'This is one queen who's learnt her lesson. Vampires and Glories are bad. Check. Ask Mischief, he'll tell you just how much I wasn't down with the Under World.' I grinned. 'This bitch is for turning.'

The Mage rose up into the night-time sky; his wings beat in flaming arcs. 'How kind, thank you for permission to torture Zophia.' Mischief rolled his eyes at me, and I shot him an apologetic glance. 'Until then, let's get you settled. The sooner you accept your life as an apprentice Mage, the better.'

I beat my wings, rising up with my hand clasped in Mischief's; he soared next to me. 'The barracks?'

I'd reckoned it'd be like a Hogwart's dormitory, rather than a military barracks. Was the Mage building an army?

The Mage swooped towards the gatehouse. 'Why would I place a queen amongst riffraff? You shall live with your brother, the prince.'

Mischief caught me, before I could fall from the sky.

I had a brother?

Was he a captive here, or an enemy member of the Legion: A Mage? And was he like me? A *monster?*

Dizzy, I clouted and booted at Mischief, but he held on, whispering soothing nonsense into my ear.

Suddenly, everything cleared; violet and black peeled back.

I had a brother: I wasn't alone.

I peered at the castle ahead. Then I broke free of Mischief's hold, my wings flaring in glory, as I soared towards the stars, swooping beneath the shimmering moon.

A royal brother and sister monster team...? *We'd be kickass...and dangerous enough to destroy the world.*

I flew towards my fam, brother, and new home. Towards magic.

The End

Ready for the next instalment in the Rebel Angels series?

Check out **VAMPIRE MAGE!**

https://rosemaryajohns.com

Did you enjoy **Vampire Devil: Rebel Angels Book Three**?

Let me know by leaving a review!

Love Reading Addictive Fantasy?

Sign up to Rosemary A Johns' *VIP* Newsletter List to be notified of new promotions, secret bonus content, and never miss out on hot new releases.

Plus you'll also receive Rosemary's FREE and exclusive novella "All the Tin Soldiers".

It's our gift to you.

Visit Rosemary's website to subscribe and become a Rebel: rosemaryajohns.com

Hooked on the *Rebel Verse*?

Series in the Rebel Verse

Rebel Vampires
Rebel Angels

Read More from Rosemary A Johns

Website: https://rosemaryajohns.com
Bookbub:
https://www.bookbub.com/authors/rosemary-a-johns
Facebook:
https://www.facebook.com/RosemaryAnnJohns
Twitter: @RosemaryAJohns
Secret Rosemary's Rebels Fan Group:
https://www.facebook.com/groups/698811356958470/permalink/867211580118446

ABOUT THE AUTHOR

ROSEMARY A JOHNS is an award-winning, #1 bestselling fantasy author, music fanatic, and paranormal anti-hero addict. She writes sexy angels, savage vampires, and epic battles.

Winner of the Silver Award in the National Wishing Shelf Book Awards. Finalist in the IAN Book of the Year Awards. Runner-up in Best Fantasy Book of the Year, Reality Bites Book Awards. Honorable Mention in the Readers' Favorite Book Awards. Shortlisted in the International Rubery Book Awards.

Rosemary is also a traditionally published short story writer. She studied at Oxford University and ran her own theatre company. She's always been a rebel...

Want to read more and stay up to date on Rosemary's newest releases? Sign up for her *VIP* Rebel Newsletter and get a FREE novella!

Member of a Book Club?

Why not share *Vampire Devil* with your group?